MURDER
AT
TOPHOUSE

OTHER BOOKS AND AUDIO BOOKS
BY CLAIR M. POULSON

Falling

In Plain Sight

Checking Out

Framed

I'll Find You

Relentless

Lost and Found

Conflict of Interest

Runaway

Cover Up

Mirror Image

Blind Side

Evidence

Don't Cry Wolf

Dead Wrong

Deadline

Vengeance

Hunted

Switchback

Accidental Private Eye

MURDER
AT
TOPHOUSE

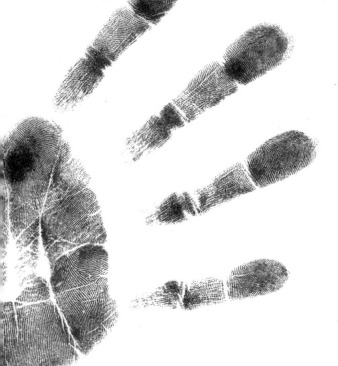

A CRIME NOVEL, FROM BESTSELLING AUTHOR
CLAIR M. POULSON

Covenant Communications, Inc.

Covenant®.

Cover image: *Handprint* © Katrina Brown | Dreamstime.com

Cover design copyright © 2015 by Covenant Communications, Inc.

Published by Covenant Communications, Inc.
American Fork, Utah

Printed in the United States of America
First Printing: March 2015

21 20 19 18 17 16 15   10 9 8 7 6 5 4 3 2 1

ISBN 978-1-68047-033-8

To the wonderful people I met in New Zealand and specifically to a wonderful guide, Jennifer Sloots, who introduced me to the TopHouse and inspired this story.

ACKNOWLEDGMENTS

I AM GRATEFUL FOR THE dedicated staff at Covenant Communications and especially for my talented and patient editor, Stacey Owen. I also want to thank my family for their constant support and assistance. Without them this book could not have been written.

PROLOGUE

I WAS IN THE MIDDLE of a difficult embezzlement investigation, interviewing a prime witness for the company, when my sergeant interrupted. "I need to talk to you for a moment, Mike."

"Can't I finish here first?" I asked.

"This shouldn't take long," Sergeant Hart, a small, slender man in his midfifties, growled.

"I'm sorry," I said to the witness. I spoke into the recorder, indicating that we were taking a break, and then I turned it off. "I'll be right back," I added as I left the interview room.

As soon as I'd shut the door on my witness, Sergeant Hart said, "Your wife has called several times. Detective Granberg says she's been bugging him for an hour, but he told her you were busy. I got the call this time. She sounded pretty upset, so I thought you should know. You may want to call her."

Macy made a habit of interrupting me at work, and everyone at the station was fed up with it, none more than my partner, Detective Cal Granberg. I didn't blame him for trying to get her to be patient after calling the first time or two, but calling for an hour should be a clue that something important was going on and maybe he should let me decide if I should return her call. Granberg and I were partners, but I couldn't say that we were friends. I didn't trust Cal, and he made no secret of the fact that he didn't like me.

Maybe it was because when we had been teamed up, I was given equal authority to him in our assignments as detectives. Or it may have been that I'd caught him doing things that, in my opinion, undermined the integrity of the department, and I'd attempted to stop him. Quite frankly, I suspected him of being a dirty cop. I hoped I was wrong but didn't think

I was. I'd noticed some things lately that made me very suspicious, and I intended to look into them when I got a chance.

He'd been passed over for sergeant several times, and having a young partner who'd been promoted to detective after only three years as a patrolman rubbed him raw. After all, he continually reminded me, he had fifteen years of experience. Since he couldn't make sergeant, it seemed his aim was to try to make me look bad. I worked especially hard to counter his attempts.

I sat at my desk, next to the one where Cal sat. He'd refused to help me with the interview, saying he would catch up on reports—normal behavior for him. I did the work; he took the credit. I didn't say anything to him as I dialed my wife's cell phone number with a certain amount of dread. She could be really hard to talk to when she felt like she'd been slighted in some way, and not calling her right back could be considered a slight, despite the fact that I hadn't known she'd been trying to reach me.

Macy answered on the first ring. I stepped out of the cubicle and away from Cal. "Where are you, Mike?" she demanded, as angry as I'd ever heard her. And that was saying something. After a few blissful months of marriage, things had deteriorated. Macy wasn't the girl I had fallen in love with and courted. Despite my best efforts, the only thing that held our marriage together at all was our son, Mike Jr., now two years old.

"I'm at work," I said, knowing she already knew that. "What do you need, honey?"

"Don't *honey* me," she snarled. "I need you to come home right now."

"What's the matter?" I asked, keeping my voice gentle and calm even as I felt the stirrings of alarm.

"Something's wrong with Mike Jr.!"

My stomach clenched. She had my full attention now. My son was the most important person in the world to me. "What's happening with him?" I asked.

"He's screaming, and he won't quit. He's burning up with fever and holding his head. You need to come and take him to the emergency room right now!"

Our apartment was closer to the hospital than the police department was. "Okay, there's something I need to wrap up here real quick. Head to the emergency room, and I'll meet you there."

"I think you should come take us," she whined.

"No, there isn't time. You're a lot closer to the hospital, Macy. You head there right now, and I'll meet you in the emergency room. I should be able to be there not long after you."

"Why didn't you call me sooner?" she demanded angrily instead of starting for the hospital with our little boy.

"That jerk Granberg didn't tell me you'd been calling. I called as soon as I heard you'd been trying to reach me. Now go, Macy. I'll meet you at the emergency room."

She grumbled a moment more and then agreed.

"Why didn't you tell me Macy called, Cal?" I demanded of my partner as soon as I was off the phone and back in the cubicle.

"I figured she could wait," he said blandly. "You need to teach that woman a thing or two. You've got a job to do. I know you think you can just drop things every time she bawls for you, but it isn't so."

His comments didn't deserve an acknowledgment. I'd long since quit responding to his criticism of either me or my wife. After all, he was the worst hypocrite I'd ever met. "She's headed to the emergency room with our son," I said. "I'll wrap up in the interview room, and then I'm meeting her there." He grunted a non-response without even looking up.

I hurried. In fact, I arrived at the emergency room only a minute or two after Macy and Mike Jr. had. But by the time I reached them, Mike Jr. was unconscious. The doctors worked on him for several hours while Macy and I waited anxiously in the waiting area. I think our marriage ended that night, when one of the doctors came out, his face long, and told us our little boy was gone.

We cried, and I tried to comfort Macy, but all she did was tell me that if I'd called her when she first tried to reach me, he would still be alive. She pounded on my chest with her fists; then finally she said, "I'll be at Mom's," and left.

Alone and miserable as I had ever been in my life, I stayed and spoke with the doctors. They explained that what had happened was beyond their ability to fix. It was an aneurism in his brain, and from the moment it occurred, it was so severe that nothing any doctor could have done would have saved his life. They let me hold his body for a few minutes. Then, at last, my heart broken, I drove to Macy's folks' home. Her mother met me at the door and informed me that I had broken her daughter's heart and that I should just go home.

So that's what I did. Macy did come home the next morning, and for the first few weeks after we had buried our son, things seemed to improve. Then I got shot in the head in an encounter with a domestic violence suspect. The bullet didn't penetrate my skull, but it was fractured, and I was in a coma for three days. When I finally regained consciousness, my widowed mother was beside my bed in the ICU along with my younger sister. Macy never did come see me, and when I was released from the hospital three weeks later, I found she had cleaned her belongings out of the apartment along with a lot of mine. Within a week I was served with divorce papers.

It felt like my life was over. But with the support of a loving mother and sister and some really good friends, I gradually put my life back together. I was determined not to the let these challenges destroy me.

ONE

SIX MONTHS LATER

"YOU NEED TO TAKE A little time off, Detective Denton," Captain Bertrand said, peering over his silver-framed glasses at me.

I sat there for a minute and stared at him, in shock. I'd had no idea why Sergeant Hart had told me to report to the captain's office when I came into the station that morning. Now I knew, and it was totally unexpected. "Is that an order, sir?" I asked, shaking my head in disbelief.

"If it has to be, but I was hoping you'd look sensibly at things and do it voluntarily," he said, raising his bushy black eyebrows and pushing his glasses up. I waited to see what else he was going to say. He waited as well, his dark eyes boring into mine.

I squirmed. I couldn't help it. Captain Bertrand was a big and powerful man. He was well over six feet in height and weighed, in my best estimate, somewhere between 250 and 300 pounds.

When it was clear he wasn't going to say anything else without some prodding, I decided to forge ahead. "Why?"

The large man shook his head with what I assumed was meant to be a look of sympathy on his face, although he didn't have a reputation of being a sympathetic man. "You need to think about what you've been through, Detective," he said, sitting back in his chair, making it groan in protest.

I chewed on my lip for a moment. I bit down, stopping just short of drawing blood. I had indeed been through a lot over the past several months—more than any man should have to go through, in my opinion—but I felt like I had weathered the storm and was doing a good job at work. The self-inflicted pain in my lip helped me to focus, to pull away from tragic thoughts, and I finally was able to offer a response. "Do you think I haven't thought about that more than anything else these past few months?"

"That's just the point, Detective. I do think you've thought about your problems. So do your sergeant and your lieutenant. They're worried about you. Your partner's worried about you." He leaned forward, making his chair groan again, and thumped a long, thick finger on the desk. "This is not meant as any kind of discipline," he said, again looking over his glasses, his dark eyes intense.

It sure felt like discipline to me, and I told him so, trying to speak softly, without anger, and without my eyes misting up. I concluded with, "So if I take time off, will it be with or without pay?"

He shook his head. "That depends. Do you have any vacation time left? I know you've taken quite a bit since your little boy died."

"And since I took a bullet to the head in the line of duty, thanks to Cal Granberg," I said bitterly. I had used all my vacation, all my sick leave, and had even been on short-term disability for a while. Captain Bertrand knew that. "So it's without pay." I tried my best to return his dark stare. "For how long?"

"I'd say at least a month," he answered. "It'll all depend on a psychological exam at that point. Then, well, we'll see how that comes out."

I thought about that for a moment, trying very hard to keep my anger in check. "So, Captain, why don't we do the psych exam now? Why do I have to wait a month, sitting around in my empty apartment going stir-crazy, waiting?"

Captain Bertrand had an answer ready for me. "To give you time to get your life leveled out," he said. "If you were to have it today, you'd fail, and we might be forced to terminate you. Now we don't want that, do we?" He leaned forward and shook his head, appearing almost sad.

I wasn't buying it. "What have I done that brought this on?" I asked. "Who says I'm not fit for duty? I've been giving it my best. In fact, I think I've been giving it more than any of the other detectives in our unit. I've darn sure done a lot more than Cal Granberg. And I do have my life back in order. I've moved on."

This time, there was no ready response. The captain sat back and wiped his brow with a handkerchief. For some reason, he was sweating, not something that happened very often with Captain Bertrand.

"I know that for a while there, I wasn't like I used to be," I admitted. "Nobody would be. But I've put it all behind me. I've accepted what's happened and concentrated on my work. I don't think I've messed up anywhere." I stopped and stared at him.

He stared back for a minute, and then his eyes shifted from mine. "I'm sorry, Detective Denton, but you're making this harder on yourself. Why don't you just do like I suggested—take some time off and try to square your life away."

"What do I need to square away?" I asked, exasperated. I honestly didn't know what more I could be doing than I already was. "If you or the lieutenant see me doing something that isn't a hundred percent up to snuff, all you have to do is point it out, and I'll correct it. What exactly have I done that isn't acceptable?"

"According to Sergeant Hart and Detective Granberg, there's practically nothing that is, as you say, up to snuff," he responded.

Anger surged in my head, and I fought to repress it. I knew that both Sam Hart and Cal Granberg disliked me. I also knew that neither were honest men. They had lied about me before, and they were clearly doing so now. But instead of lashing out like I wanted to do, I begged. "Please, I need to work. The best thing for me right now is to work. It keeps my mind off of what I've lost better than anything else I can do."

"One month," the captain said firmly. "Then we'll take it from there. That will be all."

"So I'm suspended?"

"You are being given time off," he said sternly. "When you're out of vacation, I guess it will be without pay, but your benefits will continue."

"I'm already out of vacation. I might have earned another three or four days, but that's all, Captain. I can't afford this."

He shook his head, pushed his glasses up, and said, "Be back here on the tenth of January. Come directly to my office. We'll set up the exam at that time, and if you have things straight in your personal life and if the doctor clears you, you can go back to work."

I was stunned. I sat there wanting to say more but knowing it was hopeless.

"That's all, Denton. You may go now."

I stood up and turned to the door, but I stopped and turned back at the sound of his voice. "Oh, one more thing, Detective. You'll need to leave your gun, your department ID, and your badge with me."

I turned slowly and faced him. "So I *am* suspended," I said as I reached inside my jacket, pulled my service weapon out, and placed it carefully on his desk. He didn't say a word. I pulled out my ID and put it there too. The last thing I laid on his desk was my badge. Then I left his office without another word.

I stopped at my desk to get a few personal items. My partner was at his desk, bent to whatever task he was pretending to do. "You got your way, Granberg," I said, unable to keep the ice from my voice. "I guess they'll give you a new partner now. That's what you wanted, isn't it? A partner who doesn't care that you're a crooked cop. I'll be back, and when I come, I'll be watching every move you make." I knew I shouldn't have threatened him, but I couldn't help myself. His face went purple with rage.

"You're all screwed up, Mike," he said, coming to his feet, fists clenched. "I need someone I can depend on to back me up if I need it."

That really caused the anger to boil inside of me. I forced myself to speak softly. "Feeling guilty, are you, Cal? I took a bullet because you weren't paying attention. You can lie about it all you want, but you and I both know what happened. *You* didn't back *me* up when I needed it. You're a coward and a dishonest thug. And so is your buddy, Sergeant Hart. I'm sure you two cooked up this scheme to get rid of me."

I felt a strong pulsing in my temples, and I was clenching my fists. There was a lot more I wanted to say, but I checked myself. It would do no good. I'd probably already said too much. I didn't need a physical altercation with Cal. If that happened, they'd fire me for sure. Cal Granberg was a poor excuse for an officer and certainly not sergeant material, but in some way that I didn't understand, he was good at polishing senior officers in other ways, as long as they didn't have to promote him. I guessed that his close relationship with our sergeant, another man who should never have been promoted, was the conduit he used to polish those further up the chain of command. I had been relieved of my duties because of Cal, just as surely as I'd been shot because of him. I took a deep breath, finished collecting the items from my desk, and left without another word. He was still standing with his fists balled, glaring at me.

"You'll never make it here, Denton. Hart and I will make sure of that." He shot me one last glare and turned away.

There it was. The two of them had got me where I now was, and they wouldn't quit until I was finished as a cop. Me, the one that did my job, while they, crooks, would continue working and do more harm than good. Oh, how bitter I felt as I walked out of the building and into the smog that covered the city. The smog did nothing to help my mood. It looked and smelled about like I felt.

I spent the next couple of hours trying to make up my mind what to do with the time I had on my hands. I could feel despondency setting in when I finally decided. No way was I going to let Cal and Sam have their way. I had fought back from my divorce and the loss of my son. I had fought back from the bullet that could have taken my life. And I would fight back now. I picked up the phone and made a call.

Two hours later I walked into the office of an attorney I had faced from the witness stand three or four times in the two years I had worked as a detective. I knew he was a man that, if he agreed to help me, would give it his best. And his best was as good as it came in his profession. My own profession was in jeopardy. If I lost my job—and it appeared that was exactly what was going to happen if I didn't do something—I'd never get another job for any police department in the state of California, or any place else for that matter.

Barry Tomasik represented a lot of high-profile criminal defendants, but he also took on cases such as I was about to present to him. He had helped a couple of officers I knew out of trouble they hadn't deserved. I hoped he would also help me. Barry shook my hand warmly. "What can I do for you, Detective?"

I came right to the point. "I was just suspended. I've been railroaded, and I want to do something about it."

Barry was a man of average height and weight with wide-set blue eyes that radiated intelligence. Even though he was only in his midfifties, his thick head of hair was totally gray. Despite what I thought of some of the defendants he represented, I believed him to be an honest and decent man. Those blue eyes looked at me intensely. "Tell me about it," he said.

Fifteen minutes later, I had concluded the morning's events, including everything the captain had said to me and even mentioned my suspicions regarding my partner and sergeant. He was thoughtful for a moment. "You were shot more than six months ago," he said. "Are you healed up now?"

"I am," I told him as he looked at the scar that ran along the left side of my head, about half an inch above my ear. I touched the scar. "I suppose if I let my hair grow out, it would be pretty much invisible. Anyway, the bullet didn't enter my head. It did cause a fracture to my skull, but I was back to work in three months. I used my vacation, sick leave, and some short-term disability while I was recovering."

"I remember when you got shot. Someone told me you blamed your partner for letting it happen. Is that true?" he asked.

"I thought he was backing me up," I said, feeling the old anger that welled up in me every time I thought of the incident. "We were going into a house on a domestic violence call. He was right behind me when we started up the walk. I knocked on the door, and when the suspect opened it, he had a pistol in his hand. He pointed it at me and told me there wasn't a problem, that I could leave. I could hear what sounded like a woman wailing in the background. I told him that my partner and I just needed to talk to his wife and make sure everything was okay. He said, 'What partner? You mean the guy in the car?' I looked back to see that Granberg was indeed back in the patrol car. I had no idea what he was doing, but his head was down and he was looking at something inside the car. I said to the suspect, 'Why don't you have your wife come to the door, and I'll talk to her right here?'

"The guy waved the gun at me and told me to go get back in the car and leave," I explained. "But I had a job to do, and I was convinced it was a legitimate call. The way he was waving that gun around was evidence of that. So I asked him to put the gun away and let me talk to his wife."

"I take it he didn't put the gun away." Barry shook his head.

"Nope, and when I realized he was about to fire it, I tried to duck, and that's the last thing I remembered until I woke up in the hospital three days later."

"Why were you and Detective Granberg responding to a domestic violence call?" he asked. "I would have thought that uniformed officers would have done that."

"We'd been working a drug case. Granberg told me there was a guy we needed to interview at ten thirty that morning. We stopped at a house two doors away from where I got shot. It was right then that the call came in. Cal grabbed the radio and told the dispatcher we were in the neighborhood and would handle it."

Barry nodded. "I see. So how did you get to the hospital?"

A terrible thought occurred to me in that instant, and I ignored Barry's question. Thinking out loud I said, "Cal never volunteered for anything. I don't even know if he really had an interview that morning. I did hear someone wailing somewhere in the house we responded to. But whoever it was, she didn't shout for help or anything like that, I don't think. I can't remember it, anyway."

Barry put a hand up and said, "Detective, stop right there."

"But I think I'm on to something. I need to go back to the house we stopped in front of. I need to see if anybody there had an appointment to talk to Cal that day. Why didn't I think of this before?" I said, slapping the side of my head.

"Mike, think about what you're saying," Barry said sternly. "If I'm following your line of thought, you're about to accuse your partner of not only being negligent but of setting you up to get shot. That's an extremely serious allegation."

I took a deep breath. "I know. I must be wrong. Sorry. Now, what did you ask me?"

"I asked how you got to the hospital," he said.

"Oh, yeah. I was unconscious, but from what I've been told, my partner called for help after I was shot. I was told that he was still sitting in the car when a couple of other officers got there. He claimed he had been making sure help was on the way and denied being in the car when I was shot. At any rate, he did at least call for help. The suspect was gone and has never been found. I've tried and tried to remember what he looked like, but I can't. I guess the concussion erased that. Anyway, help came, and I was taken to the hospital," I said. "And since the suspect was never found, I couldn't verify my version of events regarding Cal."

"You don't think your being shot has anything to do with your being told to take some time off by Captain Bertrand?"

"That was six months ago," I protested. "No, it's because Detective Granberg and Sergeant Hart somehow convinced him that I wasn't fit for duty. I was cleared several months ago to go back to work—by a doctor."

"So what was the captain's reasoning?" he asked. "I take it there was something more than your injury."

I nodded and spent the next thirty minutes discussing the death of my little son, Mike Jr., and the departure of my wife from my life.

When I finished he said, "Mike, I think some time off would be good for you, but only if you go somewhere and do something fun and relaxing. Sitting at home and sulking won't help you. Take a vacation. Is there somewhere you'd like to go?"

"I'm sure there is, but it would take money. I've saved a little the past few weeks but not enough for an extended vacation. If I was still getting my salary, I could probably swing it."

"Do you have alimony to pay?" he asked.

"Yes, but not for long. Macy, that's my ex, has found someone else already and is planning to get married again in a few weeks. After that the alimony will stop."

"Poor guy," Mr. Tomasik said with a perfectly sober face.

"I'll be okay," I said.

"I didn't mean you." He grinned then.

I couldn't help but smile at that. "I could warn the guy, but he probably wouldn't listen to me," I offered.

"Probably not. Now, Mike, here's what I think I'll do, if you want me to, that is. First, I've seen you on the witness stand. I believe you're a good officer. So I'll draw up some papers and have them served on the police department. Then I'll do some negotiating for you."

I held up a hand and said, "Mr. Tomasik, before you do anything, I need to know what it's going to cost me so I can figure out if I can pay for it."

He smiled. "I think I'll take this on contingency, Mike. I'll take say 30 percent of whatever I can get for you from the city. Will that work for you?"

"Sure." I thought about that for a moment and then added, "I was hoping we could get the captain to reconsider without having to file a law suit. I really don't want to do that."

"No suit yet, Mike. Just a simple little letter of intent will do for now. Here's how it'll work. When they know a suit *may* be coming, I'll tell them that all you want is your salary while you're off at their request and a bonus just to keep me and you both happy. I'll get you enough that you can go somewhere nice while I help your supervisors come to their senses," he explained. "We'll only sue if we have to. Where would you like to go?"

A thought began to form in my mind. Maybe Cal wanted me removed because I was getting close to something, something he didn't want uncovered. I thought back to a phone call I'd overheard last week. I'd left Cal in the car while I ran across the street to a store, but it was closed, and I got back to the car much sooner than Cal had expected. He hadn't noticed me at first, and when he did, he ended the call. But I'd already heard a little bit, enough to make me suspicious. Cal had been talking to someone named Hemana about guns. The guy must have been in New Zealand because they were talking about how the country doesn't allow private citizens to own guns. That was one of the things that I'd hoped to look into sometime. What possible reason would he have had for talking to someone there about guns?

Another time, I overheard him mention New Zealand to Sergeant Hart. Neither of them had ever mentioned wanting to go there, and because of what I'd overheard earlier, it made me even more suspicious.

Suddenly I knew where I was going to go. "New Zealand. That would be a good place to visit, and it would get me a long way away from my partner and my sergeant." I said nothing regarding my suspicions about Granberg and Hart being involved in something shady involving guns and New Zealand.

"Then you shall go there," he said with a smile. "Go home and pack, get your airline ticket, and let me work on my end of things."

"Airline tickets cost—" I began.

"Do you have a credit card?" he interrupted.

"Well, yes, of course, and there's no balance on it, but—"

Mr. Tomasik cut me off again. "Mike, use it and get a ticket. I'll have you some cash before you leave. You've given me a lot to work with here." He waved a hand toward the door. "Now go. Come in tomorrow morning. I'll have some papers drawn up for you to sign."

I went home to my empty apartment, suddenly feeling a little less gloomy. I'd go to New Zealand and see if my suspicions had any merit. Cal may have cost me my job for the time being, but I'd do what I could to make sure that the last laugh would be on him. I'd try to relax and have a little fun there as well. And hopefully, when I got home, I'd still have my job—and a new partner and sergeant. There was no way I could ever work with the two of them again. I placed a call and made a reservation on Air New Zealand out of LAX.

Then I picked up a framed picture of my little Mike Jr. and wept bitter tears.

TWO

I HAD NEVER CONSIDERED MYSELF a vindictive person, but I guess I am. I wanted to see my partner receive, at the least, a reprimand for what he had done in failing to back me up. More than that, I'd like to see him get fired. For that matter, it wouldn't hurt my feelings if he and Sam Hart both lost their jobs. After all, they were doing all they could to see that I lost mine. And if I was lucky, my little trip to New Zealand would help things along.

As for my ex-wife, I didn't harbor bitter feelings for her anymore. In fact, she still had a tender spot in my heart. Divorce had never been something I had considered, despite the problems we'd had. I tried to think of Macy as the sweet, pretty, fun-loving girl I had married, not the snarky, sullen girl she'd become, although it wasn't always easy.

As for my little Mike Jr.—I'll never get over missing him. I carry pictures of him in my wallet, and not a day has gone by that I haven't pulled them out and looked at them. I don't want to ever forget what his little face looked like. I'm grateful God let me have him for the short time we were father and son.

When I met my attorney the next day to sign some papers, he informed me that he'd already been in touch with the police chief. That made me wither in my chair. He'd gone all the way to the top of the huge department. "He tells me he's going to look into your matter, Mike. But in the meantime, he assured me you'll be paid your full salary for the time you are off. He didn't promise a bonus, but I got the distinct impression that he wouldn't be opposed to it to keep out of a lawsuit if he finds you really have been doing your job. And I intend to help him see that."

"I don't want anyone to get unjustly hurt over this," I told Barry. "But I hope that if they really do look into my performance thoroughly they'll also look into the way I've been treated by my partner—the lies he's told and the way he's made me do most of the work. And I think they need to take a look at what both he and Sergeant Hart do in their off time." I didn't mention my own plan of looking into that while I was in New Zealand.

"I don't know about that, Mike, but they will look closely at your job performance, and as a bonus, they'll look closer at what happened the day you were shot. That's what the chief told me," Barry said. "And I know him to be a man of his word."

That was as much as I could hope for. Even more, I admitted to myself. "Thank you, Mr. Tomasik."

"I'm Barry to you," he said, waggling a finger at me. "Now I still recommend that you visit New Zealand and that you do so as soon as you can. Have you gotten a ticket yet?"

I nodded my head. "It's taken care of. I fly out on Saturday."

"Today is Tuesday. That's several days away. I think we need to get you out of the country sooner, if possible."

"That would be great; I'll see if I can get an earlier flight," I said. "But what's wrong with going on Saturday?"

"Just take my word for it that it would be best if you leave as soon as possible," he said without further explanation.

That left me speculating. The conclusion I drew was that the department might try to stop me from leaving the country, more so if Cal caught wind of where I was planning to go. I'm sure he and Sergeant Hart would be furious if they heard I was going to New Zealand.

* * *

By the time I boarded an Air New Zealand flight at eight o'clock the next evening, I was psyched about my trip, hoping it was really going to happen. I'd been a nervous wreck since Barry had told me I needed to leave soon. I had feared and even expected to be contacted by someone from the police department before I could get aboard the plane in an attempt to keep me in the country. It hadn't happened, and in a few minutes, I would be off the ground, and no one could prevent me from taking my trip, my *vacation*, as Barry Tomasik called it.

I turned my iPhone and iPad off and settled back in my seat while I waited for the plane to move away from the gate. I pulled little Mike Jr.'s pictures from my wallet and gazed at his delightful little face. The woman in the seat next to me commented on what a beautiful child he was. I thanked her, and when she asked if he was with his mother while I was traveling, I just sort of nodded.

At last, the huge plane began to back away from the gate. I was seated next to a window, and when I saw a couple of uniformed policemen exit the terminal we had just backed away from, my heart began to pound.

The officers ran toward the plane and waved their arms frantically as they looked up at the cockpit, but the plane continued to back. It stopped and then moved forward in a long turn. I watched, praying the pilot would continue to move toward the runway. He did just that, and the officers on the tarmac finally stopped and watched us leave. It was too far for me to see their faces, but I had a feeling they were angry. A moment later, they were out of my view. I wondered what lies Cal and Sam had told the department about me that made them attempt to stop me from leaving the country.

I was still tense as we taxied out to the runway. Not until we were racing down it did I allow myself to take a deep breath in relief.

Once we were airborne, I relaxed as much as I could and watched the huge city of LA grow smaller and smaller. When it vanished from my sight, I quit looking out the window, turned my attention to the small screen in front of me, and tried to find something to watch to keep my mind occupied. I kept worrying that the captain would come on the intercom and tell us we were being forced to return to the Los Angeles International Airport. I thought that unlikely, as he had so clearly ignored the officers on the ground. But I still worried. I selected a movie and was finally able to push thoughts of my supervisors and partner to the back of my mind.

The movie was boring, and I drifted to sleep only to be awakened sometime later by an announcement from the captain. He explained that no one had any reason to worry but that we were going to have to make an unscheduled landing in Honolulu. He said there was a minor mechanical problem that needed to be addressed, that it was not threatening the integrity of the plane but that he'd made the decision to divert the flight to Hawaii out of an abundance of caution.

I suppose I shifted nervously in my seat as everyone around me was doing. That was a normal reaction. Even the bravest of fliers were probably unnerved when a plane had to make an unscheduled landing for any reason, but that was especially true when it was something mechanical.

Once we were on the ground, the captain instructed us to exit the plane while the mechanical problem was addressed. It wasn't until I was walking through the gate and into the terminal that it dawned on me that the reason for the stop might not be mechanical at all. *It might be because of me.* I broke out in a sweat when I spotted four uniformed police officers standing close to the exit. They were watching as we deplaned.

The impulse to flee was strong, but I didn't know where I'd go if I did. Another man a few steps behind me in the line of deplaning passengers apparently had the same impulse. He acted on his while I simply stood and awaited my fate. He violently shoved someone into me as he surged past. We both fell in a tangled heap on the floor, and the cause of our fall continued shoving past others. I turned my attention to the young lady who had fallen to the floor with me. With murmured apologies, we began to untangle ourselves. I heard some shouting a short distance down the concourse, and by the time I had helped the young woman to her feet, the police officers had tackled the man and were putting handcuffs on him.

"What was that all about?" she asked in a tantalizing accent as the prettiest blue eyes I had ever seen gazed into my face.

"Guess the guy was wanted by the cops," I said as she looked toward where the arrest was being made.

"He seemed nervous," she said in that wonderful accent while again looking at me with those gorgeous eyes, making my knees tremble. Well, maybe it wasn't the eyes that affected me so. I suppose it could be the relief flooding over me that it wasn't me that the cops had taken into custody.

I smiled at her as I began to brush myself off. "I'm just glad it wasn't me they were after."

"Why would they be after you?" she asked, alarm crossing her pretty face.

"Just kidding," I said, wondering why I'd said that out loud. I tried to cover it up. "Aren't you glad they weren't after you?"

She relaxed and punched me playfully on the shoulder. "Of course I am," she said. "And I'm glad they got him. He was scaring me. I noticed him watching me back in Los Angeles before we boarded the plane. He looked mean, and then he sat too close to me on the plane." Strangely, she began to tremble as she spoke.

"You must have good instincts." I tried to collect my thoughts. "He was obviously wanted for something, and I'd guess it was pretty serious if they landed the plane just to get him."

"So maybe there wasn't anything wrong with the plane after all. That was scary." Her pretty blue eyes now looked frightened.

"I think you're right. It was that guy that was the problem."

"Yeah. Hey, maybe he was who the cops in Los Angeles were after when they were waving their arms like they wanted our plane to stop." The fear in her eyes fading slightly. "Did you see them?"

"Yeah, I noticed them," I replied, not saying anything about my having thought they were after me.

"I'm Skylie Yates," she said, offering to shake my hand. Hers was still trembling slightly, but she seemed to be getting control. "Sorry about knocking you down."

"Mike Denton," I replied, accepting her slightly moist hand. "And you didn't knock me down, the perp did."

She looked confused, her hand lingering in mine. "Perp?"

"Oh, sorry, that's police lingo for perpetrator," I clarified. "He was the one who knocked both of us down. And tell me, please, what is that pretty accent of yours?"

She smiled. Oh my goodness. That smile of hers was charming. "It's my Kiwi accent," she said.

"Kiwi?" I said, puzzled.

"Yes, I'm from New Zealand. We are known as Kiwis. That's actually the state bird, but it's also what people call us. Cool, huh, mate?"

"Yeah, that really is cool," I said.

"So are you a policeman?" she asked brightly. The fear had receded, and she seemed fine now.

I hesitated only slightly. "I am. I'm on my way to your country, to New Zealand, for a bit of a vacation." I gave her the brightest smile I could manage. Wow, did she ever have my heart fluttering.

"It's nice to meet you, Officer Denton," she said mischievously. "I'm a college student on my way home to New Zealand. I spent a semester in LA." Before I could respond, the public announcement speaker came on, and we were told that the problem had been resolved and that we could now board our flight to continue on our way to Auckland. I felt relief in more ways than one.

"I'm glad it wasn't a mechanical problem, Skylie. That would have made me nervous to get back on the plane." I didn't mention the other reason I was relieved.

"I think I'll go the ladies' room before I get back on the plane," she said. "Maybe I'll see you later?"

That second sentence clearly came out as a question. "Sure, that'd be great. Maybe I'll wait to board with you."

"Thanks, I'd like that," she said with a grin and moved gracefully across the concourse.

I watched her for a moment, quite entranced. When she was out of sight, I pulled out my phone on an impulse, turned it on, and waited while it booted up. Then I placed a call. I'd promised to let my attorney know when I arrived in New Zealand, but I wanted to talk to him now and be absolutely sure that the cops at LAX had been after the perp who'd been arrested here, not me.

"Hello, Mike," he said a minute later.

"Hello, Mr. Tomasik," I responded.

"It's Barry to you," he reminded me sternly. "And I know you're not in New Zealand yet. What's going on?"

"I'm in Honolulu," I said.

Before I could explain why, Barry interrupted. "Did the internal affairs investigators have your plane diverted there?" he asked, sounding suddenly angry.

"I don't think so," I said. "But we did get diverted here." I explained what had happened and then asked, "Why did you ask if IA was involved?"

"Because the chief called to tell me that they didn't want you to leave the state during their investigation," Barry responded. "I told them you had every right to do so, but he said they had some questions to ask you before you left. He admitted they already knew you were going to New Zealand and that they'd try to stop you long enough to talk to you."

"So the officers at LAX who tried to flag down the plane were after me and not the guy that was arrested in Honolulu?"

"I think so, Mike. But don't worry about it. You just get back on that plane and continue with your plans. I'll get hold of the chief and see if he'll simply give me a list of the questions they have, and then, if I think it's appropriate, I'll call you and get your responses."

"Thanks, Barry," I said as I saw Skylie coming toward me. "I need to get back on the plane now."

I clicked off and put the phone back in my pocket as my new friend approached. "Should we?" she said, gesturing to the end of the line of passengers slowly moving forward to re-board the plane.

But before we turned toward the boarding gate, four officers approached, dragging the man who had knocked us down. He was resisting and cursing loudly. When they reached Skylie and me, the guy suddenly shouted, in a distinctive Kiwi accent, "You haven't seen the last of me, Skylie Yates!"

Skylie gasped and collapsed against me. I held her and kept her from going clear to the floor—again. I had an almost overpowering impulse to rush after the officers and find out who the man was, but I couldn't since my arms were around a frightened girl who needed me to hold her up. I did get a better look at him though. He had dark, shoulder-length hair. His eyes were dark, filled with menace, and a prominent scar ran down the left side of his face. He was probably around six feet tall, and I guessed him to be a good two hundred pounds. He was giving the arresting officers all they could handle. They disappeared from sight, but I had filed his looks in my memory. If I ever saw him again, I would recognize him.

I became aware of the long blonde hair that cascaded down my chest as Skylie's head rested against my shoulder. I cranked my neck around to where I could see her face—it was pale, but her deep blue eyes were wide open and staring in the direction the perp had been taken. "Hey, it's okay," I murmured. "He can't hurt you."

She began to shake and attempted to pull away from me, but I held her tight, and she gave in, allowing herself to relax against me. We stood that way until the announcement was made that the rest of the Auckland-bound passengers needed to board immediately. I gently guided her toward the gate, keeping a protective arm around her shoulder.

There was still a short line there, and when we stopped at the end of it, she said, "Who is that guy? How did he know my name?" Her voice was quivering, and her eyes were moist and pleading as she looked up at me briefly before diverting her eyes.

Suddenly feeling very protective of this young woman, this veritable stranger, I said, "I have ways to check. I'll make a call or two when we're back on the plane, before we have to shut our phones off. Maybe by the time we get to Auckland, I'll be able to give you some answers."

"Thank you, but you don't need to check on him. I, uh, I don't think I want to know."

Something was a little off in her answer, but I let it slide. I had a feeling she knew more about this guy than she was letting on, and whether she wanted me to or not, I had every intention of finding out all I could. Just the way he looked made me suspicious of him, and the way he had spoken to Skylie, calling her by name, as he was dragged past, had sounded very much like a threat. And though I scarcely knew this girl, I didn't take kindly to her being threatened.

The line was moving, and we were soon again on board the plane. I stopped at my seat and stood watching until she was in hers, just a few rows behind me. She gave a little wave when she sat down. I watched for a moment more before squeezing past the fellow in the aisle and taking my seat.

I pulled my iPhone out and punched in Barry's number.

"You have to turn that off now," the fellow next to me said gruffly. "I can't believe this happened. It will make us late getting to Auckland."

"Yes, it will," I agreed as nicely as I could. He was clearly put out at the delay. He'd introduced himself to me earlier as Arch Vertucci. We had visited a little after the captain's announcement had awakened me, and he seemed like a nice guy. It was a rash thing to do, but as I waited for my call to go through, I said, "Better late than hijacked. Did you see the look on the face of that guy they arrested?"

Arch's face went white. "Do you think he—" Arch began, but I cut him off by lifting up a finger when Barry answered.

"Mike, what's happening now?" Barry asked, sounding quite concerned.

"I know this is a lot to ask, but I really need to know who the guy was that was taken off the plane in Honolulu," I said.

"Why do you need to know that?"

I quickly explained about Skylie and what had happened. "She was scared to death of the guy. She said she doesn't know him, but I'm not so sure about that. He called her by name when he threatened her."

"Feeling protective, are you?" Barry asked, a tease in his voice. But before I could respond, he went on. "I'll get on it, Mike. I'll get back with you after you land in New Zealand."

"I'm sorry to put you to the trouble," I said meekly.

"Hey," his voice boomed. "What are attorneys for if it isn't to help their clients? I'll call you when I find out. If you don't have your phone on yet, I'll leave a message. You can call me back when it works for you."

"Thanks, Barry."

"Oh, and Mike, when you call, remember the time difference. Unless it's an emergency, I'd prefer not to be interrupted when I'm sleeping." He chuckled and disconnected.

The man beside me said, "Do you really know someone who can find out who that guy was?"

"I'm a police officer, a detective with the LAPD. And yes, I can find out who he is and what he's wanted for." I didn't tell him that I was currently suspended. Not that it mattered; I hadn't been fired—yet.

"Do you really think he might have hijacked the plane?" Arch asked.

"One never knows, but I suppose it could have been possible." Actually, I honestly doubted it very much. "At any rate, you and I can both feel more at ease for the rest of the trip knowing he's in custody in Hawaii."

"Yes," he agreed, "we can."

I smiled to myself and shut my phone down.

THREE

WE WERE AIRBORNE, AND THE fasten seatbelt signs had been turned off for only a couple of minutes when there was a tap on my shoulder. I looked past Arch, and my heart took a little skip. Skylie smiled at me from the aisle. But she looked troubled. "Mike, that guy's seat is empty, and the woman next to me said she'd sit there if you wanted to come back and sit by me."

"What have you got to lose?" Arch asked with a grin as he quickly got to his feet and signaled me to slip past him. "I'd go if she were asking me."

"Thanks, I think I will." I reached into the pocket in front of me and retrieved my iPad.

"Thank you, Mike," Skylie said with a weak grin.

"Let me grab my carry-on," I said, retrieving it from the bin above my head.

"Ah, look at all the room I have," Arch said. "Thanks, you two." Then he winked at me. "Lucky devil, you."

Skylie and I moved down the aisle to where she had been sitting. The lady who had been seated next to Skylie smiled up at me from her new seat and made some comment about Skylie not being separated from her guy. It made me smile, and I thanked her. Skylie blushed. I opened the overhead compartment to put my bag there. It was quite full. I began moving stuff around in an attempt to make room. One bag was a little hard to move. I read the name stenciled on it, and then asked, "Are any of you Antony Bahr?" The people in the nearby seats all shook their heads.

On an impulse, I pulled the bag out, settled mine in, and sat down with Antony's on my lap. No one except for Skylie paid any attention to what I was doing.

Her eyes were wide, and she looked frightened again. "Do you think that's *his*?"

"Could be," I whispered back. "We'll check it out in a little while." I shoved it beneath the seat in front of me and then settled back.

"Thank you, Mike," my new seat companion said, the worry in her eyes fading slightly. "You really are a cop, aren't you?"

I looked over at her. "Sure am."

She gave me a weak grin. "I'm glad. You make me feel safe."

Those words made me feel mighty good. I thought of the hours ahead of us as we winged our way to New Zealand and counted myself lucky. Being near someone as attractive as Skylie for those few hours would make the whole trip worth it. I guess I hadn't realized how starved I had been for female companionship since Macy's abrupt departure. But sitting next to a girl who seemed to like me, I felt like a hole was being filled, temporary though it may be. I wasn't so naïve as to think that I would ever see her again after we landed in Auckland. Although a guy could always dream.

As the hours passed, I learned more about Skylie. At twenty-two, she was six years younger than me, not that the age mattered. She told me she'd been orphaned as a tiny child and shifted around from foster home to foster home for several years. She didn't know anything about her natural parents, but she spoke fondly of the Māori couple who had taken her in when she was twelve and had treated her as their own child ever since. From the time she'd been placed in their home, she told me she hadn't ever wanted to go to any other foster family. "They'll be at the airport to pick me up, so maybe you can meet them." She smiled almost shyly. "I think you'd like them. And I know they would like you."

We both watched a movie—not the same one; ate a meal—identical ones; and listened to a little music on our headphones—probably radically different. We both pulled them off about the same time, and I decided to ask a question that had been on my mind. After glancing at the woman in the seat next to the window, just beyond Skylie, and assuring myself that she still had her earphones on and was engrossed in a movie on the small screen in front of her, I blurted out, "Are you sure you haven't seen that man somewhere before? He spoke in an accent a lot like yours, and he sure did know your name."

I had caught her off guard, and her face went red. I thought she was going to ignore the question when she turned her head away from me. I didn't press her for an answer, just waited, although her very hesitation told me that my earlier suspicions had been right—she hadn't leveled with me. Eventually, she turned her head back toward me. "You'll think I'm awful," she said, her eyes misty.

"I doubt that."

"I have to be honest with you, Mike. You're such a good guy. And you're a cop," she said and then wiped at her eyes. "You probably know when someone's lying to you."

She'd nailed me there. I definitely suspected that she knew the guy. I smiled. "You didn't exactly lie. I never did ask if you knew him or not."

"But I acted like I didn't know him, tried to deceive you. The Paratas, the couple who raised me, would say that is lying."

"Hey, so what?" I said. "I'm betting you wish you didn't know him."

She nodded, brushed her long blonde hair from her face and looked away. "That is so true," she said so softly that I barely was able to make out her words.

"So before we snoop in his bag, would you like to tell me what you know about him?" I asked.

She hesitated for a moment, and then she looked back at me. "He's not an old boyfriend or anything, if that's what you're thinking. He's not even someone who was ever my friend. I mean, I didn't even know his name until you pulled his bag down. But yes, Mike, even though I don't know who he is, I've seen him before—several times. That's why I'm so afraid of him. He's a very bad man, and . . . and . . ." Skylie's voiced faded, and once again she looked away, her eyes focusing on her hands, which she was wringing nervously in her lap.

I waited, trying to be patient, hoping she would say more, but the nervous wringing continued. Finally, I spoke. "Tell me what you know about him, Skylie. Tell me why you believe he is a bad person."

She looked over at me then. "He's been stalking me at school for the past two weeks. I'd never seen him before then, and that's the truth. One day I was with a guy on campus, a friend of mine. We were coming from a class we had together when this guy suddenly walked toward us, coming from the opposite direction. He stopped us and called me by name. He told my friend to leave, that he and I had to talk. When I told him I didn't even know him, Justin, that's my friend's name, told him to get lost."

I said nothing as Skylie took a deep breath. After a moment, she continued. "He punched Justin in the face, making him fall backwards. Justin hit his head on the sidewalk so hard that he couldn't even move.

He just lay there moaning. This guy, I guess his name is Antony"—she pointed at the brown bag beneath the seat in front of me—"he grabbed my arm and began to drag me off the sidewalk onto the grass. Two other guys in our class saw what was happening and came to help me. They were able to get me loose from the creep. When they did, he ran off, but he said something about it not being over. I don't have any idea what he was talking about."

She became silent, and once more she began wringing her hands.

"Did you see him again after that?" I asked.

She nodded and then looked up at me. "Several times, but I was always with other people, and he didn't try to approach me again. I saw him near my dorm several times. I didn't dare go out at night, even with friends."

"When was the last time you saw him, before this trip, I mean?" I asked.

"Two days before I left. It was the end of the semester. I had planned to stay in school, but I was so scared of him I decided to go back to New Zealand. I was just coming out of the administration building with three of my friends, two guys and a girl. They had gone with me so I could finish checking out of the university. All my friends knew how scared I was. Anyway, he was leaning against a palm tree near the door, looking right at me," she said with a shudder. "If looks could kill, I'd have been dead right then."

"But he didn't try to approach you?" I asked.

"I thought he was going to. He started walking toward us. I told my friends that he was the guy who put Justin in the hospital. One of them suggested we run back into the admin building. That's what we did, and he didn't follow us inside," she explained. "I didn't try to leave again until the campus cops came and escorted me back to my dorm. The next time I saw him was when he got on this plane."

"Oh, Skylie," I said sympathetically. "I'm sorry. But tell me, why hadn't he been arrested? I mean, if he assaulted Justin so badly that it put him in the hospital, you'd think he'd have been arrested."

Her face reddened. "We didn't tell the cops, not until after we saw him outside the admin building. Then they couldn't find him."

I must have looked at her a little too sternly, because tears flooded her eyes. They flowed freely when I asked, "Why didn't you report it?"

"We thought about it, but Justin was afraid it would only make the guy more dangerous. We were both pretty scared."

"If Justin was taken to the hospital, surely the paramedics would have asked you what happened."

"He didn't go in an ambulance. The guys that scared Antony off drove us there. They only kept him in the hospital for a couple of days," she explained.

"What about at the hospital? Didn't the doctors want to know what happened to him?"

"Justin told them he fell. They didn't question it."

"Fell?" I asked suspiciously. "How would that explain damage to his face where Antony hit him and the injury to the back of his head? He would have had to fallen twice to get injuries both front and back."

She shook her head sadly and rubbed the tears from her face. "We told them he stumbled, hit a tree with his face, then fell over backward as he tried to stand up straight. They didn't question him or any of us about it after that."

"Okay, so why do you think the cops wanted him badly enough that they got the airlines to have our plane land and have him arrested?"

She shook her head. "I have no idea," she responded. "Maybe someone else told the police about him hitting Justin and grabbing me?"

It was my turn to do the head shaking. "I don't think so," I said. "And let me tell you why. What he did was probably considered just a simple assault, not an aggravated assault."

"But he tried to kidnap me!" she protested hotly.

"Maybe, but since all he did was drag you a few feet, it might be really hard to prove kidnapping in court, even attempted kidnapping. He could say he just wanted to get you to where people on the sidewalk couldn't hear the two of you talking. After all, you did say he wanted to talk to you."

"Yes, but Mike, the way he said it was threatening," she answered.

"I believe you, but proving that in court would be difficult. No, Skylie, I think he did something else to cause the plane to make an emergency landing. Hopefully, I'll know what that is when my, uh, my attorney friend calls me after we get to Auckland." I had almost slipped and referred to Barry as *my attorney*. I didn't want to give her the wrong impression, and we weren't good enough friends that I wanted to go into an explanation of all my troubles.

"Will you tell me what you learn from your friend?" she asked, a hopeful look in her eyes.

"Of course I will." Then in an attempt to shift our focus a little bit, I reached down and pulled the brown leather bag from under the seat and lifted it onto my lap. Once again, I glanced at the lady next to Skylie. She still had her earphones on, and her movie showed two men in a heated argument. But her head was tipped back, her mouth hanging open and her eyes closed. "Must be a boring movie," I whispered to Skylie as I nodded my head in the woman's direction. She chuckled.

I glanced across the aisle and then at both the rows in front and behind. No one was paying any attention to us. I zipped the bag open, trying to appear as nonchalant as I could just in case someone did look our way. We both peered into the top of the bag, our heads nearly brushing each other's as we did so. The closeness of Skylie's face made me tingle. I pushed the feeling aside and concentrated on what I was seeing. Skylie reached over and pulled a girlie magazine out. It had clearly been the last thing the notorious Mr. Antony Bahr had shoved in the bag. "This is disgusting," Skylie said as she slipped it quickly out of sight in her seat pocket.

I mumbled my agreement and focused on what she had uncovered when she pulled out the magazine. It was a medium-sized manila envelope with Antony's name scribbled across the front. It was fairly thick. I looked at Skylie, and she asked, "Let's see what's in it, should we?"

Since that's exactly what I had intended to do, I opened the flap and reached in. The bundle I pulled out was almost a quarter of an inch thick. A folded note was stuck on top of another envelope filled with what felt like photographs. There was also a map of some location in New Zealand. Skylie reached for the map, and I let her take it.

"It's of a map of Wellington," she said. "Very detailed."

"Where's Wellington?" I asked.

"It's the city farthest to the south on the North Island. New Zealand is actually divided by the ocean. Auckland and Wellington are both on the North Island," she explained. "Wellington is our capital city."

There were some locations on the map that had been circled in red. I pointed to one of them. "Any idea what these are?" I asked.

"This is in the main business district of the city," she said, placing her finger on the area of the map I'd indicated.

"How familiar are you with Wellington? You are from Auckland, aren't you?"

She smiled at me. "What makes you think that?"

"I don't know," I replied sheepishly. "It's just that we are flying there, and I'm really not familiar with New Zealand cities."

"I grew up in Christchurch. That's the largest city on the South Island. It got hit really badly with an earthquake a few years ago. It was terrifying. People were killed. A lot of buildings collapsed; other buildings were damaged so badly they had to be torn down. Some damaged buildings are still standing, but the government condemned them, so they can't be used."

"Yeah, I remember that earthquake. It made the news in America. California is a bad area for earthquakes, so things like that get a lot of coverage there," I explained. "So you are actually headed back to Christchurch?"

"No, my foster parents moved to Wellington a couple of years ago. I'll be going back there."

"Sounds good," I said. "Let's hold on to that map."

Without a word she shoved it in the seat pocket in front of the girly magazine. I opened the note.

We read it together, and we were barely into it when I regretted that decision. She moaned and sank against my shoulder. "Oh, Mike!" she exclaimed. "This is terrible. What did I ever do to deserve this?"

"Nothing, I'm sure," I said. I folded the note back up and put my arm around her shoulder. I held her as she sobbed quietly for several minutes. Finally, I said, "Let me read the rest of the note, Skylie. You don't need to see it again."

She looked up at me, her eyes red and her face stricken. "He was supposed to kill me, wasn't he?"

FOUR

THAT WAS WHAT THE NOTE said. Someone had instructed Antony Bahr to learn everything he could from Skylie and then dispose of her. It was chilling, and my heart ached for my new friend. Giving her hand a squeeze, I said, "We won't let him. Anyway, he's in custody."

"That's not much comfort," she said. "He'll be loose again. And who knows, he probably has friends who'll do it for him." Her eyes dropped away from mine and down to the note as she spoke. I understood exactly what that look implied. Whoever wrote the note was also a threat to her.

"You close your eyes and try to relax while I read the rest of the note," I suggested.

But Skylie shook her head. "No, I want to read it all. It might explain what it is they think I've done to deserve . . . to make them want to . . . to murder me."

I shuddered at her words, and our eyes met again. I could see Skylie was made of pretty sturdy stuff. Though Antony scared her, she was obviously a brave person—and strong willed. My admiration of her grew. Together, we again began to read. I reread the offending paragraph: *Antony, when you find the girl, Skylie Yates, talk to her, make her tell you what she knows, then dispose of her. Don't let her convince you that she doesn't know, because she does. Of that I am certain.*

It was a chilling read, and it didn't get any better. In the next paragraph, the writer mentioned Skylie's brother, although it didn't refer to him by name.

Skylie looked up. "I don't have a brother, Mike. Whoever these guys are, they've got it wrong. It's all a big mistake."

I had a feeling it wasn't a mistake. Of course, I was thinking like a cop not a sympathetic friend at that point. "Maybe you do have a brother,

Skylie. Maybe you've just never been told about him. Maybe he bounced around in foster homes just like you did."

Her eyes grew wide, and her fingers grasped my arm. "I never thought of that. So maybe he's the reason I'm in trouble? I don't even know him."

That was exactly what I had been thinking. I simply nodded an acknowledgement and looked back down at the note.

What more we learned didn't help calm Skylie's frazzled nerves. The writer believed Skylie knew the location of a very large sum of money that had been taken by her brother and hidden somewhere in New Zealand. Her brother's name still wasn't mentioned, but it appeared he was suspected of having stolen from a violent Samoan gang in Auckland, and they would obviously do anything—including kill innocent people—to get it back. The note was signed with just one name—Hemana. I felt like I'd been hit by a thunderbolt as I stared at that name. Hemana was the name Cal had mentioned when I'd caught him speaking on his cell phone to someone in New Zealand.

I tried to hide my reaction from Skylie as I folded the note. "So when we get to New Zealand, we need to find out if you do in fact have a brother, and if so, who he is and where we can find him." What I didn't tell her was that I wanted to find this Hemana as well.

"Mike, this isn't your problem," she said. "You don't have to do this for me."

"No, I don't. But you won't turn down my help, will you?" I smiled at her.

Her chin quivered as she spoke. "I guess not, but it could be dangerous."

"I've been shot before," I said brashly. "I can handle danger."

"Oh, Mike. You've been shot?" she asked as her face went pale and her eyes grew big as saucers.

"Just grazed," I said, feeling foolish for mentioning it even as I touched the scar left by the bullet. "I'm okay now. But I only mentioned that to let you know that I can handle a little danger."

"You don't have to worry much about getting shot again," Skylie said. "It's illegal for people to own guns in New Zealand. The only people who have them are hunters, and they have to have special permits."

I already knew that, and it was something I personally disagreed with. If some people had their way, guns would be illegal in the US as well. But that would never keep criminals from having and using them. I suspected that was also the case in New Zealand. I said, "I would guess that criminals could get them. I don't suppose they worry about what's legal or not any more than criminals in America do."

She shrugged. "Maybe, but there isn't a lot of crime in my country. You don't read about a lot of shootings. In fact, we hardly hear of any. That's especially true outside of Auckland."

"What about cops having to shoot people. Does that happen very much?" I asked.

"No, but I wouldn't expect it to. The police don't carry guns either."

"What!" I exclaimed. "Cops don't carry guns? That's insane."

She shrugged her shoulders. "I don't think they need them much. Some police officers have them in the trunks of their cars, but they can't carry them on their sides or under their jackets like you cops in America do."

I was stunned, but I didn't say any more about it. Instead I said, "One way or the other, we'll figure out if you have a brother, and if so, we'll see if we can locate him."

She shook her head. "How can we do that? There are four million people in New Zealand."

That didn't worry me. I'd found a lot of wanted men and women in Los Angeles, and there were more people in that city alone than in all of New Zealand. I simply said, "I'm a detective, Skylie. I know how to go about it."

She favored me with a smile then said, "Sorry, Mike. And, yes, I'd like your help. Now are we going to see what's in the smaller envelope?"

I opened it and pulled out the contents. They were photographs. The very top one was of Skylie. It was a full body shot of her walking on a sidewalk with a handful of books. She gasped, clearly shaken.

"I guess that means it was taken without your knowledge. Can you tell where it was taken?"

"It's on campus, but I don't remember anyone getting close enough to me to take a picture like that without me knowing."

"It was probably taken with a telephoto lens from quite some distance."

"Oh, of course," she said. "I guess there are more like it in that stack."

She was right. Every picture was of her. All but two were candid shots. Most of them had been taken on campus. One was of her as she stepped out of her dorm room with a roommate; another had been taken as she was standing in the checkout line at a grocery store near campus.

I noticed she was wearing the same yellow blouse and tight blue jeans in each snapshot. I pointed it out to her. "Did you always wear the same clothes every day?" I asked with a grin I hoped would release some of her tension.

It didn't, for she trembled slightly. "That was a new blouse. I only wore it once before I left." She looked up at me. "These pictures were all taken on the same day, weren't they?"

"If you only wore it once, then I guess that would be the case," I agreed. "Are you sure?"

She nodded. "Yes, Mike, I'm sure. It was the same day Antony confronted me and hurt my friend. I remember because I got his blood on my blouse."

"So these others were obviously taken earlier in the day."

She rubbed her chin for a moment, her eyes seeming to focus on the seat in front of her. I watched her intently. She finally spoke slowly, without looking toward me. "Kris, my roommate, and I bought groceries that morning. Then I went to class, and it was after coming out of that class that this picture must have been taken." She pulled the one of her with books in her hand from the bottom of the pile. "After that, I had lunch at the student union building." She pulled out another of the snapshots. "This one must have been taken when I was walking toward it."

She recounted her day, determining when each of the pictures had been taken. Finally she picked up the two photographs that were professionally done. "These were taken in New Zealand. They are two of several that were taken of me and of Rongo and Marama Parata, my foster parents. Some of them were of us together, and others were of me alone or of them as a couple. But I don't know how Antony would have gotten them. We keep them in an album in our house."

"They were obviously stolen," I said. "We'll talk to the Paratas about that when we see them. Maybe their house was burglarized."

"Maybe," she said, "but surely they would have mentioned it to me in a letter or something."

We didn't get a chance to discuss it more before an announcement was made over the aircraft's sound system. "Will a passenger by the name of Mike Denton please come forward? You will be met in the front of the aircraft and escorted to the cabin. The captain needs to speak with you."

"What in the world," I mumbled. "Here, put these away," I told Skylie. "We'll explore the bag more when I get back."

Her eyes were wide, and the worry lines on her forehead were deeper. "Why does the captain want to talk to you?"

"I'm sure it's nothing," I lied, feeling a little twinge of guilt, but I felt like I needed to keep her from worrying more than she already was. There was no way the pilot would want to speak to a passenger if it wasn't something important.

She seemed slightly reassured. "Don't be long," she said. "I want to see what else is in this bag."

I touched her shoulder lightly and then headed for the front of the plane. I was met by a flight attendant and directed up the stairs to the upper deck. A minute later, I found myself looking into the dark-brown eyes of a tall, slender man of about fifty.

He smiled as he held out his hand, offering to shake mine. "I'm Captain Brandon Vaughn," he said with a twinkle in his eyes and a strong New Zealand accent. "I hope I didn't alarm you. I know it's unusual for a captain to ask to speak to a passenger."

"I've never known of it to happen," I agreed. "What's the matter?"

The twinkle left his eyes, and he invited me to sit down. "I've had my copilot take over so I could speak to you. Detective Denton, I have to tell you something that may alarm you a little bit. Your boss had a message delivered to me."

"Captain Bertrand?" I asked.

"No, the Los Angeles police chief," Captain Vaughn clarified.

"Okay," I said, trying not to let the alarm I was feeling come through in my voice. "What did he want?"

"He said you need to know that your former partner, Detective Cal Granberg, has been fired, and your sergeant, Sam Hart has been suspended pending further investigation." The pilot kept his eyes locked on mine. "Now, I don't know what that's all about, but I suppose you do."

"Yes," I said, my head spinning. "It's a bit of a surprise though. Granberg and Hart are both crooked cops. I thought they had the brass totally snowed."

"Apparently not," Captain Vaughn said. "The chief said to extend his apology to you for the way you were treated because of the two of them."

"That was all he wanted to tell me?" I asked. "My attorney could have told me that after we landed in Auckland. I was supposed to call him then."

"Actually that wasn't all. He asked me to tell you that you might be in danger," Captain Vaughn added. "That's the real reason for the unusual communication."

I clenched my fists in an attempt to keep my hands from shaking. I looked away for a moment, and then I again looked into the pilot's eyes. "What kind of danger?" I asked.

"Apparently Granberg made some calls to Auckland. The chief has reason to believe that an ambush may be awaiting you when you disembark in Auckland. At the chief's request, I'm taking measures to protect you. There will be a security team awaiting our arrival," he said. That confirmed my suspicions that Cal had shady ties to New Zealand. "He suggested you wait in the airport and catch the next available flight back to LA," the captain concluded.

I shook my head. *No way am I falling for that,* I thought with some alarm. If they wanted me back, it had to be bad news for me. The chief's apology suddenly rang hollow. "No, I'm taking a vacation, and I don't intend to return to LA until it's over."

The captain smiled. "He thought you might say that. In that case, all I can promise is that our security people will safely escort you away from the airport. I wish I could tell you more, but I don't have any information on who might be waiting there—if anyone. I'm sorry to be giving you unpleasant news."

"At least Cal got what he had coming," I said with bitterness in my voice.

"There must have been some bad blood between you two," Captain Vaughn said.

"He let me get shot," I retorted. "But he never admitted it. I guess it's caught up with him now." What I didn't say was that I wasn't reassured that the brass was ready to let me go back to work. I'd wait until I got confirmation of that from Barry before I returned home.

"Are you okay now?" the captain asked sympathetically.

"I'm fine. So is that all you know?"

"Yes, it is. But I do have a request for you. After we land in Auckland, I need you to wait while all other passengers leave the plane. That way, I can be sure you get the escort you need. In fact, I'll meet you before you leave the plane."

"Okay, thank you, sir," I said, but then I thought about Skylie and the danger she was in. I decided he needed to know about that. "Sir, there is something else."

"What's that, Detective?"

"When we stopped in Hawaii, a passenger was arrested there. Do you know what that was all about?"

"Yes. He was considered extremely dangerous and needed to be removed from the plane," he responded, eyeing me closely. "He's wanted back in Los Angeles. Do you know something about him?"

"I do, sir. His name is Antony Bahr. He threatened a passenger, a college student who's heading home to Wellington, Skylie Yates. I'll be keeping her back with me when we get to Auckland because I've promised to help her find out what's going on. I'll want to stay close to her when we get off the plane."

"So that's why you want to stay instead of returning to LA," the captain said, winking at me. He had me there. I was becoming more interested in helping Skylie than looking into Cal's activities, especially now that I knew he'd lost his job. The captain leaned back, rubbed his eyes, and then leaned forward again. "Antony Bahr is wanted in LA for attempted murder," he said. "Do you or the young lady, Miss Yates, know anything about that?"

I explained about the assault on Skylie's friend. "But I don't think that can be considered attempted murder; they didn't even go to the police for several days after the assault."

Captain Vaughn shook his head. "He was wanted for shooting a cop. He was arrested at one point, but somehow he managed to get away. Next thing we know, he's on this plane. I'm sure you can find out more about that when you talk to your attorney or your boss."

"I hope so." We both stood, and I thanked the captain.

He again shook my hand and said, "I'll see you and Miss Yates after we land in Auckland, Detective. I'm sorry about the trouble."

FIVE

TENSION SEEMED TO POUR FROM Skylie's face when I returned to my seat. "Is everything okay?" she asked.

"He's a nice guy. His name is Captain Vaughn."

"What did he want?"

"My boss at the LAPD had a message for me. No big deal," I lied. Once again, I justified the lie because I didn't want to cause her to worry any more than she already was. "Let's find out what else is in that bag of Antony's."

Skylie scowled. "Mike, there's something you're not telling me. Please."

I thought quickly and then made a decision. "I did ask Captain Vaughn about Antony Bahr's arrest in Honolulu."

"Oh, really? What did he say?" After I explained what Antony had done, she said, "He shot a cop. He really would have killed me, wouldn't he?"

"He's a dangerous man; that's for sure," I said as I picked up his bag again. There was nothing else of interest in it, but at least I had managed to divert Skylie's questions about my visit with the captain. I thought a lot about the message he'd passed along, particularly the part about Cal having made calls to New Zealand. What were they all about? Who were they made to? Could he have called the man named Hemana? When did he make the calls? I had a lot of questions, but I tried to shove them from my mind.

The rest of the flight was relatively pleasant. Skylie and I were both tired and dozed off and on. We ate our meals, chatted with each other, and watched a movie. When Skylie fell asleep, leaning against my shoulder, a couple of hours from Auckland, I relaxed and enjoyed her closeness. I wished there wasn't so much danger ahead of us. It would be nice if I could spend my time in New Zealand just getting to know this girl better.

She awoke as we were making the descent into Auckland. "Did you have a good nap?" I asked when she straightened up and began to brush her long blonde hair with her fingers.

She smiled at me, a smile I could get to like a lot. "I did. Thanks for the use of your shoulder."

"Anytime," I answered with a grin, meaning every word. Our eyes locked, and we simply gazed at each other for a moment. My spine tingled, a feeling I hadn't experienced for a long time. I liked it.

We turned our phones on after our plane had pulled up to the terminal. My stomach was rolling. The problems that lay ahead weren't what I had anticipated when I decided to fly to New Zealand. Yes, I'd wanted to try to find out what Cal and Sam were up to, but it had become much more than that now. I tried to hide my worries from my pretty seatmate. "We'll wait to get off the plane until after everyone else has already left," I told Skylie. "The captain wanted to see us before we leave. He will be waiting for us."

She crinkled her eyes in surprise. "Why would he want to do that?" she asked.

"I guess he's worried about you and wants to make sure you aren't bothered by anyone like you were in Hawaii," I suggested, keeping the real reason to myself.

"That's nice of him." She relaxed back in her seat and began to punch a number into her phone. "I think I'll call Rongo and let him know I'm here."

"That would be great," I said as I began to make a call of my own.

When Barry answered, he asked, "Did you have an uneventful flight after Honolulu?"

I chuckled. "What do you think?"

"You mean other than the police chief contacting your pilot?" he asked with his own chuckle. But then he got down to business. "Listen, Mike, even though the LAPD fired Cal Granberg, they still haven't cleared you to go back to work. They want to make sure you're emotionally and psychologically ready first. I was hoping you wouldn't agree to come right back like they want you to. You didn't agree to that, did you?"

"Definitely not. Tell me more about what to expect when I get off the plane," I said as I glanced at Skylie; she was totally engrossed in her own phone call. "What do you think Granberg has set up?"

"I have no idea. I'm not sure the chief didn't blow it way out of proportion in the hope to get you to return right away," he told me. "I'll keep working to get them to clear you to go back to work. With Granberg off the force and Hart suspended, I would think that they'd listen to a little reason now."

"I hope so," I agreed.

He changed the subject. "I've learned more about the man who was arrested in Honolulu," he said. "His name is Antony Bahr. He shot a cop who was attempting to serve an arrest warrant on him. The cop will recover, but Antony will be coming back here to face attempted murder charges."

I basically already knew that, but I didn't tell Barry. Instead I asked, "So what questions did the chief want to ask me?"

The first ones were simple questions that had to do with Cal's behavior the day I was shot as well as my feelings when I lost my son and then my wife. Barry explained that they'd already come to realize Cal had lied about the day I was shot and a lot more since then. That was the reason he was terminated. The other questions were, according to Barry, designed to see how much I liked my job and how dedicated I was to returning to work.

"Police work is my life, Barry," I told him. "I very much want to get back to work. I think I'm pretty good at what I do, and I'm working hard to improve. Will you tell the chief that?"

He agreed that he would, and then he said, "Mike, you have a good time there, and we'll keep in touch. I'm certain everything will work out with your job here. But do be careful, just in case Granberg is worse than we think he is, in case he's as bad as you suspect he may be."

After my call was finished, I noticed that Skylie was looking at me with a frown on her face. "Is something wrong?" I asked.

"You tell me, Mike," she said with a touch of anger. "Unless you're totally honest with me, I don't think I want you to help me."

"What are you talking about?" I asked, knowing exactly what the problem was.

"What did the pilot really want to talk to you about?" she asked. "I didn't mean to eavesdrop while you were talking to your attorney friend, but I know there's something you aren't telling me."

She had me. As I gazed at her, I decided I needed to be more open with her because she needed my help and because I wanted to spend more time with her. "Okay, you're right, and I'm sorry. I'll tell you, but I don't want you to worry, Skylie. There isn't time to tell you everything right now. Captain Vaughn will be waiting for us. But I promise I'll tell you everything when we get away from the airport."

The scowl remained. "I want to trust you, Mike."

"And I want you to," I responded. "So smile, and I'll tell you as much as I can before we have to meet the pilot."

She did smile, but it wasn't the bright smile I'd hoped for. People were moving slowly past us as we waited. I said, "There is a detective I worked with in Los Angeles that I've had trouble with. He was my partner. He's the reason I got shot. He's a liar and a cheat—a dirty cop."

"What do you mean by that?"

"I mean I think he's taking money from crooks—bribes. I can't prove it yet, but I suspect it. He was contacting people here in New Zealand and talking to them about guns. One man he talked to, he called Hemana."

"That's the name of the guy who wrote the letter to Antony," she said, her face twisting with worry.

"That's right. Anyway, my partner convinced my supervisors that I wasn't fit to work. So they told me to take some time off with the requirement that I undergo some psychological tests before I go back to work—but they won't let me take those tests for at least a month. My attorney friend is more than just a friend. He is actually my attorney, and this trip was his idea. My bosses didn't want me to come, although they didn't tell me I couldn't."

Skylie began to wring her hands, and she looked sad as well as worried. "They're making you go back now, aren't they?"

"Oh no, Skylie," I said firmly. "That's not it at all. They want me to go back to LA now, but they aren't telling me I have to. My attorney is advising me not to. The reason the captain called me was to warn me that my former partner has been fired and my sergeant suspended. I don't know how they did it, but they found out that Cal was lying. After they fired him, they found out that he had made some calls to here in Auckland. The chief of police thinks Cal might have been stirring up trouble for me here. My attorney thinks they've exaggerated it. The pilot has arranged for security to get you and me away from the airport safely. That's why we need to meet him."

The plane was nearly empty. "I'll tell you the rest, but it's got to be later. Right now we need to get our bags and go meet the captain."

"There's danger for you as well as for me, isn't there?" she asked.

"Maybe, but probably not. Anyway, I've got you to watch my back, if you will. And I'll watch yours," I said.

"Do you mean it?" she asked, a hopeful gleam in her eyes.

"Yes, I do mean it. If you agree, we'll be partners, or mates, as you say here, until we get through our troubles." I smiled at her.

"I'd like that, but what kind of vacation will you have? It doesn't sound like much fun for you," she said.

"Being with you will make it worth it," I said, surprised at my own intensity.

We got to our feet and began to gather our things. I grabbed Antony's bag, and she shoved the map back in it, leaving the girly magazine in the seat pocket. "We'll take this bag of Antony's with us. Do you think that's okay?"

"If you do," she said.

"I do, but we don't want Captain Vaughn to know what it is," I added.

Skylie placed her carry-on bag on a seat near us and turned to me. Impulsively, she threw her arms around me and hugged me tightly. It felt good. I mean, it felt *really* good. "Thanks for that," I said when she released me. "Let's go."

"My foster parents will be waiting for us at the baggage claim area. We can ride with them to our home down in Wellington," she said. "You can stay with us there if you'd like."

"That sounds really good," I agreed. Wow! What more could I ask?

As promised, Captain Vaughn was waiting for us when we approached the exit. I introduced Skylie to him, and he grinned at me. "She's pretty, Mike. I don't blame you for wanting to help her. Oh to be young again. Now, Detective, have you explained to Miss Yates what's happening?"

"I have," I said. "Her folks are waiting for us at the baggage claim area. They are Māori. They aren't Skylie's natural parents—in case the security people need to know that."

"I'll make sure they do, and they will be near you, both uniformed and plainclothes officers. You young people be careful now," he said as he ushered us off the plane and to the gate, where the security officers were waiting. He introduced us to them and then turned and walked back onto the plane.

I took a deep breath and looked around, hoping I could spot any lurking danger in time to avoid it. I'd be lying if I said I wasn't worried, but I felt obligated to my companion, and I didn't plan to let her down if I could help it.

When we approached the baggage claim area, I was especially alert. Skylie was watching for her foster parents. When she waved to them,

I noticed a man standing a short distance behind the couple. He kept looking at the two of them like he knew who they were. That alarmed me. He was a slender man of medium height, and something about him looked familiar. I caught the eye of one of the airport security officers. I nodded in the direction of the Paratas and mouthed, "The man in the flowered shirt. Watch him."

The officer nodded and slipped toward another officer. The two spoke briefly as Skylie pushed her way through the crowd toward the Paratas. I stayed with her, so close we were almost touching. My eyes, though still roving the crowd, were also trying to keep track of the man in the flowered shirt. When we were almost to the Paratas, I let Skylie move a little farther ahead of me, and I watched the man. His eyes followed Skylie. He didn't seem to be paying any attention to me. So with my free hand, I casually aimed my iPhone at him and snapped a picture. I put the cell phone quickly back in my pocket and hurriedly closed the gap between Skylie and me.

"Skylie, my dear!" Marama Parata cried out as she threw her arms lovingly around the younger woman. The man in the flowered shirt closed in. But just as I was ready to drop my bags and tackle the guy, two of the security men stepped in front of him, blocking his path. The guy shoved one of them. The other security guy grabbed the man's arm, twisted it behind his back, and both officers dragged him away.

It was the look of anger on the man's face that jolted me with recognition. He looked startlingly like Antony Bahr, minus the scar. I was almost certain that he had to be a younger brother to Antony. That recognition alarmed me, but rather than watching the security men hustle him away, I again scanned the people around us for others who might present a danger.

I felt a tug on my arm and glanced at Skylie. "Marama and Rongo, this is the man I told you about on the phone. His name is Mike Denton. Mike, this is my family."

The two older Māori people beamed at me and said in unison, "It's nice to meet you, Mr. Denton." Their Kiwi accents, like Skylie's, were very charming. I liked them instantly, but even as I acknowledged them, I continued to watch for danger.

Skylie must have noticed that I was distracted, for she leaned close to my ear and asked, "Did you see something that has you worried?"

"Yes, but the security officers already got to him," I said quickly.

"What was he doing?" she asked, her face going white. She had apparently been so excited to see Rongo and Marama that she hadn't noticed the scuffle.

"He was watching you and your folks. I might be wrong, but he looked like he could be Antony's brother. He's no longer a threat," I said in an attempt to soothe her. "But there could be others. We need to get our luggage and get out of here."

Her family, as she called the Paratas, picked up on Skylie's fright and closed in tightly. Rongo relieved her of her carry-on bag and said, "The young man is right. Let's get your luggage as quickly as we can and get you home. We will stay right here beside you."

From experience, I knew getting the suitcases would not be fast. It never was. It certainly wasn't an exception that day. It was ten interminable minutes before we finally spotted my one medium-sized suitcase and her two very large ones on the turntable. I was grateful when two uniformed security officers stepped close and offered to help us get our bags to the Paratas' car. I was tense the entire time and didn't relax until we were in the short-term parking area, had loaded our bags, and were driving toward the exit. Even then I stayed alert.

Once we were out of the airport parking lot, Skylie, who was sitting close beside me in the backseat and gripping my arm with one hand, said, "Do you think there was more than that one man?"

"I hope not," I replied. "I didn't see anyone else who seemed interested in either one of us—except for a few young men who couldn't keep their eyes off you." That wasn't entirely a jest. I had seen one fellow a couple of times. Both times he'd been watching Skylie, even leering at her. He was a little taller than me and a lot heavier. He had longish, bushy black hair and dark-brown eyes. He wasn't a bad-looking man, but I'd dismissed him as someone who simply looked at Skylie because she was attractive.

From the front seat, I heard a hearty chuckle from Rongo. "The young men always look at our Skylie. Do you blame them?"

I didn't—she was indeed nice to look at. I glanced at her then and said, "None of them seemed threatening, just lecherous."

She punched me lightly on the shoulder. "Well, there were plenty of girls looking at you—and glaring at me."

My cell phone rang as I grinned at her. I pulled it from my pocket and looked at the screen. It was Barry. What in the world did he have to tell me now?

"Barry, I didn't expect to hear from you so soon," I said. "Has something come up?"

"Yes, I'm afraid so. It seems that Cal Granberg has disappeared. He was supposed to come and turn in all of his equipment but failed to do so. They've been trying to call him, but he's not answering his phone. They contacted Sergeant Hart, and he claims he hasn't heard from Cal. It may mean nothing, but I just wanted you to know."

"I appreciate it," I responded as I took a peek at my watch. It was almost ten o'clock AM, which meant it was nearly two o'clock PM in Los Angeles. The diversion to Honolulu had only cost us about three hours. "He's probably sulking somewhere. And he has a habit of being late. I was always waiting for him. What time was he supposed to turn his stuff in?"

"At ten o'clock this morning. He's four hours late and not answering the calls from Captain Bertrand," Barry reported. "Bertrand called to let me know. But that isn't the only thing I called about. I spoke with the police chief just after I talked to you this morning. I gave him your responses to his questions, and he said he wanted to consider them. I didn't hear back from him, but Captain Bertrand said he, the chief, and a couple of other senior officers had a conference and decided to clear you to come back to work immediately. In the meantime, they're looking closer at the activities of both Hart and Granberg."

"Wow, that's great news," I said. "What about the psych exam?"

"You won't need it," Barry said. "They feel bad for the inconvenience this forced time off has caused you—they refuse to call it a suspension. Bertrand says they realize now that the entire problem was with Granberg and Hart, not with you. They've offered a settlement, which I took the liberty of telling them you would consider. Of course, I won't finalize things without your permission. The settlement gives you a ten thousand–dollar bonus and pays me for my time. In addition to that, they'll continue to pay you your full salary until you're back to work. They'd like you to wrap up your vacation and report for duty a week from tomorrow."

When he finished I wasn't ready to respond yet. I was still digesting everything he'd told me. Now that I was in New Zealand, I was in no hurry to go home. I really wanted time to see the country. I had already seen enough as I was riding with the Paratas to be convinced it was an absolutely spectacular place. But that wasn't all. I felt obligated to Skylie. I didn't want to leave her without helping resolve her problems and see that the danger she was in was cleared up. And I still wanted to follow up on Cal's interest in New Zealand. I had no idea how long those matters would take.

I was still mulling things over when Barry said, "Mike, are you there? Did you hear what I told you? Your job's waiting for you. You have a week to enjoy New Zealand, and then you need to report back for duty."

"I heard you, Barry. I appreciate what you've done for me. And I'm grateful for all your hard work. You must have put some pressure on them to get this all resolved so quickly."

Barry chuckled lightly. "You could say that. As I'm sure you know, I can be quite persuasive. They wanted you back to work sooner, but I convinced them that you should at least have some time to enjoy the country you flew so far to visit."

"I appreciate that," I said. "And I do want to see a lot of this country. To be back to work in a week would mean that I need to fly out of here in about five days. That's not much time. I could sure use a little more."

"Well, I can try, but I had to talk pretty hard to get you what I got, Mike. I'd be lucky to squeak out even another couple of days, but I'll try if that's what you want."

"Please, if you would do that, I'd be grateful. If you can't get those extra days, then I'll just have to see what I can do," I said, hedging a little. I would just have to work hard and see if, with Skylie's help, I could get to the bottom of things here in the next few days. If not, well, I didn't know what I'd do.

"What about the settlement money?" he asked.

"I was shot, Barry," I said. "Is that all that nearly losing my life is worth?"

"Good point," he said. "I'll see that you get the ten thousand but let them know we'll be expecting more later on. We can talk about that when you come home."

After the call was ended, I rode in silence for several minutes. Finally Skylie nudged me. "Are you going to tell me what that call was all about?"

"Sure," I said. "That was my attorney. He got me reinstated. I've been cleared with an apology from the department and have been offered a little money for the trouble they caused me. It's good news."

"Mike, I realize that we barely know each other, but I can tell something's bothering you. It's the short time you have before you have to return, right?"

"Yeah."

"And it's more than just wanting to see more of the country, isn't it? You feel like you have to help me."

"That's not it, Skylie," I said.

Before I could explain further, a flash of anger darkened her face. "So you don't want to help me? Well, please, don't mess up your career because of me."

I took her hand in mine and looked directly in her eyes. "Skylie, I know I don't have to help you. That's not the problem at all. The problem is that I *want* to help you. Your problem has become mine. There's no way I'm leaving you here to face this alone. I, uh, I like you, and I'll do whatever I can to free you of the danger you're in."

Rongo Parata looked over his shoulder at me. "And we appreciate your willingness to help our girl. Marama and I will help in any way we can." He glanced back at the road and then spoke once more. "We need to find a place to spend the night. Marama and I are quite tired. Do you young people mind if we find a motel somewhere and then drive on to Wellington tomorrow morning?"

"That's fine with me," I said.

"That would be great," Skylie agreed.

"Then why don't we spend a few hours on the road and stop somewhere along the way. When we get back home tomorrow, we need to sit down and go over everything—the four of us. Then, under your direction, we'll get to work and get Skylie out of this mess."

I wasn't sure what the Paratas could do, but I appreciated the gesture. And perhaps they could assist in some way, like making phone calls. I'd have to see. I didn't want them to be in danger too.

I was still holding Skylie's hand, and she squeezed it tightly, leaning gently against my shoulder. "You are a great guy, Mike," she said. "I am so glad I met you."

Not any more glad than I was. I really didn't look forward to wrapping things up in New Zealand and flying home in a few days—alone.

"So, if you don't mind my folks listening in, I'd sure like to hear all about you and what led to your flying down here."

I didn't mind the Paratas listening in. And at this point I was comfortable with sharing my story, sad and wretched as it was. So, starting with the illness of my son, I began to speak.

SIX

FORMER DETECTIVE CAL GRANBERG WAS a bitter man. He was sitting in his favorite bar sipping a beer in the midafternoon. His anger at his former partner was simmering in his rancorous mind. Across the table sat his best friend and cousin, Wilson Blanco.

Blanco was a sympathetic listener. He too was angry that Cal had lost his job with the LAPD. That made it much harder for Wilson to operate his *business*. He'd always been able to count on Cal to grease things for him with the department when that business drew the attention of the cops. Wilson owned and operated a body shop, but that was only a front for what made his real work lucrative. He received and altered, meaning *chopped*, stolen vehicles. He'd been at it for fifteen years, since he was twenty-three. With Cal's help he also bought and sold stolen guns on the black market. During all of those years, Cal had received a generous amount of money under the table for running interference for him and even helping dispose of stolen items at times. With Cal off the force, it was going to be more difficult for Wilson to stay out of jail. Like Cal, he blamed his troubles on Detective Mike Denton.

Both men took another sip of their beers and then set them on the table. "So when are you going to turn in your gear, Cal?" Wilson asked. "I know you said they wanted it this morning, but since you didn't do it then, when will you?"

"Probably won't," Cal growled. "They already took my badge, police ID, and service weapon. I think I'll just keep everything else."

"Don't blame you." Wilson wiped his grease-stained hand across his mouth. "Have they tried to call you?"

"Only about a dozen times. I'm not answering my phone. Fact is, I think I'll just trash it and get a new one. They could track me with this one if they wanted to, and I think I'll take a little trip out of the country. I don't want them to know where I'm going."

Wilson leaned back and rubbed his generous belly. "Could you use a traveling companion?"

Cal grinned and took another swig of beer as Wilson did the same. Then he said, "I'm counting on it."

"Sounds like fun. When do we leave?"

"Within the next day or two, if we can get a flight to New Zealand. Apparently Denton is going to be allowed to go back to work, but only if he manages to return to the states. I think you and I can see to it that he's not able to do that," Cal said with a growl. "Anyway, a trip to New Zealand would be good for business. We could check out our customers down there firsthand."

"Yeah, that would be good. We can do that and take care of Mike in one trip. We can't have him snooping around down there."

Cal scowled. "I really can't wait to get my hands on that guy. It's time his luck runs out. He should have been dead when he got shot. It was just my luck your shot was so bad. You should have killed him that day."

"I tried, and I thought I had. But some guy stuck his head out of the house across the street. I couldn't risk taking another shot, so I split. Mike was just lucky. He won't be so lucky next time," Wilson noted with a grin. "Between us, we'll make sure he doesn't ever leave New Zealand."

Cal nodded. "They don't allow guns down there, but I would guess that we should be able to find somebody who can help us overcome that little obstacle. You and I know exactly who to go to for guns in New Zealand." He chuckled.

"Shouldn't be too hard," Wilson agreed. "They'll either provide us what we need, or we'll cut off their supply from here."

A few minutes later, the men left the bar and headed to Wilson's shop. There they had Wilson's secretary make reservations on Air New Zealand for the two of them. They got lucky. Their flight left the next evening. Wilson pulled a couple of beers out of the refrigerator in his office, and the two of them went back to drinking.

Not too long after that, the secretary buzzed Wilson's office and told him that some cops were coming in. Cal said, "I don't think anyone at the department knows that you and I know each other, but just in case, I'm going to go out back until they leave. Call me when they're gone."

"Not to worry, Cal. I'll send them packing," Wilson promised as Cal headed for the door.

The officers were in fact looking for Cal. Wilson told them that they had nothing to do with each other and that he most definitely had not seen Cal. When asked, he admitted that they were cousins but insisted they hadn't had anything to do with each other for years.

The officers finally left, and Wilson gave Cal a call. "They're gone," he reported, "but I think you definitely better get rid of that phone."

"Did they track me here by the GPS on my phone?" Cal asked as he left his hiding spot behind the garage and started back inside.

"They didn't say that, but I don't know why else they thought you were here. Of course, they did know that we're cousins. They might be talking to all your relatives." Wilson put down the phone as Cal walked back in.

The two men talked for a while longer, downed a couple more beers, and then Cal got ready to leave. "Guess I'll go home and get to packing," he said.

"Ah, Cal, I don't think that'd be such a good idea. They'll probably be watching for you at your house. You're a cop. You should know that," Wilson chided.

"*Was* a cop, but you're right," Cal admitted. "I guess I'll find a hotel room. But I'll need a ride. You'll have to send someone to go pack a suitcase for me."

"That might not be such a good idea either. Your old buddies could be watching your place—" Wilson began, but Cal cut him off.

"What will they do?" Cal asked. "Arrest someone for going to my house? I don't think so."

"Maybe not, but if one of my employees goes there—and I don't know who else we'd send—they'll follow him when he takes your suitcase to you and figure out where you're staying. Are you sure it wouldn't be better to just turn your stuff in? Then they'll forget about you, and nobody will care where you go or what you do. And you and I can continue our business without pressure from the PD."

Cal thought about that for a moment. "Maybe you're right, Wilson. I'll give Captain Bertrand a call and tell him that something came up but that I'll bring in the rest of my gear in an hour or two. That should get them off my back."

Cal sat right there and made the call. When he'd finished, he said, "Captain Bertrand said that would be fine. He'll be expecting me. Now I should be able to go home without them bugging me. Could you give me a ride back to the bar to get my car? I need to go home, drink some coffee, and take something to get the booze smell off my breath. Then I'll gather up the stuff Bertrand wants."

While riding back to the bar, the two men discussed the upcoming flight to New Zealand and made a few plans.

"I hope we can find Mike," Wilson said. "New Zealand isn't a huge country, but it might not be easy finding him."

"I don't think we need to worry about that. Our customers will give us a hand. We'll find him, all right."

* * *

Sitting in jail was not what Antony Bahr had planned to be doing. He only shot that cop because he was going to arrest him. And how the cops knew he was on the plane to New Zealand was a mystery. They must have asked airport security to watch for him. At any rate, he had to find some way of getting out of jail, and he would prefer that it be while he was still in Hawaii. If they got him extradited back to California, it might not be so easy. Of course, even if he did manage to escape, traveling might be a problem. The cops in Honolulu had taken his passport. One thing at a time, he told himself. He'd gotten himself out of serious scrapes before. He could do it again.

Right now what he needed was to get in touch with his brother in Auckland. It was time to make another phone call. He'd been permitted one call when they first arrested him. That had been to his brother—collect, of course, as that was all that was allowed. He wanted to find out if his brother had managed to find the girl, Skylie, after she got off the plane. They'd taken his watch, but they hadn't yet served lunch, so he knew it was still morning. Auckland was an hour difference in time from Honolulu—an hour and a day, actually, but the day didn't matter. Perhaps Tristan would be home by now, the information obtained and the girl disposed of.

Antony rattled his cell door to get a jailer's attention. Ten minutes later he was escorted to a phone and left to make his call. He hoped the calls weren't recorded, but it was a chance he would have to take. He began to dial. If only his brother was at home.

Luck was on his side for a change. Tristan answered on the third ring.

"Did you get her?" Antony asked as soon as Tristan had accepted the charges.

"No. You didn't tell me they'd have security watching her at the airport, Antony. They grabbed me before I got to her. The old Māori couple was with her, but they wouldn't have been a problem. She didn't even see me, but the security officers did."

Antony was shaking his head. He couldn't imagine why they would provide security for Skylie at the airport. He was quite stunned. "They must not have arrested you or you wouldn't be home," Antony reasoned. "So what happened?"

"I hadn't done anything, so they couldn't arrest me, but they threatened to, held me for a half an hour, and finally cut me loose. Of course, by then the girl and the old couple were gone."

He took a moment to collect his thoughts. "Did she have someone with her? If she did, I never noticed it when she was on the plane. I was sitting close to her, and she didn't seem to know anyone."

Tristan took time to think about the question. Finally he said, "There was a guy that was sort of walking behind her at the airport. He was close at first, and then he dropped back. I didn't pay a lot of attention to him. I did notice that he was carrying two carry-on bags." Tristan paused for a moment. "Hey, did you take that brown leather carry-on when you flew to LA? You know, the one with your name on it?"

"Yes, it was on the plane when I was arrested at the airport here in Honolulu. Who knows what the airline will do with it. It had the girl's pictures in it—both the ones I took of her in Los Angeles, and the ones I took out of the Paratas' house. Why do you ask?"

"The man I mentioned, the one with two carry-ons, one of them was brown, and it was shaped like yours. What if it was yours?" Tristan asked.

"That could explain a lot if some guy had snooped in my bag. The letter from Hemana was in there. And of course, they would have figured out who I was," Antony said as he slammed his hand against the wall. "I messed up. Hemana won't like that."

"Don't worry, Antony. I won't tell him. So if that guy is with Skylie, I need to figure out who he is. Are you sure he wasn't somewhere close to the girl on the plane?" Tristan pressed.

"I'm sure, but I just remembered, she was standing by a guy when the cops arrested me at the airport," Antony recalled. "What did the guy look like, the one that had my bag?"

"I just said it could have been."

"Yeah, yeah, I get it, so describe him to me."

"I didn't look too closely at him, but he was quite a bit younger than me and had short hair, quite dark. That's about all I can remember."

"The guy I saw had short dark hair too," Antony said. "You've got to find him. He's probably with the girl and the old Māori couple. You need to head for Wellington. That's where Skylie is from. Her brother's probably from down there too. Does Hemana know I'm in jail?"

"Yeah, he knows. The whole gang knows. He's not happy."

"Call him, Tristan. Maybe he'll feel better if he gets an update on Skylie," Antony said. "Tell him that, and also tell him you're going to Wellington."

"Hemana's down there now. He and a couple of his guys were going down last night. He's going to make a visit to the couple's house."

"Good. Call him, tell him what you know, and then do whatever he asks. Got that?" Antony asked.

"Got it," Tristan said. "And you better spend your time trying to figure out a way to get out of jail."

"I know. It won't be easy, but I do have an idea."

SEVEN

SKYLIE HAD THE WHOLE STORY now. I hadn't kept anything back. She knew about the death of my precious son, the divorce from my wife, my trouble with my sergeant and my ex-partner. She knew how Cal had allowed me to get shot and how I'd been forced to take time off and then been reinstated. She had shed a lot of tears and had held my hand most of the time I spoke to her. The Paratas had listened in silence to the entire story. The only time either of them had said anything was when I mentioned that Granberg had failed to make contact with the captain. Rongo had looked back over his shoulder and asked, "Would he be the type to try to take revenge?"

"I don't know," I'd told him honestly. "I'm not too worried." Actually, I guess that wasn't entirely true. Cal had made those calls to New Zealand. He could have friends here that would do him a favor. I had tried to shrug the worry off. Surely Cal didn't have that kind of influence.

Skylie showed them the pictures from Antony's bag.

Marama gasped. "Those were in a photo album in the desk in the living room!"

"Someone's been in our home," Rongo said. "They couldn't have gotten these pictures any other way." He looked at his wife. "Did you notice anything out of order in the house, Marama?"

"No, whoever took the pictures must have taken care to make sure we wouldn't suspect anything," she said.

We talked a bit longer and then drifted into silence. Skylie dozed for a while against my shoulder. We finally stopped at a town call New Plymouth on the coast of the Tasman Sea. We checked into a small motel. Rongo parked behind the motel. "I'm parking back here out of sight just to be on the safe side. They might know what my car looks like."

I agreed that it was a good idea, although we hadn't taken the shortest route from Auckland to Wellington. We'd taken what Skylie called the scenic route, the coastal route. We'd stopped a couple times when Skylie wanted me to see a particularly spectacular view. We'd also stopped to eat lunch.

The view from the motel was wonderful, and Skylie asked if I'd like to take a walk with her. I readily agreed. I felt like we were safe for now. I couldn't imagine how any of Antony's friends would know where we were. Rongo and Marama were very tired and wanted simply to relax in their room. "You young people take your time," Rongo said with a grin. "Marama and I will get some dinner later. Enjoy yourselves."

We first walked around town. Skylie told me more about her past, being shuttled from one foster family to another. "I guess I wasn't a very nice child," she told me at one point. "I never could get along with the families I was put in, at least not until the Paratas."

"What was the difference?" I asked.

"I could tell they cared about me," she said. "No one else had really loved me. They just provided food and a place to live—and let their kids pick on me. I was always in trouble because of some kid in the families I was in. The Paratas didn't have any children. They . . . well, they loved me. And I love them."

"They seem like great people," I said.

"Oh, they're wonderful," she replied. "They let me invite friends into their home when I was growing up. I liked Christchurch, and I liked the schools there. For the first time in my life, I got good grades and didn't end up in trouble all the time. I didn't have a lot of friends, but I had good ones."

I shared more of my past with her, the good things before my marriage. I told her how I'd always wanted to be a cop. "From the time I was little, I liked to figure things out. You know," I said, "mysteries and such. I was pretty good at it. At least, I could figure things out when my friends couldn't. Anyway, being a detective was always my dream."

She smiled. It was a genuine, pretty smile. I returned it with the best smile I had. "You have many boyfriends?" I asked.

She chuckled. "Not really. I was shy. And I'd had some bad experiences with boys in some of the families I lived with when I was small."

"Oh, come on," I teased. "Surely there was at least one." We had just approached a quaint shop that looked inviting. We stopped just short of the door. "I'm sorry," I said, suddenly feeling guilty. "I shouldn't have asked you that. Should we go in here?"

She didn't answer. She was looking up the street with a frown on her face. "Okay, maybe there was one," she said, continuing to stare at something.

I looked in the direction her eyes were focused. "It's okay. It's none of my business," I said. "Let's go in here."

She still didn't move. Then she pointed and asked, "Do you see that dark-blue Honda parked up there?"

My stomach twisted uncomfortably. "Yes, I see it. What's the matter?"

She finally looked at me. "I dated a guy that drove a car like that one. I never considered him my boyfriend, but he got pretty possessive of me. I finally broke it off with him. I haven't seen him in quite a while."

"I'm sorry," I said again. "I shouldn't have asked."

"It's okay," she said, and her smile returned. "Let's go in this shop."

We spent several minutes inside. When we were leaving, I held the door for her, but she hesitated. "Just a second," she said. "Will you wait for me outside? There's something I want to get."

"Sure." I tried to read her face. I think it was something she wanted me to have but not right then. She grinned and turned back. I stepped outside and waited. Glancing up the street, I saw the blue Honda. There was someone in it now. I couldn't see the driver very well, but I could tell he had a large amount of bushy black hair. The car started toward me. The driver turned his head as he passed by, so I didn't get a good look at his face, but the hair reminded me of the guy I'd seen leering at Skylie at the airport. A moment later the car was gone. I felt that familiar nervous twist in my stomach, but I told myself it was nothing and tried to relax.

A couple minutes later, Skylie came out with a small bag and a big smile. "Okay, we can go on now," she said. She gave me no hints as to what was in the bag, and I didn't ask.

We walked through a few more shops in town. I enjoyed just looking at the items inside. The shops were all quaint. But other than some gum, we didn't purchase anything. I kept looking for the blue Honda with the bushy-haired driver. But I didn't see it, and I told myself to quit watching for it. I didn't listen to myself very well, but eventually I wasn't looking for it quite as often.

We eventually walked down to the beach. At some point, our hands came together, and we held hands most of the rest of the time we were walking. Being with Skylie felt right. It was hard to believe I'd only known her for just over a day. We talked, we laughed, we enjoyed the sights, and we avoided any talk of the trouble we faced. At the beach, she pointed to some rocks. "Let's sit there for a few minutes," she suggested, a shy grin on her face.

After we had sat down, she opened the mystery bag. "I got us a treat," she said. "I hope you like it. I wanted it to be a surprise."

It was sort of a pastry, pleasantly sweet, different from anything I'd ever tasted. I did like it, and I told her so.

"I thought you would," she said. "I never did find anything in California that I like as well as I like this." We ate slowly, and after it was gone, we walked on down the beach, hand in hand.

The evening passed pleasantly, and before we realized it, it was time to return to our rooms. We stopped on the way and had a light dinner. When we finally returned to the motel, it was after nine o'clock. I glanced around but saw nothing of the blue Honda. I tried to shove it out of my mind as I escorted her to her room. We stood for a moment outside her door, looking deeply into each other's eyes. Then I did something I hadn't done in a long time. I leaned down, she reached up, and our lips met. The kiss was wonderful. The girl was wonderful. Right at that moment, life was wonderful.

I held her for a minute or two, and finally she said, "I wish you didn't have to go back to California in a few days. I'll miss you."

"No more than I'll miss you," I told her. With her here, my old life in California wasn't nearly as attractive at it had been. We kissed again, and finally, reluctantly, I saw her into her room and then went to my own. But I was still nervous about the guy with the dark bushy hair. So I ended up leaving the room and walking alone through New Plymouth. After finally convincing myself that the blue Honda was gone, I went back to my room, where I slept uneasily.

Whenever I woke up during the night, it was either to the lovely face and sweet voice of Skylie or the sour face and threatening voice of Cal Granberg. A couple of times I saw in my dreams a dark-blue Honda and a man with dark curly hair.

I awoke early and once again walked the area near the motel. No blue Honda. I realized I was probably overreacting. A few minutes later, I met Skylie and the Paratas, and we ate a leisurely breakfast in a small café near the motel. We drove out of New Plymouth about ten o'clock.

We took our time, again stopping from time to time to enjoy the beauty of the country. By the time we reached the outskirts of Wellington, it was close to three in the afternoon.

The Paratas' house was in a rural area just to the east of the city, not far from the coast. "Here's home," Skylie said cheerfully when Rongo pulled into the driveway of a simple white framed house. The yard was large and filled with an array of colorful flowers, bushes, trees, and grass. It was well maintained and attractive. "Isn't it pretty here?" she asked me.

"Gorgeous," I said. "And you even have a view of the ocean. Wow, I like it!" I wasn't trying to flatter anyone. My reaction was genuine.

Rongo's was also genuine when he opened the front door. His dark face became mottled with anger, and he punched a fist into his palm. "Someone's been in our home again! Oh, Marama, it's a mess."

Marama's reaction was also genuine. She began to cry—as did Skylie. Skylie's enemies had been here. At least that was my conclusion.

But after we examined the house, Rongo said, "Who would do this to us? We've never hurt anyone in our lives. Every room is a mess. It's like someone was looking for something. You are a policeman, Mike. What do you think?"

"Someone was looking for something; that's for sure. And unless I miss my guess, they were looking for money," I suggested.

"We are simple people," Rongo said, his anger turned to sadness now, matching that of his wife. "We have money, but we don't keep it here. It's in the bank."

Skylie looked stricken. "This is all my fault," she said softly.

"No, my dear," Marama said firmly. "It is not your fault. You have done nothing to justify anyone trying to hurt you."

"That's right, Skylie. This isn't your fault at all, but I worry about you staying here tonight," I said.

"Do you think they might come back?" she asked.

"What do you think?" I asked, putting an arm around her shoulders and pulling her close.

"I think that since they didn't find the money in our house, they'll come back and try to force me to tell them where it is," she said. "But I can't because I don't know where it is. I don't know anything about their money."

Rongo and Marama both stepped close to us. Rongo said sternly, "I take it there is something we don't know. Would you like to tell us what this money thing is?"

I answered, "There was a letter in Antony's bag. I'll show it to you in a little while. But right now, let's call the police. While we're waiting for them, Skylie and I will explain the best we can."

"I better start cleaning up this mess," Marama said.

"No, not yet," I told her. "Don't move anything until the police have been here and tell you it's okay."

"Oh my goodness. You're right. I guess I do need to wait until the police tell us what to do," she said, her face flushed with embarrassment.

While we waited for an officer to come, Skylie and I told the Paratas what we knew. We showed them the note we'd found in Antony's bag. Rongo read it twice and then said, "I wonder if this has anything to do with the bank robbery."

"What bank robbery?" I asked.

"A bank in Wellington was robbed recently. A lot of money was stolen, but the police haven't made any arrests. That's all I know. That's all the press knows, I guess."

"That could be it," I said. "So tell me. Does Skylie have a brother she's never heard of? I wonder if the supposed brother could have something to do with the robbery."

They looked at each other in puzzlement. "We don't know anything about Skylie's parents or her family," Rongo said, looking at Skylie with a great deal of affection in his dark eyes. "I suppose we should have tried to find something out about them for her sake. All we know is that they died when she was just a baby. But we don't know if she had any brothers or sisters. Do you think we should try to find out?"

There was a knock on the door just then, but before Rongo answered it, I said, "Yes, we must try to find out about her brother, if she has one. And I have a feeling she does."

The officer was about my age, and of course, though in full uniform, he carried no gun. He introduced himself as Constable Nico Portill. He was about five eight, and I estimated his weight at around 150 pounds— slender and wiry. His short blond hair was parted in the middle, and his blue eyes shone with intelligence behind gold-rimmed glasses. "Looks like you've had a little problem here," he commented, his face serious, almost offended. "Why would anyone do this to you good folks?" He'd apparently made a quick but accurate assessment of the Paratas' character.

"That's what we're wondering," Rongo said. Then he introduced his wife and Skylie. Finally, he pointed to me and said, "This is Skylie's friend,

Detective Mike Denton, from Los Angeles. He's with the Los Angeles Police Department."

"Detective, huh?" the constable said. "And from a world-famous police force no less. Perhaps you can assist me here. We don't get a lot of serious crime in this country, so we also don't get much experience investigating things like this."

"I'll do what I can," I said. "But I think I can give you an idea right now of what happened."

"Really, Detective?" he said, sounding skeptical. "Go ahead and tell me what you think; then we can examine the house more closely. I assume the damage extends throughout?"

"I'm afraid so," I said as I moved away from where I'd been standing when Rongo had answered the door. "Maybe we should sit for a minute. I think you'll want to take some notes."

Marama invited us to sit at the kitchen table, one of the few places in the house that was uncluttered from the angry search. We all sat down together, and I said to Constable Portill, "You recently had an armed robbery in Wellington at a downtown bank. Is that right?"

"I'm afraid so. That's a very rare occurrence in our country," he said. "Nearly a million dollars was stolen."

"New Zealand dollars, I suppose," I said.

The constable chuckled. "Of course. That would be about the equivalent of, let me see—"

I waved him off. "It doesn't matter, Constable. What's important is that you did have a robbery. I'm afraid that Skylie and I might know a little bit about it. Let me explain."

After listening to our account, the constable shook his head. "This is terrible. Let me just get this straight, mate. This Antony, he's in jail in Honolulu and wanted back in Los Angeles for shooting a police officer."

"Right," I said. "I think he may have a brother, however. The man who approached Skylie in the airport yesterday resembles him. Here," I added, suddenly thinking about the picture I tried to take in the airport. "I snapped this picture just before he lunged for Skylie. I have no idea if it's any good, but let's take a look."

I opened up the photos in my iPhone and brought the man's picture up. Skylie, who was sitting next to me, leaned over and studied the image for a minute. "Oh my goodness, Mike. That guy really does look like Antony, just smaller."

I showed the picture to Constable Portill, and after looking at it closely for a moment, he asked, "Can you either e-mail or message that to me?" He pulled out his own cell phone.

After a couple of minutes, he received the photo on his phone. "I need to make a call. Someone who is involved in the robbery investigation will want to speak with you." We waited quietly while he made his call. Finally he hung up and said, "While we are waiting for Inspector Keller to arrive, I'd like to take a look through the house, Detective. You're welcome to follow along if you like."

We worked our way slowly from the front of the house to the back. Constable Portill took pictures in every room with a small digital camera. We were almost finished when the inspector arrived. The constable introduced us to Inspector Kelsey Keller, a distinguished man of about fifty, with short silver hair. He was the same height as me but was a little heavier.

"You're a detective?" he said to me. "Where do you work?"

"Los Angeles," I said.

"I assume you've had some experience handling major investigations."

"Quite a bit, actually," I responded.

"That's good. I'm grateful you have a lead on our bank robbery. Do you mind if we sit down and discuss it?" he asked.

"Glad to," I said.

So once again, Skylie and I recited our stories, and the inspector listened carefully. From time to time, he nodded. He interrupted us a couple of times with thoughtful questions. I produced the leather bag we had brought from the plane and said, "This belongs to Antony Bahr. He left it on the plane, and I took the liberty of removing it. There are some things you might be interested in."

I first showed him the map of Wellington. He studied it with a grave face and then showed it to Constable Portill. "You'll notice, Constable, that there are markings right here." He touched the spot on the map that Skylie and I had noticed when we looked at it. "This is where the bank robbery occurred." He looked up at me. "This is very interesting, Detective. It certainly ties Mr. Bahr to the robbery. This is our first solid lead on the case. What else do you have?"

I showed him the letter from Hemana; lines creased his brow as he read. Once again he showed it to the constable when he was done. After Nico had finished reading, the inspector scanned through it once more and then looked at me. "This is very likely referring to the money taken at the robbery. Apparently someone, probably your brother"—he glanced at Skylie—"made off with it. Hemana, whoever he is, and I have an idea I might know, wants it back and is willing to do whatever it takes."

I spoke up. "Skylie doesn't know if she even has a brother. She was placed in a foster home as a baby and has never known anything about her family."

"I'm sorry, Miss Yates," he said. "But I have to assume that you either have a brother who is involved in this matter or the robbers think that you do. Either way, that explains the search of this house. They probably hoped to find the money here. They thought maybe you were helping your brother."

"I guess," she agreed. "I just wish I knew if I even had a brother."

"That's something we'll want to look into, but for now, let's see what else is in this bag you so wisely snuck off the plane," Inspector Keller suggested with a little smile at me.

"These are pictures of Skylie," I said, opening the smaller envelope and laying the photos on the table in front of the inspector.

He looked through them in silence. The ones taken by the professional photographer were on the bottom. Marama got to her feet and hurried into the living room. She came back a moment later with the album, laid it on the table, and proceeded to examine it. "They were right here," she said as she lifted the book to show a page with two blank spots.

Rongo took a deep breath. "Our home seems to be a popular place for thieves," he said, trying, it appeared, to make a joke. "But when they took the pictures, they didn't make a mess like they did this time."

They looked at the other pictures, and then the inspector asked, "Is there anything else of interest in the bag?"

"I don't think so, but you'll probably want to take it," I said.

"Yes," he agreed and carefully replaced the items we had taken out. "I'll need to come up with an explanation as to how I obtained it," he said.

"I'm sorry if I messed up some evidence," I said. "But if I hadn't, we would never have seen it, and Skylie's safety was the most important thing in my mind when I decided to, uh, examine the contents."

The inspector sat back, rubbed his hands together, and said, "This is helpful. You did what I might have done under the same circumstances. Thanks to you young people, we now have an idea where to look for the robbers. One of the most powerful Samoan gang leaders happens to be a great big violent man by the name of Hemana. No last name has ever been mentioned in connection to him, but my colleagues up in Auckland have been vigorously investigating him. He is suspected of smuggling guns into the country, but so far we've been unable to prove it. But we will."

"Does Hemana have a criminal record?" I asked. "Has he ever been arrested?"

"Not for anything terribly serious." He rubbed his short silver hair. "There are a few minor charges. But besides the gun smuggling we suspect, we also believe he may have either personally murdered some rival gang members or had them killed. But this offense here, an armed bank robbery, is new."

"Maybe he needed cash to buy the guns," I suggested as I thought of the call I'd overheard from Cal to Hemana. I was suddenly convinced that Cal, and probably Sam, had been smuggling guns to Hemana and his gang. It all fit—the phone call, the name, illegal guns.

The inspector nodded thoughtfully. "By golly, mate, you might be onto something there. We'll certainly look into it."

"Thank you," I said. "I'd appreciate it."

"What about Antony Bahr?" I asked. "Does he have an arrest record?"

"Yes. He and his brother, Tristan, both."

"Tristan must be the guy who was waiting for us at the airport," I interrupted.

"They're bad ones, those two," he said with intensity. "They're not currently wanted for anything here, but it sounds like your country has Antony in custody. I hope they go hard on him."

"I think they will," I said. "He tried to kill one of my colleagues. In LA, we throw the book at cop killers—even people who try but don't succeed."

"As we do here," the inspector agreed.

I reflected briefly on the somber fact that no book had been thrown at whoever had tried to kill me, but the inspector's voice pulled my thoughts back to the present. "Now let's get back to the matter of the hypothetical brother of Skylie's. We need to find him. I suppose his last name could be Yates, but it could also be something else. He may have been adopted, or he might have simply changed his name. He might be hard to trace, especially if he's connected to Hemana's gang."

"The only thing we know," I said, "is that if there is such a person, he would have to be older than Skylie. Her parents died when she was just a baby."

"I'll have to have someone dig into that," Inspector Keller said.

"Would you object to me also trying to learn who he is?" I asked.

"I'm not sure how you can, but as long as you don't interfere with our investigation, I suppose I can't object. If you do learn anything, I would ask that you keep me posted," he said.

I noticed how Marama was wringing her hands, her eyes darting around the room. "Inspector, do you and Constable Portill care if Mrs. Parata and the rest of us start to clean up the mess?"

The two officers glanced at each other. When the constable nodded, the inspector said, "Go right ahead. I think we're finished here."

Marama went right to work, and Skylie joined her. Rongo and I followed the officers to the door, but before they had stepped outside, my iPhone began to ring. I glanced at the screen and saw that it was Captain Bertrand. "This is my captain," I said. "I better take it."

No one said anything, but all movement toward the door ceased. "Hello, Captain," I said into the phone, taking a few steps back into the living room.

"Hi, Detective," he responded. "I trust you're having an enjoyable time in New Zealand."

"I haven't been here long enough to do anything fun yet," I said in an effort to thwart any intention he might have of asking me to come home right away. As I spoke I noticed that Skylie was back in the room, watching me, and that no one else was moving. It made me a little nervous, and I resolved to be careful what I said because of my audience.

"Well, since you have a few days before you report for duty, it should give you time to enjoy yourself," Captain Bertrand said. "But let me get right to the reason for my call. You were told that Cal Granberg disappeared. That worried us since he blamed you for his troubles and we found that he'd made some calls to New Zealand. We know better now, Mike, and I apologize for the problems caused by Granberg's actions. We've conducted a thorough investigation, and the results, as I'm sure your attorney told you, have completely exonerated you. Your attorney also told us you'd like a day or two longer before you have to be back to work. Your request is granted. You don't need to be back for nine days. Does that work?"

"Thank you, Captain," I said. "That'll be great. I appreciate it. Have you heard anything from Cal?"

"As a matter of fact, we have. He called and said that he'd had an emergency and misplaced his cell phone," he explained. "He claimed that he called immediately after finding it. That may or may not be true, but he did come in and return some of his equipment."

"So he's okay?" I asked.

"He seems to be, yes. That's not to say he's not angry, especially with you, but there's no need for you to worry. He's here in LA, says he'll find a job soon, and has no plans to sue the department. Not that it would do him any good because he was so clearly in the wrong."

"I appreciate knowing that, Captain."

"I'm sorry we caused you more stress when we suggested that the calls he made to New Zealand might have been to cause you trouble. We've since learned that he's made a number of calls down there over the past few months. So it's nothing new for him. We're checking now to see if he has a relative or friend there he keeps in contact with."

I, of course, had suspicions—serious ones—but I kept my knowledge of Hemana to myself for now. "Thanks for letting me know, Captain." Then another thought flashed into my mind. "I'm down here. If you could give me the numbers he's been calling, I'd be glad to see if I can find out who they belong to." If nothing else, it might give me Hemana's number, I thought to myself.

"That's a good idea, Detective. I'll do that. You might let the New Zealand authorities know what you are doing. They'd probably help you," he suggested.

"I'm sure they would," I said, glancing at Inspector Keller.

After he read the three numbers to me, he said, "When you get back to work, you'll be given a new partner and, because of all the trouble, a pay raise. You'll also have a new sergeant. We're still looking into Sergeant Hart's activities, but we have enough now to demote him, even if we can't terminate his employment."

"I have a suggestion, Captain. You may want to see if he's made any calls to the same numbers that Cal's been calling. Just a gut feeling I have."

"We were able to get a warrant to look at Cal's phone records. It might be a little more difficult to do so on Hart, but I'll trust your instincts, Mike. I'll see what we can do."

"Can you tell me who my new partner will be?" I asked.

He told me, but I didn't recognize the name because the officer was being transferred from another precinct. "I know you'll like her, Mike. She's about your age, very smart, and as a bonus, she's quite attractive."

"Sounds interesting," I said, not at all sure if I wanted a female partner. Although I certainly was enjoying the female "partner" I had here in New Zealand. "What about the new sergeant?"

He recited another name, and I said, "Hey, that's great. He's a good man."

"Keep in touch, Detective," Captain Bertrand said. "I look forward to seeing you in a few days. Rest assured that you're fully reinstated—not that you were ever suspended, but I can see how it may have seemed that way."

"Yeah, it felt that way, but I'm glad it's over. And thanks for calling, Captain."

The phone call ended, and the people in the room began to move again. Skylie stepped over to me and asked, "Is everything okay, Mike?"

I smiled and nodded. "Everything is great. Granberg showed up in the captain's office in LA."

"Oh, good," she said. "That's one less worry anyway."

"Sort of," I said. "He's been making calls to someone in New Zealand. That worries me a little, although it's been going on for months, so it probably has nothing to do with me."

"Is that someone you put in prison, Detective?" Inspector Keller asked.

"No, Granberg is my former partner. He was dirty, and the department just fired him," I explained briefly. "We don't need his kind in law enforcement."

"That's for sure," he agreed. "I heard you tell your captain that you thought someone here could help with something. Does it have to do with the phone numbers he gave you?"

"It does," I said. "I have three numbers, all ones Granberg has been calling down here for some time now, according to Captain Bertrand. He'd like to know who those numbers belong to. I'll be surprised if one of them doesn't turn out to belong to Hemana." I explained quickly why I suspected it.

"Give the numbers to me, and I'll find out as soon as I can," he promised. "And while you're giving me those numbers, could I also get your cell phone number? I'll keep you posted on anything we learn about Hemana or Tristan Bahr as well as these phone numbers."

I gave him the information and accepted a card from both him and Constable Portill. I promised again to let them know what, if anything, I could dig up about Skylie's hypothetical brother, and they left us to the sizable task of getting the house back in order.

EIGHT

NERVES WERE HIGH AT THE Parata home. Even when the cleanup was complete, both Marama and Skylie worried about the burglars returning.

"What if they decide they didn't search thoroughly enough?" Skylie asked.

"I think we should take a little trip for a day or two and ask the police to keep a close look out on the house," Rongo suggested.

"I like that idea," I said. I did like it, but not just for the reasons the family had mentioned. The burglars may or may not come back for the money, but the odds of them coming in search of Skylie were very high. I was sure they hadn't changed their minds about using her to try to find her brother or the money or both.

"We can make phone calls regarding a possible brother from anywhere," I continued. "I want to get right on that." The deadline I'd been given to return to LA wasn't far away, even with the two extra days I'd been granted by Captain Bertrand. I had work to do.

There was a brief discussion on where we should go. "Let's make it someplace Mike will enjoy since it's his first time here," Skylie suggested.

Rongo smiled. "I know just the place, but I don't know if they'll have an opening on this short of notice or not. But we could stay in a hotel on the South Island tonight, and then maybe tomorrow we could go up to the Nelson Lakes National Park. There's a nice place near the park called TopHouse Historic Guesthouse. It's in a pretty area, quite isolated, and has nice accommodations and a lot of history."

"Yes, let's do that." Skylie was obviously excited about the idea. "I love that place."

"We will need to pack quickly," Rongo said. "We should try to get across the channel to the South Island tonight. We'll haul my car across on the ferry, and we can easily find a room in Picton. In the meantime, let's see if we can reserve a place at the TopHouse for the next couple of nights."

I had reservations—I wanted to get to work on my investigation—but I didn't have the heart to hurt the Paratas' feelings and especially not Skylie's. So ten minutes later we were on our way to catch a ferry across the channel. As soon as we boarded the ferry, Rongo called and made reservations at TopHouse.

After Rongo hung up, Skylie had second thoughts of her own. "Rongo, it is expensive. Maybe we should do something simpler."

"Like what?" Marama asked.

"Maybe we could camp, if you didn't mind, Mike."

"I'll do whatever you guys want to do," I said.

Rongo was shaking his head. "No, we'll take this trip and do it my way," he insisted stubbornly. "We're not terribly rich, but we're also not poor. And we've missed you, Skylie. We're so glad you're back. Let Marama and me give the two of you a little vacation. We could use one too."

That ended that discussion. So Skylie and I sat down and watched the dark water passing, enjoying the evening, the cool air, and each other's company. My anxiety over finding the elusive brother was stirring around in my head, and I kept thinking about Cal's repeated calls to New Zealand. I tried not to let Skylie see it, but those two things upset an otherwise perfect evening—well, those two and one more thing.

A dark-skinned man with bushy black hair. I spotted him twice on the ferry but never did get a good look at his face. What worried me was that he reminded me of the leering man at the airport and the one driving the dark-blue Honda in New Plymouth. I didn't mention him to Skylie. She was so relaxed I didn't want to upset her.

We stayed in a small motel in Picton, right across the channel from Wellington. The Paratas offered to pay for my room, but there was no way I was going to allow that. After all, thanks to my attorney, I'd received some money from the LAPD, so I could afford it. Besides, I was still drawing my salary as well.

* * *

The drive to TopHouse the following morning was gorgeous. The road over the mountain was narrow and twisty, but the scenery was breathtaking. Far below us the ocean gleamed in the early-morning sunshine. The deep but varied green of the thick foliage was gorgeous. I'd never seen anything quite like it. We passed several brave individuals on bicycles, wending their way up and down the narrow highway. Once we were on the other side of the mountains, the landscape changed but was equally beautiful. Tall mountains towered above the sweeping, grassy valley.

I was especially intrigued when we turned off the highway. We drove down a narrow dirt road, dipped through a small stream, and passed lush green pastures that grew all the way to the densely timbered mountainside a fair distance away. Then I saw the TopHouse and was unable to suppress a chuckle. It was a small white building with a dark-red metal roof, a historic building, as its full name, TopHouse Historic Guesthouse, implied. It was an old building, but it was in excellent condition. The gravel parking area had only one other car in it.

"What do you think?" Skylie asked as we stood gazing at the place where we'd come to spend a couple of days.

"The word *quaint* comes to mind." I grinned at her. "I like it, Skylie."

"So do I," she said with a smile that sent a pleasant shiver through me.

After we checked into our rooms, we ate a tasty lunch on a weatherworn wooden table a small distance from the building. On the downhill side were fields and fences and a lot of green trees, shrubs, and beautiful flowering plants. Majestic mountains rose in the distance.

"The little building attached to the end of the TopHouse is a bar, the smallest bar in all of New Zealand and some say the smallest in the world," Rongo said as he pointed at it. "Marama and I don't plan to go in there, as we are not drinkers, but you might like to."

"Actually, I don't drink either. I watched what it did to an uncle and aunt of mine. It destroyed their marriage and sent their kids, my cousins, spinning off into lives of waste. I decided it wasn't for me."

"Then you'll fit in well with us. We don't drink, and neither does Skylie . . . or have you taken it up in college?" he asked with a little concern, looking at the young lady he and his wife had so lovingly nurtured to adulthood.

"You taught me well," she said with a chuckle. "No, I still don't drink. Some of my friends in the States did, and they tried to get me to join them, but I didn't. Well, I might have tasted a tiny sip once, but it didn't even taste good. So no, I don't need to visit the bar. I do want to go to the lakes though." She turned to me. "Mike, you'll love the lakes. They're amazing. How far is it to them, Rongo?"

"About eight kilometers," he said. "We'll drive over after we finish our lunch."

So instead of doing what I should have been—searching for a brother to Skylie, who may or may not even exist—we began to hike a spectacular trail near one of the lakes. I tried to absorb the exotic beauty of the mountains, the northernmost part of the range known as the Southern Alps.

Rongo and Marama walked with us for a while, but when I told them I needed to spend some time on the phone looking for tips as to the existence of Skylie's brother, Rongo said, "I'm already getting tired, Mike. And I know that Marama is too. We're not young anymore. So if you don't mind, we'll go back to the trailhead, and I'll make some calls. You two young people go ahead and hike for as long as you'd like. You've both been through some stressful times, and it would do you good."

When I started to resist, Skylie took my arm and looked at me pleadingly with those incredibly blue eyes of hers. "Please, Mike. Rongo's right. Let's enjoy the afternoon. The weather's perfect, the scenery is spectacular, and I'd like to spend more time with you just, well, you know, relaxing and having fun."

It was hard to argue with that. I tried anyway. "I really do need to make some calls, Skylie."

She punched me on the arm, hard enough to hurt but without rancor. "Hey, mate, let Rongo give it a try. Remember, he's a native here, and he will have a better idea who to call. If he'd had any idea about the possibility of me having a brother, he'd have tracked him down years ago."

I gave up. She had me. I suspected that Rongo would accomplish more than I could over the next hour or two. "In that case, let's head up that trail."

She laughed, grabbing my hand, and we hiked rapidly on.

The afternoon ended too soon. I could have hiked with Skylie for days without end. Even though I knew I shouldn't, I found myself comparing Skylie to Macy. I had loved Macy, but in every comparison, she came up short. Skylie was, to put it mildly, incredible. And unless I was very mistaken, she enjoyed being with me. We shared a couple more kisses on our hike, and each time, it made my blood race. I was falling for this girl, falling hard. I hated to think of having to return to Los Angeles in a few days—or ever, for that matter.

When we got back to the car, Rongo was excited. "I did it!" he said as animated as a little boy who'd just hit a home run. In fact, a home run was pretty much what he'd hit. And he'd done it in just four hours. "Skylie does have a brother. Actually, she has two brothers. One of them was adopted by a family in Christchurch. His name is Josh Infelt. He's married with two kids and lives in a small town not too far outside of Auckland. And get this, he works for the police."

"You're sure of this," I asked.

"Oh, yes, mate. I'm sure," Rongo said.

Skylie was subdued at the news. Rongo noticed and asked, "Skylie, aren't you excited to hear this? You have a niece and a nephew and a brother."

"Yes, that's great, but I have another brother, Rongo. He must be the bad one," she said sadly.

"His name is Jalen Lillard. He and Josh are twins, but they were separated when your parents were killed. Jalen was also adopted, but his new parents lived in Dunedin. The father taught at the university there. Sadly, Jalen rebelled at an early age, and by the time he was sixteen, he'd left home. He'd gotten a tattoo of a snake on each of his arms, which upset his parents, and they think their reaction to it may have contributed to his leaving home. His parents haven't seen him since the day he left. He broke their hearts," Rongo reported.

"I'm impressed, Rongo," I said. "How did you learn all this?"

The old Māori just smiled. "I know a few people, Mike. As for Jalen, I talked to his father. He and his wife still live in Dunedin. When I told him who I was, he cheered. I could hear him telling his wife, and she squealed. They want to meet you sometime, Skylie."

"What about Josh's parents?" I asked.

"I have a phone number for them, but I didn't get an answer. I didn't try to call Josh. I thought I'd let you do that, Skylie," Rongo said.

"How old are they?" she asked.

"Twenty-four. They were barely three when they were separated— when the three of you were separated," he said. "You weren't even a year old yet."

Skylie walked over to Rongo and threw her arms around him. Then she did the same with Marama. "I maybe got shuffled around from family to family until I found you, but I am the luckiest of us all. I love you both more than you know." She shook her head. "To think that one of my brothers grew up in the same city I did . . ."

Rongo smiled. "Skylie, remember Christchurch is the second largest city in New Zealand, and you only knew a few of the people there."

I chuckled. "Okay, Rongo. Now that you've solved that mystery, what am I going to do?"

"Ah, Detective, that should be obvious," he said with a big grin. "I did the easy part. Now you've got to find the rebellious brother." The grin faded. "That won't be so easy."

"Maybe not so hard either," I said. "I'm betting the cops can help with that."

"He must be connected somehow with Hemana and the Bahr brothers," Skylie suggested. "So now that we have a name, I'll bet the police can help. Let's let them work on it while we spend a couple more days here. Is that okay, Mike?"

"Whatever you say, Skylie." I smiled when I was favored with a hug every bit as big as the ones she'd given to her folks. I was still anxious to get to work, but spending time with Skylie was something I was enjoying more by the hour.

We returned to TopHouse in time for dinner. After we'd eaten, I left Skylie visiting with the Paratas while I called the cell phone number Inspector Keller had given me. "I'm glad you called, Detective," he said. "I was just about to call you. I assigned one of my officers to identify the phone numbers your captain gave you. She had success, but you'll not be happy when I tell you what she learned."

I braced myself. "Okay, so tell me."

"You were right about one of the numbers your former partner has been calling. It does belong to our gang leader and gun running suspect, Hemana," he said. He paused to let that sink in. I waited for the next name. It wasn't a great surprise. "The second number is to the house where the Bahr brothers, Antony and Tristan, live. So, Detective, I suspect you'll want to get that information to your captain as soon as you can reach him."

"That's for sure," I said. "Maybe that will give them enough information to charge Cal with something."

"You suspected this, didn't you?" he asked.

"I did," I admitted. "I've known for a long time that Cal was up to something. I just couldn't put my finger on what it was."

"Well, now you know. I suppose you'd like to know about the third number," the inspector said. "This one doesn't mean anything to us, so it won't to you either. The guy is a young man known on the streets as Snake. He has a tattoo of a snake on each arm, all the way from his knuckles to his shoulders."

I felt like I'd just been punched. I gasped.

"Don't tell me that means something to you," Inspector Keller said. "We've heard the nickname, but until today we didn't have a real name to go with it."

"I hope I'm wrong, but I think that would be Jalen Lillard," I said.

For a moment there was no response from the inspector, but when he did speak, he said, "Detective, how in the world did you know that? I'm blown away."

"Don't be. Jalen is one of Skylie Yates's twin brothers. He's twenty-four years old. His parents, adoptive parents, live in Dunedin. His father is retired, but he taught in the university there."

"This is great information." The inspector chuckled. "How did you come up with it?"

"It was easy. I took Skylie for a long hike in the Nelson Lakes National Park. When we got back to the trailhead where we had left Rongo and Marama Parata, Rongo told us. He'd been on the phone," I explained. "He found out who both twins were."

"How did he do that?" the inspector asked in amazement.

"I asked him that very question, but all he would say is that he knows a few people."

"That's amazing, Detective. Tell me who the other brother is."

"You're in for a surprise," I said. "You'll either know this guy or know cops in your department who do. He's a police officer, Josh Infelt. He lives just outside of Auckland."

"Doesn't ring a bell, but of course ours is a large department," he said. "I can confirm that with a couple of phone calls in the morning, but I'll take your word for it for now. I'll find out exactly what his assignment is and get back to you tomorrow. I take it he's also twenty-four."

"Yup. Identical twins. Josh grew up in Christchurch, and his parents still live there. Rongo tried to call them, but apparently they aren't home. Rongo wasn't able to get cell phone numbers for either of them," I reported.

"Tell Rongo I'm grateful to him. I better let you go so you can call your captain."

A moment later I was dialing Captain Bertrand's number. I had checked out the world clock on my phone. It was a little past eleven at night in Los Angeles, but I didn't think this could wait. I would risk waking him up.

"Detective, what are you doing calling so late, or don't you realize what time it is here?" Captain Bertrand said. "This better be important."

"It is, Captain. Believe me," I said. "I hate to call so late, but I talked to a police officer here by the name of Inspector Kelsey Keller from Wellington. I gave him the numbers you gave me, and he identified them. Cal has been calling a man named Hemana, the head of a Samoan criminal gang in Auckland, a man they suspect is smuggling guns into the country. He's suspected of some other crimes as well, including murder."

When the captain spoke again, I knew I had his complete attention. "That's far worse than anything I expected, Detective. I'm stunned."

"Then prepare to be stunned again," I said. "The second number is to the home of Antony Bahr and his brother, Tristan, in Auckland."

"The same Antony Bahr who's in jail in Honolulu that we are trying to extradite back to LA?" he asked.

"It is. Antony assaulted a man who got between him and a woman he was stalking. When officers attempted to arrest Antony, he shot one of them. The third number is for a man who is somehow associated with both Hemana and Antony," I said. "His name is Jalen Lillard, known locally as Snake. He is, we have learned, an older brother of the girl who was being stalked by Antony in Los Angeles."

"So it all ties together," Captain Bertrand said, dragging his words out like he was thinking deeply.

"It does," I agreed. "And it doesn't look good for Cal and Sergeant Hart. There is one other thing I should tell you. I overheard Cal saying Hemana's name on his cell phone one day. They were talking about New Zealand and guns. Cal never knew I could hear him."

"So you had a reason for going to New Zealand," Captain Bertrand said. It wasn't a question. "You wanted to see what you could learn down there about this Hemana."

"That's right," I confirmed.

"I guess you're earning your salary. Keep me posted," the captain said. "And I'll do the same for you."

I rejoined the Paratas and Skylie. She was frowning.

"Is something wrong?" I asked.

"I don't know," she said. "I finally got a hold of my brother's mother. Josh's mother. She gave me the phone number for Josh. I called and talked to a woman who says she's his wife. When I told her who I was, she told me it was a surprise, but a nice surprise."

"So what's wrong?" I asked.

"When I asked if I could speak to Josh, she said he wasn't home."

"Probably because he was at work," I said.

"That's what I thought, but when I asked her when he'd be home, she acted kind of funny. I asked again, and she finally said she didn't know, that she hadn't seen him for a few days. When I asked her where he was, she said she didn't know," Skylie said. "I didn't press her, and we ended the call on that note. I think there might be trouble between them."

I tried to think of what I could say to put a positive spin on the situation, but I couldn't think of anything. So I simply said, "Let's hope not," and we left it at that.

Nearly an hour later, Bertrand called me back. "Granberg's gone. As near as we can tell, he flew to Hawaii this morning. But watch yourself down there. I think he's more dangerous than any of us suspected."

"Not any of us, Captain. I still think he wasn't just negligent the day I got shot. I think he was behind it. I can't prove it, but I believe it." And I did, although the feeling wasn't something I'd had until I came to New Zealand. He might have had reason to get rid of me. He might have figured out that I suspected him of being more than just lazy, which it turns out was right. He was a dirty cop.

"After what you've told me tonight, I'll see that your suspicions are looked into closely, Detective. And once again, you watch yourself. I wouldn't put it past Cal to show up there."

NINE

Antony Bahr was a free man. Not that the authorities had intended
for that to happen. In fact, they were extremely angry. His escape, the
brainchild of former LAPD detective Cal Granberg, had been quickly but
carefully planned and then meticulously carried out.

Cal's experience and expertise as a detective served him well in his
planning for the escape of his friend. When he heard that Antony was in
jail, Cal called Hemana in New Zealand and told him he had a plan to get
Antony out of jail but that he needed Hemana to have one of his contacts
in Honolulu fix some forged papers for Antony so he could continue on
to New Zealand under a false name.

The passport was ready by the time Cal had succeeded in orchestrating
Antony's release, and the three of them, Antony, Cal, and Wilson, were
away before the authorities realized Antony's release had been accomplished
with forged documents, including a court order from a judge in Los
Angeles—a real judge, just a forged signature and fraudulent paperwork.

When, as anticipated, the jail personnel told Cal—artfully disguised
and carrying his own forged papers—they needed to call the judge's
office for confirmation, he provided a phone number, and they unwisely
called that number. It was answered by the wife of Sergeant Sam Hart.
She pretended to be the chief clerk of the judge's court, and when she
"confirmed" that the judge had ordered the release, they simply complied
with the order. Antony and Cal were picked up at the jail by a taxi and
whisked to the airport. Wilson was waiting for them there with the forged
documents and other necessities.

They went into a men's room, where those items were quickly put to
use. Antony donned a wig and false beard, applied makeup to hide the
scar on his face, and was given a change of clothes. The old clothes, the

ones he'd been wearing the day he was arrested, were stuffed in a trash can. He was also given some glasses to wear. The picture on the forged passport had been photo shopped, and when they left the men's room, he was a very close match. An hour later, the three men were on a plane, and before anyone knew Antony had been erroneously released, they were winging their way to Auckland.

* * *

I was enjoying myself. Skylie and I were sharing a picnic lunch beside Lake Rotoroa. We had once again been hiking and were eating our lunch on the bank of the lake in the shade of a large pine tree. It was another beautiful day. We hadn't mentioned anything about her troubles or her newly discovered but mysterious brothers. It had simply been private time between us.

My phone rang, and I pulled it from my pocket, looking at the screen. Thanks to a satellite connection, I could use my phone anywhere in the country. I found myself wishing that wasn't so at that moment. The instant I saw who the call was from, I had a disturbing feeling that my tranquil day was about to be turned on end.

"Detective Denton," Captain Bertrand began, "I'm afraid I have some bad news."

"Can it wait?" I asked with a forced chuckle, knowing full well that if he was going to the trouble of calling, it was something urgent.

He also chuckled. "Good try, Detective," he said. "I'm sorry to disturb your vacation again, but there's something you need to know. Antony Bahr escaped from jail in Honolulu. It was discovered less than an hour ago, but he's been free for several hours."

I'd been leaning back against the tree, but when he made that shocking announcement to me, I sat upright and gripped the phone. Seeing my reaction, Skylie grabbed my arm, her eyes wide. "How in the world did he manage that?" I asked.

"He had help—smart, capable help," the captain said with a growl. "Someone, and we have our suspicions who, presented a cleverly forged order from a superior court judge in LA ordering Antony's release. An officer called the number provided by the man presenting the order, and the woman on the other end identified herself as the chief clerk for the judge. She confirmed that the order was legitimate, and the inmate was released."

"Could Cal have been behind it?" I asked.

"The description of the officer who presented the order doesn't fit Cal, but he could have been in disguise. We checked the phone number he gave the officer, and it turns out to be a number that's not listed anywhere. We're assuming it was a disposable cell," Captain Bertrand explained.

"I don't suppose we have any idea where Antony and Cal, or whoever it was, were going after leaving the jail?" I asked as Skylie's grip on my arm tightened. I looked at her and forced a smile, but it didn't seem to provide any comfort. It was quite apparent that she'd figured out what had happened. Her face was pale, and she was trembling.

"I have no idea," Captain Bertrand responded. "They're searching all over the island right now, and the airports are covered. We faxed photos of both Cal and Antony to the airports, bus depots, and so on. They would both have to have false passports and be in disguise in order to leave the island. I suppose such documents could be obtained with the right connections, but it should take some time to get it done. And hopefully the disguises won't be good enough to fool the security teams at the airport."

"Could Cal have had the passports already prepared?" I asked.

"That's a possibility, but it doesn't seem likely."

To me it seemed very likely. Cal wasn't honest, but he was smart—or *cunning* might be the more correct word. "What do you need me to do here?" I asked.

"I know you've made contacts with the local police. Will you call and let them know about Antony's escape, just in case he does show up in New Zealand? And would you have someone in charge call me as soon as they can so I can establish my own link with them?"

"Actually, I can do that right now. I met an inspector, the man who got the information on the telephone numbers, Inspector Kelsey Keller. Let me give you his number," I said. After I had done that, I added, "I'll call him right now and tell him to be expecting a call from you."

"Thanks, Detective. That'll be great. Now, as to your status—you're on the payroll, so we'd like you to be available to help us down there over the next few days if we need it."

"I'd be glad to do that, Captain," I said.

"It may mean extending your stay a little longer if we don't find Cal soon. We'd like you to work with this Inspector Keller to build a case against Cal on the matter of the gun smuggling. We're quite convinced that's exactly what he's been doing."

"And who knows what else," I said bitterly.

"I'm afraid you may be right, that he might be involved in other illegal activities. We've already been looking at his bank accounts, and he has far more money than he could have ever earned as a cop."

"What about Sergeant Hart?"

"We're looking into his activities as well," he informed me. "At this point I trust your instincts," he said. "I'm sorry I ever doubted you."

"Well, I don't blame you, Captain. Cal and Sam knew what they were doing, and I can understand your doubts. After all, they were both experienced and trusted men," I said.

"You're a good man, Detective," he said, making me feel pretty decent. It sure beat the feeling I had when I'd left the captain's office without my gun, badge, and ID a few days ago. "I hope we don't have to keep you in New Zealand too long, but until we wrap things up, I'd like you to consider yourself on assignment there for however long it takes."

"Not a problem," I said, grinning to myself. I was in no hurry to leave this place or the girl holding so tightly to my arm. "Is there a chance I could get you to send my ID and badge down so I look official?"

"I'm sure it'll take a bit to reach you, but if you'll give me an address, I'll get it on the way," he said.

"Um, I don't really have an address," I said as I tried to figure out how to have him send it. I supposed he could use the Paratas' address, but their place didn't seem to be very secure. "Why don't you send it to Inspector Keller. He can give you an address when you talk to him."

"That'll work," the captain agreed, and we ended our call.

I immediately called Inspector Keller and informed him of what had happened. He was outraged. Not that I blamed him. "My captain would like you to call him," I said. "He wants to coordinate the investigation on the gun smuggling. We believe that Cal Granberg and some others are the ones who have been dealing with Hemana. I also suspect that Cal was somehow involved in Antony's escape."

"Thanks, Detective. Instead of waiting for him to call me, I'll call Captain Bertrand right now," the inspector said.

"Before you do, you need to know that he's asked me to stay here and represent the LAPD until we wrap this thing up. He'll be discussing that with you," I told him. "If that's a problem, let him know, and I'll back off."

"I can't see why that would be a problem, Detective Denton," Inspector Keller said. "For right now, as far as I'm concerned, I'd like you to keep an eye on Miss Yates."

"You know I'll do that," I said. "Also, when you talk to Captain Bertrand, can you give him your mailing address so he can send my ID and badge down here?"

"Sure," the inspector agreed. "But if you'd like, I'd be glad to furnish you with a temporary ID associating you with the New Zealand police."

"That would be great. In fact, if you're willing to do that, I probably won't need Captain Bertrand to send anything."

"I'll have ID for you the next time I see you, Detective."

"Thanks. I appreciate it," I said.

"Oh, by the way, Detective, I've learned a little more about Skylie's brother, Josh," Inspector Keller said. "It seems he's currently working on an undercover assignment. I'm not sure exactly what his assignment is, but I'll find out. He's an outstanding officer, from what I've been told. He's going to call me at some point so I can personally fill him in on the matter of his brother and sister. I expect he'll be very surprised, but I also think he'll want to meet Miss Yates as soon as it's practical."

"I'm relieved," I said.

"Why's that?" he asked. I explained about Skylie's call to Josh's wife and what our concerns had been. Skylie was watching me with large, expectant eyes.

When I had finished, the inspector said, "She was doing exactly what she would have been told to do with her husband undercover. By the way, other than the Paratas and Miss Yates, I will expect you to keep that bit of information confidential."

After that call was finished, I filled Skylie in. "So my brother's marriage isn't falling apart," she said with a sigh. "I don't even know him, and the thought was eating on me."

"Of course it was," I said, lightly touching her cheek. "Oh, and get this. I guess I'll be working with the New Zealand police here for a while."

"Does that mean you don't have to leave next week?"

"That will depend on how quickly things move in the investigation, but there's a good chance I'll be here for a little longer."

With that, she threw her arms around me and buried her head against my chest. "I'm so excited," she said. Then she pulled back, a worried look replacing the excitement. "Do you have to leave and go work with the police now?"

I chuckled. "Not yet. We can spend a little more time together here. Right now, how about if we do a little more hiking?"

She was agreeable to that, and we had an enjoyable afternoon, despite worrying about Antony Bahr. When we got back to the TopHouse and told Rongo and Marama what had happened, they were both worried.

"We should be okay here," I told them. "No one knows where we are, do they?"

"I hope not," Rongo said.

We had a nice evening, and when I had received no orders to report to the inspector or anyone else with the New Zealand police, we kept our rooms and went on a sightseeing road trip. But by the time we sat down to eat dinner that evening, I was getting very tense.

Skylie seemed to sense my mood. "Are you worried that Antony and your old partner could be in New Zealand by now?"

"I am," I said flatly. "I'm sure the police have been watching for them, but if they're disguised well enough and have really good forged IDs, they could have gotten off the plane and made it to wherever they decided to go."

"Wouldn't they just go to Antony's house?" she asked.

"I doubt it. I think there's a good chance the police are watching his place closely. If the cops know where Hemana lives, they probably have his place staked out as well."

"Why don't you call Inspector Keller and ask him?"

I had been thinking about that but had put it off, reasoning that if the inspector had anything to tell me, he'd have called me by now. I pulled out my phone. "I think I'll do that, Skylie."

The inspector's answer didn't surprise me. "Our people haven't seen either Hemana or Tristan Bahr. We have both of their homes under surveillance, but there's been no one at either place since we established the stakeouts. That's not too surprising, especially considering the fact that Samoan gangs are quite fluid. The officers in Auckland tell me we really don't know where a lot of them stay much of the time."

"Okay, I'm just trying to decide what I should do, and what Skylie and the Paratas should do as well," I said.

"We have officers periodically checking the Parata residence," Inspector Keller said. "So far, we don't believe anyone associated with the gang has shown up there, but I think it would be wise for them to stay away for a little longer." He didn't ask where we were, and I didn't offer. I wanted our location to be secret; although, I was thinking that maybe it would be well if we moved on, maybe farther south, the next day. Until there was something I could do, I'd just as well see as much of the country as I could with Skylie.

After I'd finished talking to Inspector Keller, I told Skylie, Rongo, and Marama what I was thinking, and they agreed. We were up late that night, watching the stars and visiting on chairs outside of the TopHouse. It was a beautiful, cool, moonless night, and the stars were shining brightly. It was an enchanting place, and we were all able to relax despite our worries.

When we did finally retire to our rooms for the night, I grew restless and was unable to fall asleep. I kept looking at my watch as the minutes and hours dragged on. As much as I wanted to drive south in the morning, I was having second thoughts. The likelihood of Antony and Cal being in New Zealand was very high. I felt like I needed to go to Auckland and help the officers there locate the two fugitives. The more I thought about it, the more I wanted to do just that. I finally concluded that I would do so, but I would also insist that Skylie and the Paratas stay out of sight and out of Wellington. I didn't look forward to sharing my plans with Skylie the next morning. I knew she wanted to be with me as much as I wanted to be with her.

I did eventually get to sleep, but I couldn't have slept very long before I was awakened by voices outside my window. They were fairly loud and sounded angry. I couldn't make out the words, but for some reason, it was unsettling to me. I tossed and turned a few minutes, thinking about getting up but feeling foolish, not having any idea what I would do if I did.

The voices drifted away, and for several minutes it was quiet outside my window except for the normal, soothing sounds of night. I finally got out of bed and put my clothes on. I wasn't soothed, and I couldn't sleep; even though I had no reason to think the voices had anything to do with me or the good people I was with, I couldn't lie there any longer.

I stepped outside and walked around the TopHouse. There were a couple of cars parked at the edge of the graveled parking area that hadn't been there when we had gone into our rooms. I walked over, but clouds had moved in and hidden the stars, making it too dark to see much of anything. Using the flashlight app on my iPhone, I passed the cars and started walking up the road, thinking maybe a little exercise would tire me out and that when I got back, I might be able to get some sleep.

I'd gone maybe a half mile when I decided to turn back. I hadn't walked but a few hundred feet after turning back when I heard an engine start up back in the direction of the TopHouse. I thought I heard a muffled scream, but I couldn't be sure. It might have been a wild animal. I hurried my steps when I heard the distant engine grow louder. Then I saw headlights coming my way. I stepped to the side of the road and began to jog. My eyes had adjusted to the darkness, and I put my cell phone in my pocket. I didn't need the flashlight at the moment. There were two ways to enter and exit the TopHouse from the highway. Apparently I had chosen to walk the same way the departing car had chosen to drive.

In a matter of seconds, the vehicle was almost to me, going at a dangerously high speed for the narrow dirt road. I stopped and watched it approach. It suddenly swerved right at me. I jumped back and rolled to the fence as the car passed by, missing me by no more than a few inches. I jumped to my feet and watched the tail lights disappear in a cloud of dust. Whoever was driving that car had meant to hit me, and at the speed it was going, that could well have proved fatal.

I reached for my cell phone, but it was no longer in my pocket. I realized it must have fallen out when I fell. I dropped to my knees and began to search, but it was very dark, and the grass was long and thick. I spent a couple of minutes searching then gave up, thinking I'd have to come back after the sun came up.

I began to run along the road back toward the TopHouse. And I mean I was *running*, not just jogging. After the attempt that had been made on my life, I had a sinking feeling that I *had* heard a scream. I was out of breath by the time I reached the TopHouse. I had stumbled and fallen a couple of times, and I was sure I'd scraped holes in the knees of my jeans.

There were lights on, and the Paratas were standing near the front door. As I ran up they turned to me.

"There you are," Rongo said. "We've been knocking on your door and shouting for you."

"Is Skylie okay?" I asked urgently.

"She isn't answering her door either," he said as he hurried back inside. I followed right behind him as he approached the door to her room. "We woke up when we thought we heard a scream."

"I heard it too," I said as I raised my hand to knock on the door. I knocked and waited.

Rongo asked, "What were you doing out on the road?"

"I couldn't sleep. Someone was talking really loudly in the parking area, and I finally got up and went outside," I said. "I'm not sure what I was going to do. I suppose I would have asked them to be quiet. But by the time I went out, there was no one there." I knocked on the door again. "Skylie. Open up. It's Mike and Rongo."

Marama and the manager were standing right behind us. Marama was wringing her hands and had tears in her eyes.

"Did you see the car that sped away from here?" Rongo asked as he pounded on the door.

"Yes," I said. "Whoever it was tried to run me down. I was able to leap out of the road, and he missed me, but just barely."

"Your clothes are torn, and you have some blood on your knees and elbows," Rongo said. "Are you hurt?"

"I'm fine. We need to get in there." I turned to the manager and asked her to open the door for us. She hesitated and said something about privacy. I pointed my finger in her face. "I work with the New Zealand police. I'm telling you to open that door and open it now!"

She finally did as I asked, and when the door swung open, I stepped inside and stopped, staring at the body on Skylie's bed. There was a lot of blood on the pillow, and the long hair was soaked. Rongo gasped, and Marama pushed in beside us and promptly fainted. Rongo and the manager attended to her as I stepped to the bed and confirmed my suspicions. There was no life in the body on the bed. Someone had bashed the back of the head.

"Skylie's gone," Rongo said as he looked up from where he was now holding his wife on the floor. "What are we going to do?"

TEN

Skylie wasn't there. I was sick to my stomach, like I could pass out, but I made myself take a deep breath and buck up. "I lost my phone," I said. "We need to call the cops right now. Does someone have a phone I can use?"

Marama was coming around now, and Rongo helped her to her feet. "Where is Skylie?" she asked. "Who is that on the bed?"

I didn't have an answer to the first question, but to her second one, I did. "That's Skylie's brother, Jalen, the one they call Snake."

Rongo nodded slowly.

"Please, I need a phone."

Marama pointed to the nightstand beside the bed. "Is that Skylie's?" she asked in a wavering voice.

"It is," I said. It was plugged in, charging. "Now everyone step back in the hallway. We need to avoid touching anything else. I'll grab the phone and call the police."

I called a number the manager provided for me since Inspector Keller's was in my phone. As soon as I'd succeeded in getting officers on the way and alerted them to the kidnapping of Skylie by someone in a small, dark-colored car, I hung up. Turning to the manager, I said, "I need a flashlight. My phone is down the road where I was almost run over. I need to call Inspector Keller. He'll want to know what's going on."

The manager found me a flashlight. Rongo gave me the keys to his car, and then, after Rongo had taken Marama back into their room, I asked the manager to lock and stand by the door to Skylie's room.

I drove down the road to the spot where I'd been attacked. It took me a few minutes to find the exact area, but once I did, I spotted my phone fairly easily. It had bounced through the fence and landed a couple of feet on the other side. I retrieved it, got back in Rongo's car, and dialed the inspector's number as I rode back to the TopHouse. It rang several times before I heard his groggy voice on the line. It was just shortly after four o'clock now.

"I'm sorry to wake you, Inspector," I said. "This is Mike Denton."

"What's the matter?" he demanded. "Why are you calling me at such a terrible hour?"

"Skylie Yates has been kidnapped," I reported. Before he could respond, I went right on. "Snake has been murdered, Jalen Lillard, Skylie's brother."

"Yes, I know who you mean." He sounded more alert now. "Where are you?"

"Are you familiar with a little place on the South Island called TopHouse Historic Guesthouse?" I asked.

"Yes. At the Nelson Lakes National Park," he said. "Is that where you are?"

"I am. We are. Skylie isn't now," I said, feeling a little rattled and scared out of my wits for the girl I had become very fond of over the past few days.

"Okay, Mike," he said calmly. "Here's what we need to do. I'm going to get someone from Picton headed your way. You secure the scene. Are you sure it's a murder?"

"Yes, I'm sure. Someone bashed the back of his head in. I checked to make sure he was dead and found the wound. I haven't looked for the murder weapon," I said. "The scene is secure, and you don't need to call the cops in Picton. I already did that."

"I'm going to come, but it'll take me a while," he said. "I have access to a helicopter, but I'll need to get the pilot out of bed. And I want to bring the inspector from Picton with me."

After the call was over, I sat down on the floor outside Skylie's room. The manager asked if she needed to stay with me beside the door. I told her I'd take care of things now. When she was gone, I dropped my head into my hands and fought to keep control of my emotions. The death of my little Mike Jr. came flooding back as I struggled with another loss. I shook it off and got a grip on myself. What could I do to find Skylie rather than just considering her lost?

I was relieved when a police car finally rolled up outside and two uniformed constables stepped into the building.

"Are you Detective Denton?" the older of the two asked, a husky man of medium height, who appeared to be in his midthirties.

"I am."

"I'm Constable Andy Hodges," he said, "and this is Constable Tracy Sipe." He nodded toward a man who was about my age, tall and thin with a long nose and narrow-set eyes. "We talked to Inspector Keller from Wellington. He said you're here on loan from the Los Angeles Police Department in the United States."

I guessed that was right, though I hadn't thought of it that way. "That's correct," I said. "But I'll let you fellows take the lead here."

"Actually, we just want to take a quick look," Constable Hodges said. "Inspector Keller and Inspector Elliott Pearlman are on their way via helicopter."

The sun was unable to peek over the mountains that morning. Not that it didn't rise; it was just that the sky was cloudy, threatening rain. Within a couple of hours, it began to drizzle, and then the rain came harder. The wind also blew, and for the first time since arriving in New Zealand, I wasn't enjoying the weather. Of course, even if the sun was shining and the day was perfect, I still wouldn't enjoy the day. Nothing but finding Skylie, uninjured and smiling, could salvage this day for me.

I helped where I could as the investigation proceeded, but even though there was a murderer to catch, of more importance to me was the kidnapping. And no one believed that Skylie left the TopHouse of her own free will.

The murder weapon used against her brother, a man Skylie hadn't even known existed until a couple of days ago, was found at the edge of the parking area. Blood and hair covered the end of a foot-long hard stick, a club of sorts. We all agreed that the murder had taken place inside Skylie's room and that the murder weapon had been carried outside and abandoned there.

Fingerprints were lifted from various surfaces in the room. We hoped that more would be found on the club, the murder weapon, and that it would lead to the killer. I was feeling guilty. If I had gone outside earlier, I might have been able to save Snake's life and prevent Skylie from being kidnapped.

Before the two inspectors left, we had a conversation. Inspector Pearlman said, "I think the investigation must focus on those involved in the bank robbery, whoever they are. We must at least consider Hemana and the Bahr brothers."

"If Antony's back in the country," I said.

We were seated around a metal table on metal chairs, sheltered from the rain by the roof of the porch. Inspector Keller leaned forward and caught my eye. "Detective," he said, "we're proceeding on the assumption that both your former partner and Antony Bahr succeeded in getting into the country. Antony must be considered a suspect. After all, he had planned to kill Skylie, so it doesn't take much of a leap to figure he'd kill her brother if Snake didn't tell him where the money was hidden."

"But why take Skylie?" I asked. "I think we can safely assume that the killer and the kidnapper are one and the same."

Inspector Pearlman was leaning back in his chair, apparently thinking deeply. He looked over at me. "I don't believe we can assume any such thing."

That rocked me. "Are you saying there were two people here besides Snake?" I asked. "Or are you suggesting Skylie's kidnapping and Snake's murder are unrelated? I would take serious exception to that. The victim's body was found on Skylie's bed. That links the two crimes."

Inspector Pearlman glanced at his colleague and then back at me. "Actually, what I'm suggesting is that the killer and Skylie know each other and were together on this thing. Skylie could be the killer herself, or she could be in league with whoever it was."

I was so stunned I couldn't respond.

But Inspector Keller could. "I've met Skylie, and I don't believe that is the case. But for the sake of argument, let's say she was involved. That would rule Antony Bahr out, and by ruling him out, I think we would effectively be ruling out Hemana, his people, and Antony's brother, Tristan."

Inspector Pearlman leaned back again. "Okay, I see your point, Kelsey, but I don't think we should rule her out until we know more."

I shoved my chair back and surged to my feet. "She's a victim! And while we sit here and consider her as anything else, she's out there some-where with a killer, and her life is in jeopardy. We need to get busy and find her, not accuse her."

Before either inspector could respond to my outburst, I hurried inside, where Rongo and Marama were sitting at the long dining table, quietly talking.

"How's it going?" Rongo asked as I came in.

"We need to leave," I said. "There's nothing more to be accomplished here. Will you take me back to Wellington? I need to start looking for Skylie. I'm sure Inspector Keller and his officers will too, but Inspector Pearlman won't."

"We've just been trying to decide what to do," Rongo said. "We don't feel safe returning to our home right now. Marama's sister lives in Christchurch. She wants to go stay with her."

"I think that's what you both should do," I said.

Rongo shook his head. "No, I want to help you, Detective, if you'll let me. I know a lot of people, and I can be of assistance. If I get in your way, then I will back off, no feelings hurt."

I stared at him for a moment and considered his offer. It didn't take me long to conclude that without his help I wouldn't know as much as I did now. "That would be great," I said. "It would be nice to have a partner so we can bounce ideas off one another. But if it gets dangerous and I ask you to step back, I will expect you to do so."

"I accept your terms," Rongo said without hesitation. "We need to call Marama's sister in Christchurch. If she and her husband will meet us, it will save a lot of time. You and I can get back to Wellington in order to do some work this evening."

I handed my phone to Rongo to make the call, and a few minutes later, we had our bags and Skylie's loaded in the car. The two inspectors were still at the black metal table, deep in conversation. They stood up and followed us to the car. "I'll be in touch, Detective," Inspector Keller said. "We'll find her. I'll keep you advised of our efforts and hope you will do the same."

"Of course," I said sharply, glancing at Inspector Pearlman, who simply looked the other way. I felt like asking him how many homicides or kidnappings he had investigated. Even though I was young, I was sure I'd handled more than he had.

As if reading my thoughts, Inspector Keller said, "We don't have much experience in this sort of major crime. Any ideas you have, I would be glad to hear. Call me anytime you think of anything."

I nodded at him, grateful for the show of confidence, and then ducked into the car. The two men got in the helicopter as we drove out of the parking area.

* * *

After leaving Marama with her sister and brother-in-law we drove back to Picton, pulled the car onto a ferry, and settled back to make the painfully slow crossing to the North Island. Despite my worries, I made up for some of my loss of sleep during our travels.

It was about six o'clock when we arrived at Rongo's house. We went inside and were relieved to discover everything as we'd left it. Rongo opened a can of stew and heated it while I sat and wrote myself a few notes.

We were eating the stew when there was a knock on the door.

Rongo called the visitor by name and invited him in. Turning to me, Rongo said, "This is Keenan Chestain, a neighbor."

I was startled when I saw the man. I could have sworn I'd seen him before. He was about six feet tall and at least 220 pounds. His black, bushy hair came to his shoulders and covered his ears. He looked at me through very dark brown eyes.

Keenan acted friendly enough, sticking his hand out for me to shake, but there was something deep in those eyes that was unsettling. The feeling that I'd seen him before intensified. "So you're the American cop that's getting cozy with my girl," he said.

So that was the problem, and I knew why he seemed familiar. Even though I'd only seen him for a short time at the airport, I knew he was the man who had been leering at Skylie. And I was almost certain he was also the one driving the dark-blue Honda in New Plymouth. And unless I was badly mistaken, he had been on the ferry when we crossed over to Picton. "She's your girl, is she?" I asked, trying to disguise my distrust.

"That's right. So you need to back off," he said, fire burning in those disturbing eyes of his.

Rongo had watched the exchange, but he'd apparently heard enough. He stepped between the two of us, looked up at Keenan, and said, "Detective Denton is a guest in this house, so please be civil with him."

"I am being civil," the young fellow said. "He just needs to have an understanding of how things are."

Rongo turned to me. "Keenan and Skylie began dating when we first moved here. They continued dating until she left for California."

As I watched him now, I couldn't help but wonder if he was the reason she left. "She didn't tell me she was spoken for."

Rongo stepped in again. "Keenan, she told Marama and me that she wasn't going to date you anymore. She said she would still be your friend, but that's all."

"When did she say that?" he demanded, his otherwise handsome face turning ugly with anger.

"Just before she left for college in the states," Rongo said. "But I'm sure that's not why you're here. Is there something I can do for you?"

For a moment, Keenan stared at me like he thought he could make me wither. I didn't wither, but I did feel a shiver run down my back as I stared back. Finally, he looked at Rongo. "There was a man here. He was looking in your windows and even tried to get the door open. I just thought you should know."

"That's very good of you. When was the man here?" Rongo asked.

"Early yesterday morning," he said.

"Could you describe him to us?" I asked.

"He's about as tall as me," Keenan said, glaring at me with a fixed frown. "If you see him, you won't miss him. He has snakes tattooed on both of his arms."

"Snake," I said to Rongo.

"Yes, I said snakes," the bushy-haired neighbor growled at me.

"I'm sorry," I told him. "It's just that I know who he is." I nodded toward Rongo. "We both know who he is. His nickname is Snake. His real name is Jalen Lillard. He's Skylie's brother."

"That's a lie, and you'd know it if you knew my Skylie," Keenan said angrily, his eyes casting darts at me. "She doesn't have a brother. Rongo, you need to set this hotshot American straight."

"He's right. She has two brothers, Keenan," Rongo said evenly. "We only learned that two or three days ago."

Keenan shook his head. "I don't believe it. He must have some reason for making that claim. And it couldn't be a good reason."

"Keenan, why don't you sit down?" Rongo offered. "It appears there are a few things we need to explain to you." I was surprised at his self-control. I was seething.

"Like how some guy you never heard of comes around claiming to be someone he isn't?" the angry young man asked. He made no move to sit down, and I hoped he wouldn't. I wanted him out of here.

"He didn't come around *claiming* anything. As you know, Rongo and his family haven't been home for several days," I said tersely. "Rongo discovered who he was. There's also a second brother, a twin. Rongo also discovered him."

Keenan looked back and forth between Rongo and me. He ran his hand into and out of the bush of hair on his head. "Okay, supposing that's true, I don't think he should be coming around your house, and I told him so," Keenan said.

"You spoke to him?" I asked in surprise.

"Of course I did. My girlfriend lives here, and I'm not letting anyone come around causing her trouble," he said. The prolonged look he gave me left no doubt that his *anyone* included me.

"What did he say was his reason for being here?" I asked as I glanced briefly at Rongo, who was clearly shocked.

"He said he was looking for Skylie, that he had an important message for her. He didn't tell me he was her brother or what the message was. He asked where she was and when she'd be back."

"And what did you tell him?" I asked.

"I told him it was none of his business," he said. "I told him, *just like I'm telling you*, that she is my girl and no one else is going to be sticking their noses into her business."

"I suppose he took that well," I said facetiously.

"Not really," Keenan said clenching his fists. "He kept asking. And I kept telling him I wasn't going to tell him. Until he pulled a knife on me."

"He pulled a knife on you?" Rongo asked, his brows furrowed with worry. "Where did this happen?"

"Behind your house—out there," Keenan said, pointing toward Rongo's plush backyard. "I caught him trying to force the door open."

"So what did you tell him since you didn't know where she was?" Rongo asked.

"I knew where she was, and so I told him."

"You told him what?" I asked suspiciously. I was more certain than ever that Keenan had been on the ferry with us and probably overheard what we were talking about.

"I told him she was taking a short vacation at the TopHouse and that—"

I interrupted with, "How did you know where she was?" Although I was sure I knew.

His dark face grew darker and his eyes narrowed, but he didn't respond.

Rongo looked like he was finally losing his patience. He asked in a low, determined voice, "Keenan, please, it's important. How did you know where we were?"

"I overheard you mention it," he finally said.

Rongo looked at me. "We didn't talk about it, did we, Mike? Not here, anyway."

"We did on the ferry, and this guy," I said, stabbing a finger toward Keenan, "was on that ferry."

Rongo looked at him sharply.

"That's right. I didn't say it was here," the neighbor said. "I had some business in Picton. I overheard you talking about it on the ferry."

I shook a fist at him and said angrily, "She's in serious danger because you told him where she was. If you cared for her like you claim, you wouldn't have done that. A brave man, an honorable man, would have refused to tell him despite personal danger."

"He would have killed me," Keenan said, his face suddenly filled with shame. "But next time, he won't get the advantage on me. I can use a knife too."

"Are you saying you would hurt Snake?" I asked.

"Or whoever he was," he said darkly. "But I did warn her."

"You warned Skylie?" I asked. "How?"

"I texted her," he replied.

"When?" She hadn't said a word to me about it.

"Right after the guy left here," he said.

"Are you sure she got the text?"

"She always gets her texts," he retorted. "Of course I'm sure."

"She texted you back and told you she did?" I pressed.

"Well, no," he said, refusing to meet my gaze. "But I'm sure she did."

"Did you follow up with a second text and a third?" I asked. "Did you make sure she got your warning?"

"It wasn't really a warning. I was just letting her know the guy claimed to have a message for her and reminding her that she was my girl," he said.

"If you care so much for her, weren't you worried he might hurt her?" I asked. "After all, he threatened to hurt you."

"He wasn't going to hurt her," Keenan said flatly. "It was me he threatened. I just didn't want him to see her—just like I don't want her to see you again. And she won't, Mr. Hotshot California Detective. Believe me, she'll have nothing more to do with you if I can help it."

That statement and the chilling look he gave me set alarm bells ringing in my head.

ELEVEN

RONGO'S FACE TOLD ME HE, too, had bells going off in his head, and it appeared he had reached a similar conclusion to what I had. "Where is she, Keenan?" he demanded, his fist clenched. He stepped close to Keenan and looked up at him. "You better tell us."

But Keenan didn't. He just turned and walked back to the door. Before he could get through it, I leaped over and blocked his way. "You're not going anywhere until you tell us where she is."

"That means you don't know," he said with a smirk. "That's good. I'll be going now."

I didn't move, and he shoved me. That was too much. I swung a bunched fist and connected solidly with his chin, knocking him into the doorframe. Then I grabbed him by the front of his brightly colored shirt and held him there. "Where—is—Skylie?"

He shook the fogginess out of his head and tried unsuccessfully to shove my hand away from his shirt. "I don't know, and if I did, why would I tell you?"

I let go of him. "The cops will be talking to you, and you better come clean with them or you'll be sitting in a jail cell."

"You don't scare me," he said, backing through the door. "She's my girl, and I'll take care of her."

"We'll see about that," I said. Seeing that he was going to get away from us, I grabbed him once more, and he ducked his head like I was going to hit him again. That was not my intention, but I had more questions for him. "Keenan, where did Snake park his car, and what did it look like?"

"I didn't see a car. When he left, he walked to the street."

"Which way did he go?" I pressed.

"I don't know. I stayed back here for a few minutes."

"You were afraid he'd hurt you," I said. "What were you doing back here while you waited?"

"I just checked to make sure he hadn't done any damage to Rongo's house." Thinking he caught me by surprise, he turned and walked swiftly toward his own house.

I made no effort to stop him.

"He's involved," Rongo said flatly, his black eyes filled with anger. "He took our Skylie and killed her brother. I've worried about him for a long time. He used to be a nice young man, but I think now he's become unstable and dangerous."

"I'm calling Inspector Keller," I said. "If Keenan took her, the inspector and the New Zealand police will get her back."

Keller answered quickly, and I told him what had just happened.

"Keep an eye on the guy until I can get there," he said. "If he leaves his house, follow him. Don't lose track of him."

"Believe me, Inspector," I said darkly, "he won't get away from us."

"I'll cover the back of his house," Rongo said to me. "You watch the front." He didn't wait for a response before hustling away.

"He's just about to enter his house now," I said as I watched him walk by the dark-blue Honda parked in the driveway. "Rongo is going around back to watch there," I continued. "I'll wait for you here unless he leaves."

"I'll hurry," the inspector promised.

Even hurrying, it took him thirty minutes, but Keenan hadn't left the house. Keller was accompanied by a couple of constables. I pointed out the house, told them about Keenan being at the airport, in New Plymouth, and on the ferry, and then reminded Keller of the veiled threats Keenan had made when he came to the house.

Rongo joined me in time to see the officers escort Keenan from the house several minutes later. We watched as Keenan was placed, in hand-cuffs, into one of the police cruisers. A minute later, the constables drove him away.

Inspector Keller came back inside. "I'll let you know what we learn, but she's not in that house. He's denying knowing anything about where she is."

"I suppose he would," I said. "By the way, we didn't say anything about her having been abducted. All we did was ask him where she was."

"You didn't mention that Snake was murdered?" he asked.

"That's right, but I suspect he might already know that," I responded.

"You could be right. Thanks for the help, gentlemen," Inspector Keller said. "Oh, before I forget, I have something for you." He fished in his pocket for a moment and then handed me a laminated card with my picture and name on it. It identified me as a member of the New Zealand Police Force with the rank of constable.

"Thank you, Inspector. Where did you get the picture?" I asked.

"Captain Bertrand texted it to me," he responded. "Oh, and by the way, an informant claims to have seen Antony Bahr in Auckland. We're following up on that."

If Antony was back, then Cal Granberg was probably here in New Zealand too.

Rongo must have been thinking the same thing. "Mike, you need to be very careful. If that corrupt partner of yours is in this country, he'll probably try to hurt you."

I didn't deny it; it was true. "I'll watch for him."

"We shouldn't stay here tonight," he announced. "My house seems to be a magnet to the crooks."

I couldn't argue with that. "Whatever you say, Rongo. But while we wait for the inspector to get back with us, how would you feel about the two of us going door-to-door around the neighborhood and see if any of your neighbors can add to what we already know."

"That's a good idea," he said.

Rongo was well liked by his neighbors. They all wanted to visit with him, which slowed us down considerably. After a few unsuccessful attempts, we finally talked to someone who was able to tell us something of significance.

The neighbor, who lived about two blocks from Rongo, was a widow by the name of Victoria Staffon. She appeared to be near fifty and was short and quite heavy. She looked at Rongo as she spoke. "I saw a man with tattooed snakes on his arms. I was sitting right here in my chair on the porch when he parked his car right across the street." She pointed toward the small blue house directly opposite of hers.

"Can you tell me what he was driving?" I asked eagerly.

She turned from Rongo and said, "I don't know much about cars, young man, but I can tell you it was small and it was black."

That was helpful. It had been a small car that tried to run me down, and it had been a dark color. Could have been black—or could have been dark blue. "What did he do after he got out of the car?"

"He walked that way," she said, pointing.

"And, of course, Rongo and Marama live that way," I commented, mostly to myself.

"That's the way he went," she reiterated. "And when he came back, it was from that direction. Aren't you going to ask me about the others?" she asked, looking at me with that *for a cop you aren't very smart* look.

"What others?" I asked.

She smiled, her dark eyes crinkling at the corners. "The man and the woman who were with him." She had my full attention now.

"What did the man and the woman do?" I asked.

"Not much. They both stayed in the car while the snake guy was gone."

"Tell me about them," I encouraged her. "Even though they stayed in the car, it's been quite warm lately. They must have had the windows rolled down."

"That's right. They did."

"Where were they seated?"

"The girl was in the front; the guy was in the back," she answered. "They talked most of the time the other guy was gone. She kept turning and looking at him, and sometimes he would lean forward, toward her. But of course, I couldn't tell what they were saying from here."

"Of course not, but I'd guess you did get some idea what they looked like. Tell me first about the man in the backseat," I requested.

"He had dark hair. His arms were skinny, and his face was thin."

"How was he dressed?" I asked.

"I think it was a flowered shirt, a lot like the one the snake man had on. That was all I could see," she responded.

"Thank you, Mrs. Staffon."

"You may call me Victoria."

"Of course, Victoria. Now what did the girl look like?"

"She was pretty in a pasty sort of way," she said.

"Pasty?" I asked.

"Yes. Too much makeup. Long hair, reddish colored. She was, as I said, attractive. I would say she had a nice figure, a lot like mine used to be." She paused and smiled. "You don't believe I used to have one of those hourglass figures, do you?" she asked.

"Of course I believe it," I said, trying to keep her focused. "Is that what the girl in the car had, an hourglass figure?"

"I couldn't see her except from her chest up, but that part was definitely hourglass," she said with a twinkle in her eye. Then the smile faded, and she added. "Unlike me, her arms were thin and so was her face. And that's all I can tell you about her."

"When the other man came back, what happened?"

"They left." She shrugged. "One strange thing, though," she added after a short moment of thoughtful silence. "He was carrying a knife when he came back. It was a large knife. He stopped and shoved it down in his pants. I guess he had a sheath of some kind hidden there. Anyway, it was out of sight when he got back in the car. He said something to the other two, and then he drove off."

"Which way did they go?" I asked.

"The way he came from," she answered, again pointing a thick finger in the general direction of Rongo's house. "He drove back that direction."

* * *

We knocked on one more door but learned nothing more. It was getting close to sunset by then, and the sky was dark and threatening. "Should we go before we get wet?" I asked.

Rongo said, "Let's do. We can drive to a hotel somewhere and spend the night. Unless you think there's more we can do first."

"Perhaps we could talk to someone who knew Snake. Do you have any contacts that could help with that?" I asked.

"He grew up, as I told you, in Dunedin, but we could make some phone calls." He sighed. "I wish Inspector Keller would call you back. I'm praying that Keenan will tell him where Skylie is and that she's okay."

I'd been praying too. I'd never prayed much. I did believe in God, and I'd told Him that I sure wished he'd lead me to Skylie before it was too late.

My phone rang.

It was as if Inspector Keller could read the old man's mind. "Mr. Chestain says he doesn't know where Skylie is and seemed quite upset when I told him she'd been kidnapped. I can't tell if that means he didn't have anything to do with it or not. We're going to hold him tonight, and we'll be searching his house in an hour or two."

"I was hoping he'd confess and that you'd have found her by now," I told Keller honestly. "But I guess that would be too easy." I told him about our canvas of the neighborhood and of Victoria Staffon and what she'd observed.

"A man and a woman," he mused. "We need to figure out who they are."

"Rongo and I will work on that tonight," I said. "Although I don't know how much we'll be able to learn."

"I have an address for Snake," he revealed. "He has an apartment in Wellington. Would you like to meet a couple of my officers there? You could observe the search."

"That'd be great," I told him. "Just tell me when and where."

He did that and then said, "I learned something rather interesting, Detective. In his undercover operation, Skylie's other brother, Josh Infelt, has infiltrated Hemana's gang. Even though he's not Samoan, he's managed to get in with them quite comfortably. He knows now that Antony is back in the country, and he'll be watching for him and Cal Granberg."

* * *

An hour later, Rongo and I were waiting in front of some large apartments when four officers drove up. We joined them and introduced ourselves. Constable Nico Portill seemed genuinely happy to see us again, and he said, "I'm sorry about all that's happened. We'll do all we can to find Miss Yates. I know she means a lot to the two of you."

We watched Nico knock on the door to Snake's apartment. When there was no answer, we waited while one of the other officers got the manager, showed him their warrant, and instructed him to unlock the door.

The four officers were very thorough, but I felt helpless just watching as the others did the work. I stuck close to Nico while Rongo wandered back and forth between officers. Nico was working in what appeared to have been Snake's bedroom. It was a two-bedroom apartment, and the other bedroom didn't appear to be used much. Even the bed was bare, no sheets or blankets.

Nico searched the drawers, but he didn't find anything of interest. He tore Snake's bed apart. He looked under the bed and beneath the mattress. He found nothing. The closet was a mess. Snake had things shoved in it, some clothes on the floor, some hanging. It took Nico quite a while to sort through everything, checking the pockets of clothing, looking inside shoes, and sorting through junk.

"I'm going to see if the others have found anything yet," he said, shoving everything back in the closet and swinging the door shut. I followed him into the living room. "Anything yet, Kiana?" he asked.

"Yeah, look at this." The young female constable picked up a plastic bag. Kiana Lever was a slender woman who I guessed to be in her early-to-midtwenties. She had expressive blue eyes and short blonde hair. She was holding a photograph. "Is this who I think it is?" she asked, eyes twinkling. She knew exactly who that was a picture of.

The young lady whose face was smiling broadly in the picture, a glossy four-by-six, had stolen my heart.

"Where was that?" Nico asked.

"In this drawer," she said, pointing to a small end table beside the sofa. "So was this one."

The second one was an eight-by-ten, full-length photo of an attractive redhead with a pasty face and hourglass figure, as Victoria Staffon would have said.

"I suspect that's the woman who was with him the day Keenan confronted him behind Rongo's house," I said.

Constable Portill took the picture of Skylie, still in its plastic bag, and turned it over. On the back, in very neat handwriting, someone, probably Jalen Lillard, had written: *My sister, Skylie Yates. She's pretty. Someday I plan to meet her.*

Well, he'd met her.

TWELVE

"THERE'S ANOTHER PICTURE HERE TOO," Constable Lever said.

I knew who that was too. The flipside had an inscription. It read, in the same handwriting as on the back of Skylie's picture: *Josh Infelt. My cop brother.*

Rongo had joined us. "It appears Jalen knew he had siblings, even if Skylie didn't. I wonder if Josh knew. Surely he would have contacted her or at least tried to find her."

"Maybe he tried," Kiana said, "and couldn't find her."

"He's a cop," Nico reminded her. "If he wanted to find her, he'd have found her. I'm thinking he didn't know, even though Snake did."

I wanted to know who the redhead was. Nico picked up her photo and turned it over. *Sage Decorte. My soul mate.*

The search continued for another hour. Rongo and I were both extremely tired. It was hard to bounce back from what we'd experienced the previous night. I was anxious to continue the search for Skylie, but I needed sleep in order to do it.

Nico, Kiana, and the other two officers gathered up the evidence, which included the three pictures, a laptop computer, some illegal drugs in small quantities, and a small .38 caliber revolver. The gun and the drugs would have landed Snake in jail, but since he was in the morgue, that wasn't an issue.

What we didn't find was the missing money which Antony Bahr and Hemana seemed so sure Snake had taken. And Nico, Kiana, and the others were meticulous in their search for the loot. We also didn't find his car, which the search warrant included.

"The killer probably has his car," I suggested to the others. "Someone rode with him to the TopHouse, and whoever it was drove his car away, taking Skylie with him."

* * *

I talked to Inspector Keller again late that night. I called him from a small motel room on the outskirts of Wellington. "Is there any chance that Josh Infelt has the money?" I asked. "All that Hemana wrote in the note to Antony was that Skylie's brother had the money. There are two brothers."

"No," the inspector responded slowly. "If Josh had it, it would be evidence that Hemana and his people were involved, and arrests would have already been made. I suppose it's possible that Snake has it hidden somewhere else. Or the girlfriend could have it—or the other man Mrs. Staffon saw in the car."

I wasn't convinced. I didn't know Constable Infelt. For all I knew, he could be a crooked cop—like my former partner. I didn't press the issue but asked instead, "Did you find anything in Keenan Chestain's house?"

"Actually it's his parent's home, and they weren't at all happy with us conducting the search," he reported. "Of course we did it anyway. However, we didn't find anything of interest anyplace but in his bedroom."

"What did you find there?"

"Lots and lots of pictures of Skylie," the inspector reported. "The man is obsessed with her. It goes far beyond any normal relationship."

"Was that all?"

"No, there was a shoebox almost full of letters," he said.

"From Skylie?" I asked, even as I felt a sinking in my stomach.

"Only one was from her, and it was pretty blunt. She wrote it sometime after she arrived in Los Angeles. She was very direct." He chuckled. "She told him that there was no relationship and that she didn't ever want to see him again. It was a short letter, very much to the point."

I was glad he couldn't see me; my legs were weak with relief. He had struck a sensitive spot in my heart, one that was either falling or had already fallen in love with Skylie. "So who were the other letters from?" I asked.

"They were from him," he said and paused for effect. "He wrote one every week she was in America, and every one of them was returned unopened. I guess he refuses to get the message."

"Do you think he knows where she is?" I asked.

"It's possible," he said. "But if he does, I don't know how we're going to get him to tell us."

"Let me have him alone for an hour," I suggested hotly. "I'd find out."

"The thought crossed my mind," he said with a chuckle. "But we both know we can't do that."

Yes, I knew that, but it didn't change the fact that I would like to have the chance. "Could he have killed Snake? He sure is the jealous type."

"Yes, he could be the killer, but there is one thing that bothers me about that idea," Inspector Keller said.

"What's that?"

"I don't see any way that Keenan and Snake would have ridden in the same car to the TopHouse, especially if it was Snake's."

"Yeah, that's been bothering me too, but I suppose Snake could have forced Keenan to show him where Skylie was; then Keenan could have killed him there and taken Skylie away in Snake's car," I suggested.

"You may have something there, Detective," Inspector Keller said. "I should have thought of that, either me or Inspector Pearlman; although, Pearlman is stubbornly hanging onto the idea that Skylie could be the killer. What you just told me, however, throws a whole new light on the matter."

"That's just one theory," I said. "I can't help but think of others as well. For example, since we know that Antony's back in the country, it could have been him. He and Snake could have gone there together, either willingly or not, on Snake's part," I suggested. "Antony might have decided that Snake gave the money to Skylie and that she had gone to the TopHouse to hide it."

"Or it could have been Tristan or Hemana or any number of other gang members," the inspector said. "The only thing I think we can be sure of is that they went in the same car."

We talked for a few more minutes, but my eyes were heavy, and the inspector's must have been as well. It had been a very long day for both of us. As worried as I was about Skylie, I fell asleep quickly and slept soundly for several hours. I awoke to my ringing phone.

"Here's another possibility, Detective," Inspector Keller said almost as if we were picking up the conversation where we'd left off. "I just got a call from Inspector Pearlman. He received a call from the manager of the TopHouse. If you remember, there were other cars there besides Rongo's."

"There were other guests," I said.

"Those guests are gone now, but one car isn't. Pearlman's checking it out. That could be the car Snake came in," he said.

"Or it could be the car someone else came in. And then that person could have stolen Snake's car to kidnap Skylie," I theorized.

"Either way, the killer didn't necessarily come with the victim," Inspector Keller pointed out. I had already processed that very thought as well as what he said next. "That puts Mr. Chestain very high on our list of suspects."

"His car is at his house—not that he couldn't have stolen one. I suppose Inspector Pearlman will figure out if it's stolen. Somehow, you've got to get Keenan to talk. He might think he loves Skylie, but people with sick obsessions like that can turn love to kidnapping and then to murder." The worry I was feeling for Skylie was intensifying.

"We'll try again, but unless we find more evidence, we're going to have to release him, Mike."

"I suppose the car, stolen or not, is going to be impounded and processed for evidence," I said.

"Yes, that's already underway. I'm hoping we find Keenan's fingerprints in it. If we do, we'll have something to hold the guy on. If not, we'll have to release him."

I thought about that for a moment. "You know what, I might be okay with that. If he gets out, someone could follow him. He might lead—"

"Us to Skylie," the inspector broke in. "Good thinking, Detective. We'll do that if the car doesn't implicate him. If it does, we can apply a lot more pressure."

"Or you could release him anyway but not let him know it isn't for very long," I suggested. My biggest priority was to find Skylie, alive and well, as soon as possible.

"I'll give it some thought," the inspector said, "but I'm not promising anything."

"Also," I said, "I've been thinking about the gun we found in Snake's apartment last night. The number is filed off. Is there any chance your lab could restore it? These crooks don't realize that the number stamped on the gun actually penetrates deeper into the steel. If the lab can even just get a partial number, I could have it entered into our database at the LAPD. If we find it listed, then we'll know it came from there."

"And that would help us in our smuggling case," Inspector Keller said thoughtfully. "Yes, we'll get right on that, Detective. We're also trying to find Snake's girlfriend," the inspector added. "She might be able to add some insight into who might have wanted him dead. Who knows, there may be someone out there who had a motive we haven't even thought of yet. By the way, did I wake you up, Detective?"

"Yes, but that's okay. I feel rested now, and I have a couple of things I'd like to do." My mind was churning the possibilities.

"Related to the murder and kidnapping?" he asked.

"Possibly, and to the gun smuggling."

"What do you have in mind? Is it something I can help you with?"

"I don't know for sure, at least not quite yet. I'm hoping to somehow find Cal Granberg, and I've been thinking that the best way to do that is to try to draw him out," I said. "I'm sure he's looking for me. Maybe I can bait him somehow."

"You *will* need help for that," the inspector said sternly. "Don't try anything until we have some backup in place for you. There's something I want you to do today if you can find the time."

"What's that?" I asked. "I'll do whatever you need me to."

"Good. I'd like you to meet Skylie's brother Josh. It may mean either you going to Auckland or, if he can without risking his cover, him coming here. I'll see what I can arrange and get back with you. And if he'd like to, Rongo can go with you. I'm sure he'd like to meet Josh."

I welcomed the chance to meet Josh. I hadn't ruled him out as a suspect. Perhaps meeting him would help me to do that—or cause me to consider him more seriously.

Rongo was up and knocking on my door shortly after I'd showered. We went out and had some breakfast while I brought him up to date.

"So what do we do today?" he asked.

"The local police are going to try to find Sage Decorte, Snake's girlfriend, but I thought you and I might try as well. I'm guessing there's a good chance she lives in or near Wellington. We could ask around, I suppose. Snake probably worked somewhere. We didn't find any paycheck stubs in his apartment, but we still might be able to figure it out. We could try the same with Sage."

"Okay, I'm fine with doing that," Rongo agreed.

"If Inspector Keller gets a meeting set up for us with Josh, we'll have to drop what we're doing and go meet him."

Rongo was good with whatever we did. His concern, like mine, was that we find Skylie, and other than attempting to locate anyone connected with Snake, we didn't know what else to do.

We hadn't even begun when Inspector Keller called again. "I have a meeting set up. Josh would like to meet you closer to Auckland. He suggests a place called Waitomo Caves."

"I've heard of it. Skylie told me that some people refer to it as the Glowworm Caves since it's full of glowworms."

"That's the place. But he actually wants you to go just beyond it. There's a nature walk that goes deep into a narrow canyon, a place called Ruakuri Bush Walk. He'll meet you there, and the three of you can find some privacy," Inspector Keller said.

"What time should we be there?"

He answered and then said, "You need to leave now. It'll take you several hours to get there."

We did as instructed and drove north, keeping to the Tasman Sea side of the island until we reached Wanganui. Then we stayed inland all the way to the caves. We passed by them and soon found the trailhead. I glanced around just as a car door opened. A man about Josh's age and description stepped out of a beat-up, older-model white Toyota. I leaned back against Rongo's car and waited.

The fellow didn't even glance at us as he walked by, but he said softly, "Give me five minutes then come. Follow the trail, and I'll be waiting for you."

My stomach flipped, and Rongo and I exchanged glances. "I hope he's the kind of man they say he is," he said softly, echoing my own concerns.

But we did as instructed. When we saw Josh again, he fell in step with us and, after looking around cautiously, said, "I know a place off the trail where we can talk. It's not too far. Keep me in sight. I'll signal you when I'm ready to turn off." Then he walked quickly ahead, putting some distance between us.

I was nervous, hoping we weren't being set up for an ambush. Despite my worry, I allowed myself to be taken in by the splendor of my surroundings. I don't ever remember being in a more wondrous and beautiful place in my life. I promised myself that Skylie and I would come to this place, this Ruakuri Bush Walk, and experience it together—if and when I found her.

The trail dropped rapidly into a narrow, deep canyon. The vegetation was thick and green. Some trees grew all the way up from the bottom of the rift—and it was a long way to the top. A rugged stream coursed through the canyon. There were strong bridges with sturdy railings and lookout areas all along the trail, but we didn't have time for those. I again promised myself that I would come back here before I left New Zealand, but today, we were here on police business. The trail eventually started back up on the opposite side of the canyon. We followed it for a while, and then suddenly, Josh signaled us and disappeared from the trail. We waited until a couple speaking a foreign language passed by, and then we cautiously followed him.

He was seated on a rock not too great a distance away. His hands were clasped in his lap, and he was staring down at the water below. We were almost directly above the stream. The rushing water was loud enough that I wasn't worried about being overheard. In fact, we had to speak well above a whisper to even hear each other. Josh stood up, looked at us, and held out his hand to Rongo. "I'm Josh Infelt," he said. "And you must be Rongo Parata."

"I am. Very pleased to meet you," Rongo said.

"And you're the detective from Los Angeles," he said as he offered his hand to me in turn.

"Mike Denton," I said. "Thanks for taking the time to meet with us."

He smiled, a smile that was so much like Skylie's it made my heart ache. "I understand I have a sister I'd never even heard about," he said. "I'll help you find her, and when we do, I pity the man who took her."

I pitied him too. But I didn't say so. I just listened as Rongo said, "She's the sweetest, most beautiful girl you'll ever meet. And your smile is very much like hers. You look a lot like her in other ways too."

"Except for the beard and long hair," Josh said. "I've had to grow my hair like this in order to do my undercover work. When you infiltrate the scum, you have to look like them. Tell me more about my sister and what you know about our brother."

So we began to talk. Rongo's voice cracked from time to time, and I also had a hard time keeping my emotions in check.

Finally, when we finished, Josh said, "We'll find her, and we'll find the man who killed my brother. He might not have been a good man, but he was my brother. I've heard of him, by the way. I just never met him and had no idea he was my twin. The only name I heard was Snake. I wish I could have met him. Maybe I could have helped him change."

"Maybe," I said doubtfully. My reservations about this brother, Josh, were slowly evaporating. He certainly seemed like a good man.

"Let's talk about how we're going to find Skylie. If I have to blow my cover, I'll do it, but I'd rather not until we get Hemana and the Bahr brothers in jail."

THIRTEEN

WE TALKED FOR NEARLY THIRTY minutes. The more we talked, the more I felt I could trust him. He felt like a brother officer, something I'd never felt with Cal. Josh and I agreed we needed to find Antony Bahr, that he might prove to be the key to locating Skylie. "I think Cal Granberg could lead us to Antony," I said.

"So how do we find Cal then?" he asked.

When I told him what I had in mind, he said firmly, "That sounds risky to me, Mike. You'll need someone there to cover you when you meet him. I'll help if there isn't anyone else to back you up." He gave me a cell phone number and said, "If you need me, call this number. But refer to me as Gunner. If I can't talk, then I'll just ignore the call. If I do answer and then suddenly change the subject, just play along."

"I can do that. I've done it before," I assured him.

"Good. So let's come up with a code name for you."

I thought about it for a moment, and then I said, "Call me Otis. That's a nickname I had in junior high school."

"Let's have a last name, too, just in case," Josh suggested. "Make it something short."

"How about Leek?" I asked.

"Otis Leek. I've got it," he said. "Now, I better get back. It's been nice to meet both of you. I look forward to getting to know you both better. Let me leave first. Give me maybe ten minutes, and then go ahead and complete the loop if you like. Take your time. I'll hurry and be long gone before you get back to the parking lot." With that he slipped into the thick foliage. We listened to him for a minute; then he was back on the trail. His footsteps receded and then faded away.

"What do you think about him?" I asked Rongo a moment later.

"I like him, Mike. He seems so much like Skylie. I feel like we can trust him," he replied.

"I feel the same. Let's continue to be cautious, just in case he's a great actor," I said.

Rongo and I took our time for the rest of the trek. I tried to enjoy the splendor of the place, the ruggedness, the way the sun filtered down through the towering trees from so far overhead. But all I could think about, as I looked at the beauty and peacefulness around me, was Skylie and how I wished she were with us. As we neared the end of the trail, Rongo said, "Sometime soon you must bring Skylie here. She's been here before. It's one of her favorite places. She also loves the caves, but I think she would like both places even more if she could share them with you."

"We've got to find her first," I said, feeling depressed at the thought of what a difficult task that was.

"Keep your chin up. We'll find her, Mike. You're a smart and determined man. And I really do like Josh. I'm glad he's on our side and is as determined as you and I."

I felt even better about Josh. Rongo seemed like a wise man, a good judge of character. I was glad he was with me.

We were soon back at the parking lot. As expected, Josh's old Toyota was gone.

"Let's find some lunch," Rongo said as he pulled his car onto the road.

We stopped at a restaurant a short distance from the caves, and I let Rongo talk me into trying a lamb burger. "You'll like it," he assured me. And I did. It tasted nothing like hamburgers from the States, but it was excellent. Not only was the meat good, but the dressing they used in place of ketchup and mustard was superb.

After lunch we climbed back in the car. As we drove south toward Wellington, Inspector Keller called. "The lab was able to restore the serial number on that pistol from Snake's apartment," he said and then gave me the number. I promised to call him back as soon as I learned anything from the LAPD. "This could be a major break for us on this gun smuggling case, Detective. How did your meeting with Josh go?"

"Great," I responded. "Thanks for setting it up. He seems like a good man."

"His superiors have nothing but good to say about him," Inspector Keller confirmed. "I think he'll prove to be valuable to us as we work to find Skylie."

Next I placed a call to Captain Bertrand. I was told he was in a meeting but would be given the message to call me. I hoped it wasn't too long of a meeting. I was anxious to see if the little .38 had a history in LA. My gut told me it did.

We were almost halfway back to Wellington when I finally got the call from Captain Bertrand. "Is everything okay, Mike?" he asked.

"Not really," I said, and I brought him up to speed on what had happened at the TopHouse and everything since. I didn't enlighten him on my growing personal relationship with the pretty Kiwi girl who was missing, but I did tell him it was critical that we find her soon.

"I know finding the girl and the killer are important, but don't forget why you're there," the captain reminded me sternly.

Finding Skylie was more important to me, but I didn't tell him that. "Actually, the reason I was calling does have to do with the gun smuggling," I said. "A pistol was found in the apartment of the murder victim. It's a snub-nosed .38 Smith and Wesson revolver. The serial number was filed off, but the lab in Wellington was able to restore it. I'd like you to have someone check the number they found against our database."

"Do you think it may have come from here?" Captain Bertrand asked, suddenly sounding very interested.

"It may have. I'm actually hoping so. This fellow who was killed at the TopHouse may be tied in with the gang they suspect of gun smuggling," I said. "The bank robbers, if they're the same as the gun smugglers, probably stole the money to pay for the guns. Skylie, the young woman who was kidnapped, is the murder victim's sister. We think he was killed for refusing to disclose what he did with the money. We don't know that he ever had it, but the Samoan gang's leader thinks so. Now they expect Skylie to tell them where the money is, but she doesn't know. Anyway, that's the connection to the gun smuggling. And that's why I think the .38 could be one of the ones smuggled from LA."

"It sounds like you're probably on the right track. I'll run the number and get back with you as soon as I can," the captain promised.

A few hours later, as Rongo drove the last few miles to Wellington, I considered what I might do to get a message to Cal. I finally came up with a plan, and I called Inspector Keller to see what he thought.

"I think that might work," he told me. "Are you back in Wellington yet?"

"Almost," I said.

"Maybe we could meet somewhere. I want to discuss this with you in detail—and also some other things," the inspector told me.

"You say where."

"Let's meet at Rongo's house," he said. "I need to come to the neighborhood anyway. I want to talk to the witness you found, the one who saw Snake."

"Victoria Staffon," I said. "I can introduce you to her if you'd like."

"That's what I was hoping. Why don't we meet at Rongo's house in about an hour. Can the two of you be back there by then?"

I asked Rongo, and he said, "Easily. Tell him we'll be there."

* * *

We arrived at Rongo's house before Inspector Keller. It was almost five in the evening, which made it eight in the evening in Los Angeles, so the captain was working late when he called me with results on Snake's revolver shortly after we arrived. "You hit it right on the nose, Detective," Captain Bertrand said. "Good work."

"Was it stolen then?" I asked.

"Yes, twice. It was one of a number of guns that are missing from the evidence room downstairs," he said.

"Our evidence room?" I asked in surprise as I pictured Cal and our former sergeant, Sam Hart.

"That's right, Mike. The question is how they were taken without us knowing it. But I have a theory, and I suppose you do too."

"Cal and/or Sam," I said. "Only police officers could have pulled it off."

"That's what we're afraid of," he confirmed.

"Captain, you said it was stolen before that?" I began. "How did it end up in evidence?"

"It was stolen during a house burglary in Ventura and then used in a crime in our area," he said. "Would you care to guess what the crime was?"

My mind was going a thousand miles a minute. I slowed it down and thought. Why would the captain ask me to guess? It had to mean that he knew I'd be familiar with the case. It seemed like a crazy thought, but I suddenly had an idea. "I was shot with a .38," I said as Inspector Keller entered the house and stepped toward me. Trailing close behind him were Constables Nico Portill and Kiana Lever.

"Do you mind if we listen in?" the inspector whispered.

"Of course not," I said. "We're talking about the pistol we found in Snake's apartment." Then to Captain Bertrand, I explained, "Inspector Keller just arrived. He and two of his officers wondered if it was okay to eavesdrop. I told him it was."

"Tell him I'd like to speak with him when you and I are done," Captain Bertrand said.

I relayed his message and then said, "As I was saying, I was shot with a .38 caliber weapon. And even though I never saw it, or rather, don't remember it, it seems like someone mentioned it was a snub-nosed Smith and Wesson revolver."

The two constables' eyes opened wide in surprise. I touched the scar on the side of my head, and they both nodded in understanding.

"The gun must have been recovered at the scene," I said, "although I wasn't around to witness that."

"It was recovered," the captain confirmed. "And at that time the serial number was intact."

"The gun we have down here was stolen then used to shoot me."

"Exactly," the captain said. "It was originally stolen in Ventura."

I thought for a moment. "Cal stole it from the evidence room and sold it again—sent it to his customer in Auckland. And it's my bet that he provided it to whoever shot me." I was guessing now, but I had a feeling I was right. "He probably knew he could get it back and send it here. I doubt it would have occurred to him that it would ever be traced back to LA from clear down here, especially after he thought he'd removed the serial number."

Captain Bertrand cleared his throat. "I'm afraid you may be right. Cal was likely involved in the attempt on your life, the theft of the gun in Ventura, and the theft from our evidence room. I'm not saying he personally stole it in Ventura, but he obtained it from whoever did. That's the theory I'm working on, and if we can prove it and you can find Cal down there, we'll attempt to extradite him back to LA."

"I think we'll find him," I said. "That's one of the reasons Inspector Keller's here. I have an idea of how to get Cal to come to me."

"Be careful, Detective," the captain cautioned. "If he attempted to have you killed once, he'll certainly try again if you let him."

"I'll have backup. Is Sergeant Hart still on administrative leave?"

"Yes. We've been trying to contact him, but he's not answering."

"Have you talked to his wife?"

"We can't find her either."

"Sam's part of this, Captain," I said. "And so is his wife."

"I agree that he may be involved, but his wife? That seems like a bit of a stretch," the captain said. "Why do you say that?"

"A woman pretended to be a clerk of the superior court when the officers in Hawaii called to confirm the judicial release order on Antony Bahr," I said. "She was well coached and very convincing."

"I follow your thinking," Captain Bertrand said. "But we can't find her. I have to assume she's with Sam somewhere. Okay, Detective, we will proceed on the theory that Sam's wife took that call. And if she did, that means she's involved. I'll assign a team to it first thing in the morning."

"I wonder if by any chance Sam and his wife are in New Zealand now too," I said, thinking out loud. "Of course, if they are, I suppose they may have false papers."

"We'll check it out," he promised. "Do you have anything else?"

"Nope, that's about it," I said.

"Then put the inspector on."

While Keller talked to the captain on my iPhone, Nico and Kiana had several questions for me. "When were you shot?" Kiana asked, her expressive eyes wide. I told her. Then she asked, "Did I hear correctly? You were shot with the same gun we found in Snake's apartment?"

"It appears that way," I answered.

Nico asked the next question. "How did that gun get to New Zealand? Do you think your former partner was behind it?"

I assured him that I did think that. Then, while we waited for Captain Bertrand and Inspector Keller to finish their conversation, we discussed several theories as to who might have killed Snake and kidnapped Skylie. After the inspector handed my phone back, he joined our discussion. "I like your captain," he said. "He thinks you're on the right track about the guns, and I agree with him." Before I could respond, he changed the subject. "The abandoned car at the TopHouse was stolen in Christchurch," he said. "A few fingerprints were recovered, but we're afraid they'll all match the owner and his wife. Whoever stole it wore gloves, I suspect. However, the questions of how the car got to the TopHouse and who drove it there are things we need to figure out to solve both the murder and the kidnapping."

"It could have been any number of people, including either of the Bahr brothers, Antony or Tristan, as well as Hemana or any member of his gang," he said. "And I certainly wouldn't rule out your neighbor, Rongo."

The inspector looked at Rongo, who nodded in agreement. "So we have Keenan Chestain on the list. And there are the two people who were in Snake's car when he came here to break into the house."

Nico spoke up. "We don't know who the man is, but the woman is almost certainly Snake's girlfriend, Sage Decorte."

"We have yet to find out where she lives or works, but when we do, I'm sure she'll be a big help to us," the inspector said. He paused and looked thoughtful for a moment, rubbing his chin and shaking his head. The rest of us waited for him to speak again. He finally did. "There's one thing that puzzles me a great deal. So far, everything we know about the bank robbery and the gun smuggling is tied to the North Island, here in Wellington and up in Auckland. So why would someone steal a car in Christchurch and drive it all the way to the TopHouse from there?"

He glanced around Rongo's living room at the four of us as if he hoped one of us could provide an answer. When none was forthcoming, he shook his head again. "Which of our suspects have ties to Christchurch? That could prove to be helpful."

"So far," Constable Portill said, "all the people we're considering are either from here in Wellington or up in Auckland."

"So are there others?" Kiana asked. "Maybe there's someone we aren't considering who has ties in Christchurch."

The inspector leaned back in his chair and said, "That, Constable, is a very good question. *Who else?* That's one of the things Captain Bertrand of the LAPD and I were just discussing. Detective Denton, now that we've found a link between your former partner and Snake, the captain thinks we may want to include Cal Granberg on that list. Of course, we don't know of any connections he may have in Christchurch." He turned to his two constables. "Granberg is the man we now suspect of having attempted to have Detective Denton murdered. If in fact the money stolen from the bank was taken for the purpose of buying guns, then it could be argued that Granberg had a beef with Snake if he thought Snake had the money hidden and Hemana wasn't paying because of that."

My head was spinning, yet it all made sense. I threw another idea into the thought stream. "Inspector, Christchurch is one of the larger cities in your country. Could there be anyone there receiving guns? I mean, could Granberg have connections there because of his smuggling?"

The inspector slammed a hand onto his knee. "The same thought occurred to me. Yes, Detective, that would be possible. Maybe your partner knows someone over there, and maybe that's where he is now rather than in Auckland, like we've all been thinking."

We discussed the pros and cons of the various suspects and then decided to go over to the house of our witness, Victoria Staffon. But before we'd even left Rongo's house, I got another call from Captain Bertrand.

"Mike," he said as I calculated in my head. It was getting close to nine o'clock in Los Angeles, an unusually late hour for the captain to still be working. "Cal has a cousin who runs a body shop, which has been used for some time to chop stolen cars. I've had a couple of detectives working on it, and they just reported to me that the cousin, Wilson Blanco, the one running the stolen car ring, is nowhere to be found."

"Are you suggesting he might be down here with Cal?" I asked.

"Yes, and I wanted you to know that," Captain Bertrand said. "Wilson has served time for aggravated assault and has other arrests on his record. Our guys persuaded one of his employees to talk, so we know now that Wilson's been receiving, chopping, and selling stolen cars. And get this. Granberg was working against us to keep his cousin out of jail, and he was being paid handsomely for it."

"So he knew what his cousin was doing?"

"Oh, yes, he certainly did."

"Can you give me a description of Cal's cousin?" I asked.

"You bet I can. He's thirty-eight years old, six-foot-one, 240 pounds. His hair, the last we knew, was long, greasy, and brown. He usually has a stubby, unkempt beard, and his face is pockmarked," the captain said. "I'll text you a picture, a mug shot from about three years ago. The detectives with me now tell me it's pretty accurate."

"Okay, I'll alert the officers here and pass the picture around. While you're at it, can you also text me a picture of Cal?"

He agreed. "I'll just send the one that's on his ID, since I have that here in my desk."

"Thanks, now let me make sure I have Blanco's description right," I said and then recited back what I'd written.

"That's right," the captain confirmed.

"Okay, I do intend to lure Cal into a trap, and hopefully, when I do, we'll be able to get Wilson Blanco as well," I said.

"If there are two of them down there, you need to be doubly careful. Make sure you have plenty of backup. I sure hope you find them," the captain said. "Hang on a sec. These detectives say they have something else."

I listened to mumbling in the background.

Then the captain came back on the phone. "This is huge, Detective. It is these officers' belief, based on what their informant told them, that Wilson Blanco may have been the man who pulled the trigger on you."

My heart skipped a beat. "I wish I could remember the face that was looking at me just before I was shot, but try as I might, that's one of the things that hasn't come back."

"Well, you can be assured we'll be doing more investigating up here. We'll question everyone in that neighborhood again, and we'll show them the picture of Wilson Blanco," the captain promised. "Surely someone will remember seeing him."

Just then I recalled something else. "Captain, the call I was responding to was supposed to be a domestic disturbance. And I do remember that there was a woman in the house. I heard her scream when I first got to the door. And I remember her sort of wailing when the perp was telling me it was all okay," I said.

"Then we need to find the woman who was part of Cal's setup," Captain Bertrand confirmed.

"Yes, and again, it could be Sam's wife," I said. "I know that's just speculation on my part, but I still can't help but wonder. What do we know about her background?"

"Nothing," he said. "But we'll certainly look into it. We'll find a picture of her and show it around in the neighborhood as well. Mike, I'll get back with you tomorrow. It's getting late here, but we'll follow up very thoroughly. And remember, Cal and Wilson tried to kill you once. They probably have every intention of trying again."

A chill ran up my spine.

FOURTEEN

SKYLIE SLOWLY CHEWED ON THE hard piece of stale bread her captor had given her. Her hands were bound in front of her, and it was awkward both to eat and to drink the tepid water she was offered from time to time. She was told she'd get a decent meal when she disclosed the location of the money taken from the bank robbery.

She was also told she would suffer the same fate as her brother did if she didn't cooperate. Several times, she desperately told her livid captor, "I would tell you if I knew. But I don't know."

That only got her a swift kick to the ribs and another to her tightly bound legs. A couple of times she was even kicked in the head. She had passed out on two different occasions and awoke with no idea how long she'd been unconscious. At this point, she had no idea what day it was, let alone what time of day.

She didn't know where she was, although she was quite sure she was on the South Island. Unless she'd been taken by ferry across the channel while she was unconscious, she was somewhere within a few hours' drive of the TopHouse. She remembered much of the ride, but she had no idea the direction her captor had driven her. She'd been bound and forced into the backseat but had been unable to sit up. She'd tried to decipher the general direction of travel, but with all the twists and turns in the road, she was soon totally disoriented. Still, she felt that the odds of her captor taking her across the channel were slim. She couldn't imagine how that could have been done without raising suspicion unless—she might have been left in the car when it was driven onto the ferry and no one would have been the wiser. Suddenly she wasn't so sure she was on the South Island. She could be anywhere in the entire country.

She had been moved a couple of times while unconscious. Both of the times she awoke, the immediate surroundings were different. Currently, she was in a dark, dank place she thought might be a basement. Once she had been in a bedroom. She assumed it was a bedroom because it had a bed and a dresser. But the blinds were drawn, and she couldn't see outside at all, no matter how much she squirmed. Nor had she been allowed to lie on the bed, just the cold, filthy floor.

The first place she had been taken had appeared to be a kitchen, but not one in current use. She'd been bound to the leg of a heavy wooden table. She hadn't once seen a bathroom in any of the three locations but was forced to use a bucket when the need arose, which it didn't much anymore, as she'd had so little in the way of food or water.

The pain she was suffering was intense. She hurt from the times she'd been kicked by leather-booted feet. She also hurt from being forced to lie for hours in the same position, always an unnatural one that strained the muscles of her body. The ropes that bound her hands and feet had caused chafing to the point of bleeding.

She thought constantly about Mike and wondered what he was doing. She was certain of one thing: he would attempt to find her. But that didn't encourage her much, as that seemed like it would be impossible. She prayed for such a miracle and hoped for help to come. She was determined not to give up as long as there was life in her body.

She squirmed again, trying to get into a less painful position. It didn't help much. She chewed at the hard crust of bread, finally managing to choke the last of it down. She had considered not eating it at all, but she needed what little strength it would give her. She drank the rest of the tepid water and watched her captor. It was difficult to see the hate filled face because the only light in the room was from the open doorway. For the entire time Skylie was eating, neither of them had spoken a single word. They just stared at each other, but now, the captor spoke a few words, threatening words that chilled Skylie to the bone. She made no response. She couldn't say a word as much as she wanted to scream out in anger.

The two glared at each other a moment longer; then a twisted smile crossed the face of the captor, who turned and left the room, slamming the door and plunging Skylie's dungeon into total blackness.

* * *

As Rongo and I followed the three officers to the home of Victoria Staffon, I watched the old man from the corner of my eye. I was concerned about him. His dark skin had developed a gray pallor, and at times he seemed to be breathing abnormally heavily. I knew he was worried, as only a parent can worry over a much-loved child. I also knew Rongo was concerned about his beloved Marama. I'd overheard him talking to her on the phone before the officers had come, and from something he said, I thought Rongo was afraid she might be in danger. He'd told her to keep a close watch around her at all times and to make sure her sister and brother-in-law never opened the door to anyone they didn't know.

We got out of the car and followed Inspector Keller and the two constables to Victoria's door. Rongo seemed to stumble, but as I reached out to him, the old man caught himself and said, "I'm fine, Mike. I'm just tired. I haven't been sleeping well." That was certainly understandable.

Victoria answered the door and politely invited the five of us to enter. The inspector made introductions all around, and after we were all seated and offered tea, which we declined, he began to question her.

"Describe the man who was driving the car you saw, the man with the snake tattoos," he said.

The description she gave was quite detailed and fit the murder victim right down to what he was wearing when he died, which she described as either a blue or purple flowered shirt.

"Describe the woman who was left in the car," Inspector Keller asked next.

"She never got out of the car," Victoria said. "So I can't tell you how tall she is, but like I told Detective Denton, she had a pasty face. I think it was plastered with makeup." She went on to describe what she saw of the hourglass figure and then said, "That's all I can tell you. I wish I could tell you more."

"Think about her for a moment," the inspector coaxed. "Think about her arms, for example. Can you tell us more about her arms or any other part of her body that you could see?"

She closed her eyes and squeezed them tightly as she considered the inspectors question.

Finally, she opened her eyes. "She had strong arms, I think. They had more muscle than a lot of women."

"Any tattoos?" Inspector Keller asked.

"I don't think so."

"Her ears, did you see them?"

"No, her hair covered them. Her hair was sort of red, I do remember that."

"Good. Did she wear glasses?" he asked.

"No, no glasses," Victoria responded.

"Anything else?"

"Wait," she suddenly said, her chubby face brightening. "I just remembered. There was a tattoo. It was on the back of her neck. I saw it when she turned to talk to the man in the backseat and her hair fell to one side."

"Could you tell what it was?" I asked. She hadn't mentioned this when I'd spoken with her earlier.

She again closed her eyes in concentration, and then she said, without opening her eyes, "I think it was a kiwi. Yes, I'm sure it was. It was kind of gray. It covered most of the back of her neck, and its beak wrapped around her neck toward her throat."

I hadn't seen a real kiwi, but I had seen lots of pictures of the national bird of New Zealand. I guessed kiwi tattoos might have been popular.

Victoria opened her eyes and smiled at us. "Why didn't I remember that earlier?"

"That's very common, Mrs. Staffon," the inspector said. "That's why I asked you those specific questions."

"I'm glad you did. Maybe that will help you," she said, looking quite hopeful.

"I'm sure it will." Inspector Keller smiled. "Can you think of anything else?"

She again shut her eyes, but when she opened them, she said, "I guess not, but I'll keep thinking, and if I remember something, maybe I can call you."

"Okay, I have a picture here," he said. "Will you look at it and see if you recognize the person?" He handed her the picture of the woman from Snake's apartment.

Her face brightened. "That's the woman I saw. I'm certain of it." She touched a barely visible gray spot on the girl's neck. "This could be the tip of the kiwi's beak. The rest of the tattoo is covered with her hair. It's the same girl."

I had wondered why the inspector didn't show the picture to Mrs. Stafford before he coaxed a description out of her. As I thought about it, I realized it was a smart move. The photo, had it not been of the girl she saw, might have skewed her thinking and caused her to identify it wrongly. I vowed to remember that. If I was observant, there was a lot I could learn from the New Zealand officers.

"Now, you mentioned the man in the backseat." The inspector switched gears. "Let's talk about him for a minute."

Victoria nodded, her heavy cheeks waving back and forth as her head moved. "Like with the woman, I couldn't tell how tall he was, but he had dark hair. I'm not sure how long it was. He seemed thin," she said. "He wore a flowered shirt, mostly yellow, a lot like the one the snake man had on except that the color was different."

"Now, once again, think hard about the man. Is there anything else you might remember?" Inspector Keller asked.

Once more she closed her eyes tightly, even balling her fists where they lay on her ample lap. She finally opened her eyes and frowned. "I'm sorry. I can't remember anything else," she said. "He was in the back, and I couldn't see him very well."

"Mrs. Staffon," I said as I thought about how closely her description, limited though it was, reminded me of Antony Bahr. "Did you see any scars on his face?"

She looked at me and shook her head, sending her jowls swinging gently back and forth. "No, but I could only see the right side of his face. If there was one on the left side, I wouldn't have seen it."

The inspector's eyes met mine, and he nodded. He knew exactly what I was thinking. Antony Bahr had a scar, a prominent one, but it was on the left side of his face. I was hoping for something that would nail down that second person as Antony Bahr, as unlikely as that seemed, for he had sought out Skylie to help him find Snake. It didn't fit. I related my feelings to Inspector Keller, who agreed with my assessment. "But the description could also fit his brother, Tristan," I suggested.

It was my turn to show her a photo. I pulled up the picture on my phone of the man in the airport. I handed her my phone without a word.

She looked for a moment. "That could be him, but I'm not certain."

The inspector again had Victoria describe the car. Finally he stood up. "We thank you for your help, Mrs. Staffon. I'll leave one of my cards with you. You most certainly may call if you remember anything else, anything at all."

The rest of us stood as well, except for Rongo. He was sitting with his head in his hands. I stepped over to him. "Let me help you, Rongo."

He shook his head without a word and struggled to his feet. But he had only moved a couple of steps toward the door when he suddenly collapsed. I was able to catch him and soften the fall, but his body was limp in my arms. Constable Kiana Lever had her phone out in a second and said, "I'm calling for an ambulance."

* * *

The opening of the door to her dungeon awoke Skylie from a light sleep. She groaned and shifted slightly. She looked up, expecting to see her brother's vicious killer, but all she saw was the shadowed outline of someone in a long, loose dress being shoved through the door. The woman stumbled and fell near Skylie, and the door closed again, enclosing the two of them in total darkness. She never saw the other person.

* * *

After the ambulance left with Rongo, I drove the old man's car to the hospital with a promise to keep Inspector Keller informed. I nervously paced the hall for close to thirty minutes before a doctor stepped out to tell me that Rongo was going to be okay. He'd suffered a mild heart attack that didn't appear to be life-threatening. The doctor explained that they planned to keep him in the hospital for a few days for observation and to get him adjusted to some medications.

A few minutes later, I entered the room where he was being treated. I was glad to see that he was awake.

"Mike," he said in a weak voice. "Would you please call Marama's sister's house and tell Marama I'm in the hospital? Tell her I'll be okay and that I love her."

"Do you know the number?" I asked.

Rongo recited it from memory, and I wrote it down in the little notebook I carried in my pocket. "I'll call her in a minute or two," I said. "First I want to spend a little time with you."

"Thank you, Mike," he said with a weak smile. "You're a good man. I'm happy that my Skylie found you."

I nodded bleakly. I would be happy—we'd all be happy—if we could find Skylie. "I'll keep looking for her, but I want you to get better fast. I'll have a hard time without your help."

"Take my car," Rongo said. "And you get busy and find our girl."

I promised I would find her. I just prayed that it was a promise I wouldn't be forced to break. Rongo closed his eyes, and I said, "I'll call Marama now, my friend, and then I'll get back to work." I don't know if he heard me, as it looked like he had already fallen asleep.

I dialed the number of Marama's sister in Christchurch and waited while the phone rang. I finally gave up after a dozen rings. I then called Inspector Keller and gave him a brief report on Rongo. "I'm glad to hear that he'll recover. Keep me posted," he said.

I promised to do that, and then I said, "Rongo told me to use his car while he's in the hospital. I think I'll drive up to Auckland and put some feelers out to see if maybe I can get Cal Granberg to try to make contact with me."

"You be careful, Detective," the inspector told me, his voice raised. "These are dangerous people we're dealing with."

"I know, but I've got to do something."

"What exactly do you plan to do?" he asked me.

"Well, I'm not sure; I thought about putting a note on Antony's front door. Is that a bad idea?" I asked.

"Actually, it's not, Detective. The only one who will see it is Tristan. I'm told by my colleagues up there that they've kept close surveillance on the house and that the only one who ever comes and goes there is Tristan. But my guess is he'll get the message to Hemana, and if he does, it will eventually reach Granberg," he said. "I'll make a call up there and let them know what you're planning. Our officer, the one watching the house, can keep you covered."

"That would be great," I said. "I'd appreciate that. I'll just go, leave the note, and then head back down here."

"Wait, Detective. This still concerns me. Without Rongo to keep an eye out for you, I think you need to have someone else with you. If you don't mind, maybe I'll have one of my officers go with you."

"Are you sure?" I asked. "I hate to cut you short of officers down here."

"That's not a problem," he said. "Wait at the hospital, and I'll have someone there in the next few minutes. I'll have the officer go out of uniform. And if you want, instead of using Rongo's car, we'll send you in one of our undercover cars." He chuckled. "That way you won't have to drive. I suspect that driving on the left side of the road is probably not easy for you."

"That's for sure," I said. "I'll leave Rongo's car here and then pick it up when we get back. I'll be outside the main entrance when your officer gets here."

As soon as the call was finished, I tried once again to reach Marama's sister. This time someone picked up, and the lady at the other end sounded distraught. I had a hard time understanding her, but I caught the drift of what she was trying to say between sobs and broken words. My stomach was churning when I finally ended the call and prepared to make another one to Inspector Keller.

FIFTEEN

I HADN'T YET MADE THE call to Inspector Keller when a car pulled to the curb near where I was standing. The driver tapped on the horn. Looking up, I recognized Constable Kiana Lever. I hurried over and climbed into the passenger side of the car, the left side, something I was having a real hard time getting used to.

Kiana smiled. "Is Mr. Parata going to be okay?"

"Yes, I think so," I responded.

"But it leaves you without a partner, right?"

"That's right."

"Well, not anymore. Inspector Keller says I am to help you anytime you need until this thing is solved," she said. "I hope you don't mind."

"Of course I don't," I said. "I appreciate the company and the help, but the inspector didn't tell me it was for more than just this trip to Auckland. By the way, did he tell you my plan?"

"He did," she said, putting the car in gear and pulling away from the hospital. "It looked like you were about to make a phone call when I pulled up. Go ahead if you need to."

"I was going to call Inspector Keller again. Marama Parata is missing," I said.

Kiana's short blonde hair flipped as she snapped her head toward me. "What do you mean?" she asked.

"Her sister was so broken up that I couldn't understand most of what she was trying to say, but I did get the impression that Marama is gone and that it wasn't voluntary," I said.

Kiana shook her head and then signaled as she prepared to change lanes. "You better call Inspector Keller right now."

A minute later, I had brought the inspector up to speed on everything I knew. "That's right. She's not at her sister's home. But I can't tell you more than that."

"Okay, I'll call over to Christchurch and find out exactly what's happening. Are you with Constable Lever now?" he asked.

"I am, and again, thanks for the help."

"You'll like Kiana," he said. "She's a bright, hardworking officer. Let her help you."

"I'll do that." I looked over and realized she was watching me. She smiled, her cheeks turning a light shade of pink, and turned her eyes back to the road again.

"I like Inspector Keller," I told her when I was off the phone.

"We all like him. He's a good man," she said. "And he likes you, Detective. He told Nico and me that he wished you worked for him instead of the LAPD."

"That's nice of him," I said, feeling awkward but also flattered. "Right now, I guess I sort of do work for him."

"I'm sure he'll find out what's happening with Mrs. Parata and let us know shortly," she said. "And by the way, when we're not with other officers, would you mind if we use first names? Mine is Kiana, and I already know yours is Mike."

I already knew hers was Kiana too. I was glad for her company. It would have been a long and stressful ride for me alone.

* * *

It hadn't taken Skylie long to realize that the woman who had been shoved into the dank, dark room with her was Marama. She hadn't been able to see her or move close enough to touch her, but the old woman was sobbing and praying, and Skylie recognized her voice.

"Marama?"

"Skylie, you're alive!"

Skylie's voice was raspy, her throat sore, and it hurt to speak. For a short time, she said nothing as she worked her mouth, trying to get some saliva flowing. "I'm so sorry this is happening, Marama," Skylie finally said as she felt fresh tears flow down her face and onto the cold, hard floor. "These are terrible people."

"We must have faith, Skylie," she said. "Are you okay? I'm so glad to see you're still alive. At least you won't be alone now."

"You're an amazing woman, Marama, but we'll both suffer now. They think we know something we don't."

"How would we know where their money is?" the old lady said as she moved her bound wrists back and forth. "I don't even know who *they* are. I don't even know who that awful person is who kidnapped me and threw me in here."

"Maybe we can figure it out. As near as I can tell, the people who robbed the bank in Wellington somehow allowed one of the gang to take all the money, and they don't seem to be able to get it back," Skylie explained. "They think Snake, my brother, is the one that took it. He told me he didn't, just before he was murdered. He said he didn't have anything to do with the robbery, that he only learned about it afterward."

"I'm so sorry. I wish I could see you, my dear. It is so terribly dark in here. Come closer, and then you can tell me more," Marama said softly.

"I can't move. My hands are tied to a rope around my stomach; I can't move them. When I eat or drink, the rope is loosened around my stomach, but my hands are still tied together. My feet are tied and bent behind my back. I can't move." Skylie's voice choked with emotion.

"Well, only my hands are tied, and they're in front of me," Marama said as she crawled toward the sound of the girl's voice. "I'll come to you."

A moment later, the old lady's hands touched Skylie's legs, then her stomach, and finally, her face. A surge of hope filled Skylie at the feel of the old woman's fingers. "Marama, maybe you can loosen these ropes. Maybe if we're untied, we can somehow get away."

"I'll try," Marama said, strength and courage evident in her voice. "But it'll take a long time for these old fingers of mine. You must be patient."

"Once my hands are free, I'll undo you, and then we'll untie my feet," Skylie said. Soon, Marama was working on the knots at Skylie's wrists.

"You were saying that your brother said he had nothing to do with the stolen money. What was his name?" Marama asked. "I don't remember."

"Snake," was Skylie's reply.

"No, I mean his real name. I don't like that ugly name. No brother of yours should be called Snake."

"His real name is Jalen."

"Then we'll call him Jalen," the old lady said firmly.

"Yes, you're right," Skylie agreed. "I'd never met him until he came to me that night at the TopHouse, the night I was taken. He wasn't all bad; there was a lot of good in him."

"But you were kidnapped because of him," Marama said.

"No, Jalen came to try to save me," she said. "He told me he knew they were after me, that they wanted to force me to tell them where he was and where he had hidden the money. But he didn't have it."

Marama's fingers, bound though her wrists were, worked at the stubborn knot as the women continued to talk. "And you believe him?"

. "I feel it in my heart, Marama," Skylie said simply. "He came to warn me, but he trusted his killer, and that was his mistake. They don't believe I don't know where the money is, any more than they believed Jalen."

"How did Jalen find you?" Marama asked, resting her fingers for a moment.

"He said my boyfriend told him where I was."

"Your boyfriend? Did he mean Keenan?" Marama asked. Skylie felt her shudder. "We know he's an awful person."

"I'm sure he meant Keenan. And yes, I think he might be worse than I thought. He told Jalen he'd overheard us talking on the boat as we crossed the channel," Skylie explained.

Marama gasped.

"I told him to leave me alone when I went to America, but he won't. I'm so afraid of him now." It was Skylie's turn to shudder. "Anyway, Jalen said he came to find me at the TopHouse because he knew I was his sister, and he didn't want me to be hurt. What he did was brave. I wish I could have known him better. I think we could have been friends and that I could have helped him get the bad out of his life and replace it with good."

Marama was busy working the ropes again. As she did, Skylie explained how their captor had suddenly struck Jalen over the head, killing him, and how the murderer believed Skylie knew where the money was, obviously not believing that Jalen and Skylie had never met before.

The women continued to talk, but having had so little to drink, Skylie's voice became very weak.

"Save your voice, my dear," Marama said. "We'll talk more later."

For the next few minutes, Marama struggled with the knot in silence. Finally, she said, "I think it's finally coming loose, Skylie. I'll have these off in a minute or two now."

A moment later they heard a voice beyond the door. Skylie whispered urgently, "Move away from me, and act like you're helpless."

Light flooded in as the door was pushed open. The rope around Skylie's stomach was removed, and she and Marama were allowed to take a few bites of bread and a small amount of water. Then the rope was again tied tightly around Skylie's stomach. The entire time, Skylie had prayed that the loosened knots on her wrists wouldn't be noticed, and they weren't. The captor hesitated at the door for a moment and reminded the two of them that freedom would only come when the money was recovered.

Both women again denied any knowledge of the money. Skylie braced herself for another fierce beating, but it didn't come this time.

When the door was again shut, total darkness once again enveloped them. Skylie listened until the retreating footsteps could no longer be heard. "Okay, Marama, you can finish now."

It only took a few seconds for Marama to finish untying the knot and remove the rope from Skylie's wrists. Skylie struggled for a moment but soon managed to pull her hands under the rope tied behind her back. "Okay, now let's get your hands free."

It was excruciating work for Skylie's hands, which were so stiff and painful from the ropes that they didn't respond well. But as she worked at Marama's rope, her fingers gradually loosened up. She gritted her teeth, ignoring the pain, and in a few minutes, the rope fell free from the old lady's wrists. "Now your feet," Marama said.

It was hard to estimate the amount of time they spent trying to get her legs free, but Skylie was quite certain it was over an hour before they were successful. She then spent the next hour getting her severely cramped muscles to work again. She was eventually able to get to her knees, and then gradually to her feet. With Marama's gentle coaxing and help, she was soon able to move around the room reasonably well.

"I suppose the door is locked," Skylie said when she finally found it in the darkness. She grabbed the handle and pulled, but as she feared, it wouldn't budge. "We need to see if there's anything in the room we can use as a weapon."

The two of them then spent the next few minutes on their hands and knees, crawling around the room. It was filthy, larger than Skylie had at first assumed, and it wasn't entirely empty. They found a wooden chair in a far corner but nothing else of any use. "Maybe we can break this and use the rungs as clubs. They feel pretty sturdy," Skylie said hopefully. "If I have the strength to even lift the chair. I'm so weak."

"I'm old and weak," Marama said with a chuckle, "but between us we can do it. We must do it."

They did do it, and soon both were armed with two strong clubs each.

"The only thing we can do now is wait," Skylie said. "At least we now have the element of surprise on our side."

The two of them sat down with their backs to the wall near the door. For a few minutes, they simply sat silently. Then Skylie said, "When we get out of here, we need to figure out where we are. I have no idea."

"I was blindfolded, but I know this city well. When we get outside, I'll be able to find my way," Marama said.

"You mean you know what city this is?" Skylie asked, her spirits lifted.

"Of course. I didn't realize you didn't know. We're in Christchurch. I was taken from my sister's house, forced into a car, and driven here. It only took about ten or fifteen minutes if my estimation is correct," Marama said.

"We're in Christchurch," Skylie said. It wasn't a question, just a surprised utterance. "So what is this building we are in? Is it a house?"

"I didn't see it, but I think it must be one of the houses that was damaged in the earthquake and condemned," Marama explained. "The city has many such buildings."

Skylie explained to Marama how she had been knocked unconscious twice and awoken in different places. "But maybe I was simply moved from one room to another and then into the basement," she said.

"That's probably what happened," Marama said. "My dear, we will get out of here. Now why don't you let yourself fall asleep, and I'll keep watch. Then later, I can nap while you listen."

"That's a good plan," Skylie said. "If I can sleep. But I'll try." She closed her eyes and tried to slow down the only part of her that was still working—her mind.

SIXTEEN

I WAS DOZING WHEN MY phone began to ring. I woke up and looked out the window at the sweeping green farmland we were passing. "This is beautiful," I said to Kiana, pointing out the window with one hand as I pulled my phone from my pocket with the other. A long line of black-and-white cows were being driven up a narrow lane next to the highway. Beyond them, leading clear to the tree-covered hills, were bright green pastures. Strong fences surrounded the fields. A neat farmyard with barns, sheds, and a house, all nicely painted, stood at the end of the lane. I remembered Skylie explaining to me that sheep, which were still plentiful in New Zealand, were being replaced by milk cows, mostly Holsteins, now the strongest agricultural industry in the country.

I glanced at the phone and recognized Captain Bertrand's number. "Hello, Captain," I said.

"Detective, how are things going down there?" Captain Bertrand asked.

"Slowly, I'm afraid."

"Inspector Keller tells me that your Māori friend had a heart attack and that you have a constable assigned to work with you."

"That's right," I said. "We're on our way to Auckland now to see if we can lure Cal into contacting me."

"Be careful, Mike," the captain cautioned. "Inspector Keller told me your plan. It sounds like a good idea, but don't expect it to work perfectly. Also, he mentioned that the Māori woman has apparently been abducted."

"It looks like it, yes. She disappeared from her sister's house. Constable Lever spoke with the inspector an hour or so ago, and they have no idea yet what happened. They're doing a house-to-house search of the neighborhood, hoping to find someone who saw something," I explained.

"It sounds like you and the New Zealand Police have a full plate. Just remember what your primary focus is," he reminded me.

"Of course," I said, feeling a little irritated. "That's what I'm working on now."

"I know you are, and I appreciate it," he said. "The reason I called is to tell you that once again your instincts were good. Sam Hart's wife has worked in the past as an actress. She and Sam are still unaccounted for."

"So do you think she might have been the one who pretended to be a court clerk?"

"We're working on that, but that's the theory we are going on now. We've been able to look at the Harts' bank accounts. It appears their money has been moved. Their accounts are empty."

"They're probably bringing their money down here," I said.

"Could be, Detective. I'll let you know if we learn more, but in the meantime, I'm going to text you pictures of both of them as well as ones of Cal and his cousin Wilson Blanco," he said.

After I hung up, I explained to Kiana that I'd be sending the Harts' pictures to the inspector.

"Send them to me, too," she said.

They came within five minutes, and I immediately forwarded them on. When that was done, I said, "Kiana, we need to find someplace to buy a cheap cell phone. I don't want to give my number to Cal or any of the gang he's working with."

* * *

By the time we arrived in the neighborhood where Antony and Tristan Bahr lived, it was late in the afternoon. I had a handwritten note, some tape to attach it to the door, and a cheap cell phone in my pocket. The sky had been turning dark the past hour, and a few errant raindrops hit the car's windshield.

"I think you might get wet," Kiana said as she dialed the number of the officer currently on surveillance at the Bahr residence.

"Looks like it."

She waited for a minute or two, shaking her head. "He isn't answering. I hope they didn't pull him off the surveillance without letting Inspector Keller know."

"Well, we've come all the way here; I'm going to put the note there like I planned," I told her.

"But there could be someone in there, Mike."

"I'm trusting you to watch out for me, Constable," I said seriously. "If you see someone around the house, honk the horn with two quick taps, and I'll get away."

She took a deep breath and looked at me, worry in her eyes. "I don't know, Mike. Maybe we should wait. I'll keep trying the officer's number."

"Try once more, and then I'm going," I said firmly.

"That's the house right there," she told me a minute later.

"Okay, drive past and let me out a short distance up the street, but not so far that you can't keep an eye on the house. I'll walk back, put the note on the door, and then rejoin you," I said. As we drove by, I inspected the house she had pointed at. It was a white, wooden house with peeling paint and an unkempt, badly overgrown yard. It sat in stark contrast to the nice homes and yards surrounding it. As I opened the door to get out, I said, "I sure wish you guys carried guns. I'm sure the bad guys do. I feel very exposed without one."

She nodded. "I'm afraid you're right. I wish they would arm us, especially when we're working on cases like this. I do have a stun gun if you want to borrow it."

"No, that's okay. Just honk if you see anyone who could be a danger to me."

"I will."

I went directly to the white house and approached the front door, looking around for signs of anyone lurking about. There was a porch with steps made out of lava rock. I stepped onto it, taped my note securely to the center of the door, and hurried back into the rain. It was starting to come down hard now, and by the time I got back to the car, I was soaked.

"Sorry about that, Mike," Kiana said with a mischievous grin. "If we'd been five minutes earlier, you wouldn't have gotten wet."

"That's okay," I said. "I love the smell of the rain, and without it, this country wouldn't be so gorgeously green. And I still got the note there without being interrupted."

She drove a couple of blocks and then stopped and once again tried to call the officer who was supposed to be on surveillance. When he didn't answer on her fourth attempt to contact him, she called Inspector Keller. When she finished her call, she said, "Inspector Keller said he'll contact the officer's supervisor in Auckland. He wants us to head back to Wellington."

The rain was coming down hard as Kiana drove out of the neighborhood. I admired the homes we passed. Very few were neglected like the Bahr house. The yards were filled with colorful flowers and well-trimmed shrubs as well as a huge variety of trees, both deciduous and evergreen. It was a pretty area.

Inspector Keller called a few minutes later as we were driving south. I turned the speakerphone on so Kiana could hear. "They can't locate the officer who was on surveillance, but a pair of replacements has been sent. They've been instructed to call Constable Lever or you immediately if anyone pulls the note off the door."

"Is there any idea where the officer has gone?" I asked.

Inspector Keller's voice was serious when he answered. "No, but they found his car. It's still near the Bahr home. Frankly, we're worried something has happened to him. That's why they sent two replacements to take over the surveillance. They'll be watching out for each other as well as watching Antony's house. In the meantime, they're searching for the missing constable."

"I hope he's okay," I said after we disconnected. "Now I guess we wait for a call from one of the officers. They'll let us know when my note is found."

I thought for a moment then called a number on my iPhone, hoping I would get an answer.

"This is Gunner," Skylie's surviving brother answered.

"Otis Leek," I responded.

"Good to hear from you, Otis," Josh said. "I'm alone at the moment, but I expect others to join me at any moment."

"I'll keep this short," I promised. "I left the note for Granberg on Tristan's door. I didn't bother you because I had another officer with me."

"Excellent. Keep me informed," Josh said. "I have yet to meet Granberg, but there's talk of him and another man named Wilson."

"Have you heard the name Sam Hart mentioned?" I asked.

"Yes. I understand he's here somewhere."

"I was afraid of that," I said. "What about his wife, Jeanette Hart?"

"She's not here," he said. "At least not that I've heard."

"Have you heard anyone mention Skylie?"

"Not a word," Josh said. Just then I heard a voice in the background, and Josh said, "Talk to you later, Otis. I need to go now."

"Call me back when you get a moment," I said.

"Okay," he agreed.

And with that he was gone. I hadn't even had time to tell him about the missing officer. That was why I'd asked him to call me back. I hoped he would be able to do so before long. He needed to know that the officer was not only missing but might have been harmed in some way.

I slipped my phone back in my pocket and looked over at my partner. "Let's find someplace to eat," Kiana suggested.

* * *

We had eaten and had started the long drive back to Wellington in the pouring rainstorm when my iPhone rang. I spoke to a constable for a moment, and when we had disconnected, I said to Kiana, "Tristan has my note. He stood on his porch while he read it, then he went inside. I guess the question now is whether or not he'll see that Cal gets it."

We were nearly halfway back to Wellington when I got another call. "Tristan left his house a few minutes ago," I told Kiana as soon as the call had ended.

"He's probably going to let Granberg know," she said.

"I hope so," I agreed. "When do you think this rain will end? It's been raining nonstop since I put that note on the door."

She grinned. "I have no idea. It will end when it ends. What do you want to do now?"

"I want to go rescue Skylie," I said.

She shook her head. "You like her a lot, don't you?"

"She's a good friend, and . . . and more," I agreed. "I just wish I knew where she was and if she's okay. I hope I can get Cal to help me find her."

"If he knows," Kiana cautioned. "He might not be that tight with Hemana's gang. They may only use him to get guns."

I felt my shoulders slump. "I know you're right, but I don't know what else to do."

"How about if we spend some time in the morning asking around Wellington to see if we can learn anything more about Snake's girlfriend, Sage Decorte," she suggested. "I wish we had time tonight, but it'll be way after midnight before we get back to Wellington. At least we know she has that tattoo on her neck. Maybe that'll help us. And we have a copy of her picture we can show people."

"I do keep thinking she might know who went with Snake to the TopHouse. Finding her could be the key, more so than getting Granberg to meet with me."

"Sage might know who went with him or who met him there," she reminded me. "Remember, someone drove there in that car that was stolen in Christchurch."

"I can't say how many people were in the car that tried to hit me." I thought for a moment and then added, "I'm sure Skylie was in it. There was no other way they could have gotten her out of there."

* * *

Many hours had passed since Skylie and Marama had managed to free themselves of their ropes, but no one had appeared to feed them again. Both had slept fitfully from time to time, but they were weak and discouraged.

Skylie had drifted into a light slumber when Marama suddenly shook her. "Someone's coming."

Skylie could hear the footsteps, and her heart began to race. There was more than one person out there.

Marama heard it too. She whispered, "I don't know if we can hit them both."

The footsteps stopped before they reached the door, and an argument ensued. Skylie gripped both of her clubs tightly as she listened. She couldn't make out what was being said, but whatever it was, both people were angry. The voices beyond the door became louder, and suddenly there was a thump followed by a second one. There came a gurgling sound, and then it was quiet.

Skylie's heart pounded in her chest like it was trying to escape. She tried to calm it and listened again. Footsteps again approached the door, but there was only one set as near as she could tell. The door handle shook slightly, but the door didn't open. Both of her clubs were held above her head. She was quite certain Marama was in a similar position beside her.

The footsteps receded then approached again with a dragging sound of some kind. A moment later, the door opened, and Skylie prepared to bring her clubs down with all the force her weakened body could muster. Suddenly, a body hurtled through the door. The women stared in shock as the body hit the floor, bounced a little, and then became still.

Someone was breathing heavily just outside the door. Then someone spoke, saying he'd be back and would expect answers when he came. Finally, a head appeared in the light of the open doorway, and a man reached for the doorknob. With all her strength, Skylie brought both of her clubs down on the back of the man's head. He grunted and fell forward.

"Let's go," Skylie cried to Marama, and the two of them stepped across the man lying in the doorway. Moving as quickly as they could—which was painfully slow in their weakened state, even with adrenalin flowing—they headed for a stairway about twenty or thirty feet from the door. At the top, they fled through another open door and headed for the nearest exit on the far side of the kitchen.

Suddenly, there were lumbering footsteps behind them. Skylie screamed as her hair was grabbed, and she was jerked backward. She clubbed at her attacker, who had blood streaming down his face. Marama clubbed at him too. Skylie knew they couldn't beat him, and she screamed, "Run, Marama. Save yourself and get help."

"I can't leave—" Marama began.

"Go!" Skylie screamed as the attacker jerked her off her feet and began to drag her back to the basement. Marama fled.

The attacker threw Skylie through the door. As she stumbled over the other person, the man jerked the door shut, plunging the place into darkness. Skylie lay on the floor, her hands throbbing from breaking her fall. She kept listening, and then she heard steps approaching again. The door opened. Something was thrown into the room, and a voice called out, "That's to keep you alive until you tell me where the money is. After this there will be no more." Then the door slammed shut again. The time passed slowly, and nothing more happened. She could only hope Marama had gotten away.

Finally, Skylie willed herself to get to her knees and crawl over to where the other person was lying. She felt around and realized in horror that her hands were covered with blood. She almost retched but was able to control it. She found the person's face and then put her fingers where the carotid artery should be. It only took a moment for her to realize that she was alone in her dungeon with a very bloody and very dead body.

She backed away and bumped into something that hadn't been there before. A box. That must have been what the big man threw in the door. She opened it and discovered a couple of bottles of water and two sandwiches. Apparently he was serious about keeping her alive until she told him where the money was. For now at least, the captor didn't want her to die. It was the first decent food she'd seen since her captivity. She briefly considered using some of the water to wash her bloody hands, but that would be foolish. Who knew when she would get more—if ever? It wouldn't matter if Marama was able to get help, but otherwise she would need every drop. Shuddering, she finally rubbed her hands on her pants to get some of the blood off.

She opened one bottle of water and took a small drink then closed it again, forcing herself to ration it. She next opened one of the sandwiches and took a small bite. Ham and cheese. She'd never tasted anything so good in her life. But she forced herself to only eat a small portion of it, wrapping it back up and placing it in the box.

She waited for several minutes while the small meal settled in her stomach before once again willing herself to move. When she did, it was to get to her feet. She swayed unsteadily for a moment then moved cautiously toward the dead body. She found it again and began to explore in the pockets of the body's jeans. They were empty. She didn't know what she had hoped to find, but finding nothing was discouraging.

She shuddered. Then, picking up the box of water and sandwiches, she moved into a far corner, as far from the body as she could get. There she felt around and found what was left of the chair she and Marama had broken apart. There were more rungs, so she armed herself once again with a strong club and then sat in the dusty corner. She closed her eyes and attempted to pray. But mostly she cried desperate tears. After a while, she drifted into an uneasy sleep.

SEVENTEEN

BOTH OF MY CELL PHONES—MY iPhone and my cheap phone—were on
the stand beside the bed in my hotel room. I had placed them there after
dragging myself in at about two o'clock that morning. Kiana and I had
worked for an hour or so after getting back to Wellington, deciding that
late at night would be a good time to hit the bars and talk to patrons and
workers there. But we were still planning to do more in the morning. We'd
been excited a couple of times when someone remembered seeing a young
woman with that distinctive tattoo in company with a man with snake
tattoos on both arms. The people remembered them calling each other
Snake and Sage, but they knew nothing more about either one of them.

As we'd worked, I had received a very disturbing call from Constable
Josh Infelt. He'd sounded very anxious as he had delivered the news that
he'd overheard a member of Hemana's gang bragging that he and another
gang member had killed a cop who was hanging around the Bahr brothers'
home. They had apparently stabbed him and disposed of his body. "Call
someone," Josh had said urgently and ended the call. I was sure he'd been
interrupted.

I made a call to Inspector Keller, who grumbled about being awakened,
but the grumbling turned to anger and concern when I told him about
the possible murder of the missing constable. He thanked me and said
he'd let his counterpart in Auckland know. Before disconnecting, he'd
added a stern warning. "You and Constable Lever watch each other's back,
Detective. We've lost one officer. We mustn't lose any more."

I trusted Josh and was worried about him. He was working within a
gang who were not averse to cold-blooded murder of the police. It was
very sobering. Both Kiana and I had been discouraged and saddened at
the news, but we kept at our search for information. Surely someone could

tell us more about Sage—where she worked or where she lived. Right now, finding her seemed like the only way to find any information—unless I got a call from Cal.

Despite the hour, I kept hoping for a call from Cal. I finally drifted into an uneasy sleep.

One of the cell phones rang, and I was disoriented for a moment, grabbing blindly as I struggled to wake up. I finally managed to turn on the light. It was my iPhone, not the cheapie, that was ringing. I dragged it to my ear. "Hello."

"Mike, this is Kiana. I'll be there to pick you up in ten minutes."

I shook my head and looked at the clock on the bedside stand. It read 3:15 AM. "Kiana," I said, "do you know what time it is? We both need some—" She cut me off before I could say sleep.

"I know, but we need to go," she said urgently.

"Why? Where?" I asked, swinging my legs over the edge of my bed.

"Christchurch," she said. "Someone found Marama Parata. She's alive but in bad shape. Inspector Keller has arranged for a department plane for us. I'll pick you up, and we'll meet the plane at the airport."

I dressed as quickly as I could and was outside the hotel entrance when Kiana pulled up. As earlier, she was dressed in plainclothes. I hopped in, and she tore away.

She drove rapidly, as she had much of the way to and from Auckland. As she drove, she filled me in on what was going on. "Marama was found by a young couple who had been out late with friends. They were driving down a city street when they saw someone lying in the roadway. They stopped, discovered it was an elderly Māori woman, and called for help. She was unconscious but alive. An ambulance took her to a hospital. She's still unconscious, but the inspector wants us there so when she wakes up we can find out where she's been."

"I don't get it," I said. "Someone kidnapped her and then just dropped her off on the street, or did she somehow manage to get away?"

"Or had she been wandering all day?" Kiana asked. "She was about a fifteen-minute drive from her sister's home, but she could have wandered to where she was found, as many hours as she had been gone."

"Has she been hurt?" I asked.

"They say she has a few bruises but nothing that can't be explained by her stumbling and falling."

When we reached the airport, the plane was ready and waiting for us. Five minutes later we were winging our way across the channel. Both of us fell asleep on the flight and only awoke when the pilot shook us and said we were on the ground. There was a patrol car waiting for us, and we were whisked to the hospital.

We found Marama attached to as many tubes and instruments as Rongo was in Wellington. She was either still unconscious or in a deep sleep. She did not respond to my touch or to my voice. A nurse came in, and I asked if they knew anything about what kind of condition Marama was in.

We were told that it appeared she might have suffered a stroke but that a neurologist would be coming in soon and they would learn more then. She was apparently breathing well, and her heart seemed to be strong. We settled down in the bedside chairs and began what we decided could be a very long wait. Kiana dozed off first, and then I must have done the same thing.

When I awoke it was to Marama's voice calling out, "Skylie. Where are you, Skylie?"

I jumped to my feet and stepped to the side of her bed. The lights in the room were set very low, but additional light was leaking in through the blinds of the window on the far side of the bed.

"Marama," I said. "It's Detective Mike Denton."

Her eyes fluttered open. "Did you find her?" she asked.

"Do you mean Skylie?" I asked as Kiana stepped beside me.

"Yes. Did you find her? I've been looking for her," the old lady said, and then her eyes closed and she drifted to sleep again.

I touched her arm, but there was no response. I looked at the instruments on the wall. Everything looked normal to me, but what did I know?

Kiana sat down, and I joined her. "She must have been out looking for Skylie," she said.

"It seems so unlikely that she would just wander around the city looking for Skylie when none of us have any idea even what part of the country she might have been taken to. She could be anywhere on either island." I sighed. "But I agree with you, I guess. That must be what happened. The stress must have gotten to her."

We sat there for the next two hours. Occasionally a nurse would come in and check on her. A doctor—the neurologist, I assumed—finally arrived, and they wheeled her out, telling us only that they'd be running some tests. We went to the cafeteria for breakfast and then walked outside to get some fresh air. When we finally returned to Marama's room, her sister and brother-in-law were there. We visited with them for a few minutes, and then the hospital staff wheeled Marama back in.

She was awake but totally incoherent. After about a half hour, Kiana and I once again stepped outside. I was leaning against a tall palm tree, looking out over the parking lot, when I noticed a man get out of a black van. He looked familiar, and I stepped behind the tree and peered past it, watching him. Kiana had walked a short distance away from me, but when she saw me move behind the tree, she started back my way.

The man was walking toward the hospital, and I felt a jolt run through me when I realized that he looked like Antony Bahr. He stopped and looked around, turning his left side to me. That was when I saw the scar— Antony's scar.

I started moving slowly in his direction, hoping to get closer before attracting his attention. But he saw me, and recognition flashed across his face. He turned and ran back to his van. I ran for all I was worth but not fast enough. He had the van started and was pulling out of the parking space when I reached him and tried to open the van door. He stomped on the accelerator, and the car fishtailed.

I lost my grip on the door handle and was thrown into a nearby vehicle. The jolt knocked me to my knees, and by the time I was able to gather myself up, he had struck two vehicles and was sliding onto the street.

"Who was that?" Kiana shouted as she ran up to me. She followed as I dashed toward the street.

"Antony Bahr," I called back, winded but running as hard as I could, feeling what I knew were going to be some nasty bruises down my right side and leg. Kiana sprinted past me.

She reached the road and stopped, looking both ways. When I reached her, I looked both ways as well, but the black van was nowhere to be seen. Kiana got on her phone and called for assistance. She described the vehicle to whomever she had called, ending with, "It has damage to the front right fender and the rear right fender."

She paused for a moment, listening, and then said, "The driver is Antony Bahr. He's wanted for attempted murder in the United States, for shooting a police officer."

She listened again and then said, "Call Inspector Keller in Wellington. He'll fill you in on everything. But right now, can you have officers begin searching for the van?"

"You probably ought to have someone come here as well," I said to her. "There's damage to two cars in the parking lot."

She complied. When she finished her call, we headed back to the hospital. "What was he doing here?" she asked. "Could he have known Marama was here?"

"If he did, that could mean he thinks Marama knows where the missing bank loot is," I said. "And that puts her in danger."

* * *

The search for Antony and the damaged black van turned up empty. Inspector Keller called me on my cell phone, and we discussed the implications of Antony's visit to the hospital. "It appears we need to provide some protection for Marama and probably for Rongo," he told me.

"Or we could move them to the same hospital and maybe save you some manpower," I suggested.

"That can be arranged, I'm sure, Detective. But either way, as long as she's there we need to keep someone at that hospital in case Antony comes back. If we catch him, we might be able to discover where Skylie is being held—if she's still alive," he said, causing my stomach to roll.

"Constable Lever and I will stay here with Marama for now. If she wakes up, we'll see if she can tell us what happened to her while you decide what to do."

"I think we'll bring Marama here to the same hospital that Rongo is in," he said after a thoughtful pause. "Then you and Kiana can come back here as well. In the meantime, if she does wake up, let me know what, if anything, she says."

I had already checked on Marama a couple of times since losing Antony. She'd slipped back into unconsciousness within only a few minutes of being returned to her room following the tests. Kiana and I once more entered her room. Marama's sister and brother-in-law were sitting faithfully by her bed. They told me there had still been no signs of her waking up again. They decided to go get something to eat while Kiana and I watched Marama.

We once again sat down. My phone rang again.

It was Inspector Keller. "A medical transport helicopter is flying down to get Marama. The plane you and Constable Lever came in will be ready to bring you and Kiana back here as soon as Marama is on her way. There'll be a car there to pick the two of you up in a little while. Is there any change in her condition?"

"Not so far," I answered.

"I suppose you haven't had any contact from Cal Granberg."

"Nothing. But I'll let you know if I hear from him."

After finishing my call with the inspector, I told Kiana I needed to walk around a little.

She gave me a worried look. "We should have them check you out here, Mike."

"I'm okay," I said. "I just don't want to get too stiff."

"You took a pretty hard jolt," she went on.

"I'm okay, really. I'll be back in a minute or two."

I took a walk to the hospital's pharmacy, where I bought some pain pills. The pills hadn't kicked in yet when I got back to the room, but I expected they would pretty soon. I was surprised to see Kiana leaning over the bed. "She's awake," she said, "and she's trying to talk."

I leaned over the other side. "It's Detective Denton and Constable Lever," I said when her eyes fluttered open and darted back and forth between the two of us.

A nurse came in, a grumpy woman with poor bedside manners. She told us to step away from the bed and leave her patient alone.

We ignored her, and I said, "Marama, can you hear me?"

"Yes," she said very softly. "I saw Skylie."

"Where?" I asked urgently as my heart began to pound. "Is she okay?"

"They have her. I got away. We've got to go back."

"Tell me where she is."

"I can't, but I think I can show you," she said.

The nurse grabbed my arm. "You're upsetting her. Her blood pressure is rising."

"Just a moment," I said, jerking my arm away. "This is important."

"Relax, Marama," Kiana said. "Close your eyes and think for a minute. Maybe you can give us some idea where to look."

"How far did you walk?" I asked after allowing her to close her eyes for a short period. The nurse grabbed me again, and once more I shook her off.

"I don't know," Marama finally said. "I can't remember."

"How did you find her?" Kiana asked.

"I think someone took me there," she said as her eyes again fluttered open.

"Officers, you must let this woman rest," the nurse said angrily, "or I will have you thrown out of here."

"Please," Kiana said, "don't cause us to lose the one chance we have of saving a woman's life, the life of this woman's daughter."

I looked at the nametag. *Eleanor Key.* "Eleanor," I said, "Constable Lever is right. A young woman by the name of Skylie Yates was abducted. We've got to find her. Mrs. Parata is in this hospital because she was trying to find her daughter."

Eleanor looked at me then, indecision on her face. "But we mustn't make it worse for our patient," she finally said with less potency.

"We'll be gentle. Anyway, she won't be your patient for long," Kiana said. "There's a medical plane on the way to take her to a hospital in Wellington, near her home."

"Are they taking her to the same hospital her husband is in?" the nurse asked.

Marama gasped. "Rongo! What's wrong with Rongo?" she asked in a strangled voice.

We had hoped not to alarm her about her husband, but the damage was done. "He's fine, Marama. He wasn't feeling well, so we took him to a hospital to be checked out. He's going to be just fine."

"And so are you," Kiana added gently. "Now, can you tell us which way you walked after you left Skylie?"

Marama was shaking her head. "I don't know. I don't know! I don't know!" she cried out. "My Rongo. Take me to my Rongo. Please find my Skylie. She's hurt. Take me to my Rongo. Take me to my Rongo."

Her blood pressure was continuing to rise. "We'll take you to Rongo," Kiana said gently. "Now you must rest. We'll go look for Skylie."

We left without further prodding from Nurse Key. Marama's sister and husband had not yet returned. "We can't leave here," Kiana said. "We've got to stay in Christchurch. I believe Skylie is here."

"You're right. We've got to do something."

"Marama said Skylie is hurt, that she saw her," Kiana said. "I wonder if any of it is true or if she is delusional from worry and stress."

"I think she must have seen Skylie." I looked at Kiana for a moment, and then a hopeful thought occurred to me. "We've got to proceed on that assumption. If she did, maybe Skylie got away too."

"But we only have Marama here," Kiana reminded me gently.

"Yes, but maybe they got separated. Maybe that's why she feels so strongly about finding Skylie. Maybe she thinks Skylie's lost in this city," I argued.

"Maybe, but I don't know," Kiana said, shaking her head. "She was raised here, so she should know her way around."

"We've got to talk to Marama again. Maybe she can tell us more," I suggested.

After Nurse Key left, we slipped quietly back into the old woman's room. She seemed to be sleeping better now. The instrument that was keeping track of her blood pressure was showing a reasonable reading. We again approached her bed.

"Marama," I said, loud enough to be heard but not so loud as to alarm her. "It's Mike again and Constable Lever."

Just at that moment, the door opened, and Marama's sister and brother-in-law came in. Marama made no response to my voice, so we moved back and whispered to the two of them, explaining what had happened while they were gone. "Skylie could be somewhere either lost or disoriented," I said.

"And she could be hurt," Kiana hypothesized.

"Mike," the weak voice of the old lady in the bed said.

I whirled around and stepped over to her. "I'm here, Marama. What do you need?"

She was breathing deeply, and her eyes were wide. I glanced at the blood pressure indicator. It was rising again to dangerous levels. I leaned in close. Her eyes met mine for a moment. "We got away. Skylie was fighting him, but she made me leave without her. I must go find her. I must. I must. I . . ."

She made a strange strangled sound, and Kiana and I exchanged alarmed glances. Her sister crowded close. Then suddenly Marama convulsed. Kiana rang for the nurse. Her sister grabbed her hand. Marama's eyes closed, and she convulsed again. The blood pressure indicator was going off the charts.

Eleanor Key bustled in, followed by a doctor. "You people get out of here!" Nurse Key shouted.

All four of us headed for the door. Marama's voice followed us. "You must find her," she pleaded in a broken voice. I looked back, but she once again convulsed, and her eyes rolled back into her head.

EIGHTEEN

ONE SANDWICH AND ONE BOTTLE of water of what she'd been told was her final supply was gone. Skylie desperately wanted to make the food and water last longer—she hadn't meant to eat so much—but she seemed unable to stop herself. All she'd done is nibble and take sips of the water, and when she discovered that she was down to the last bite of the sandwich, she'd been shocked. With a shrug, she ate that last bite, drank the rest of the water, and then put the box with the remaining sandwich and water bottle in the corner of the room, promising herself not to touch it for a long, long time.

She dozed for a while after that, leaning against a hard, cold wall. When she awoke, she found that some much-needed strength had returned to her body. Feeling ahead of her with her hands, she crawled around the room for a few minutes. She finally found the nerve to examine the dead body. The blood had dried now, and she felt compelled to find out where it had come from—how the person had died. She carefully ran her hands over the body, which was lying face down. She touched something sharp, so sharp that it pricked her finger. She withdrew her hand for a moment and then, more carefully, found what she believed was the tip of a knife blade sticking out of the body's back. *A knife.* She shuddered at the thought of pulling it out of the chest, but she also realized that if she could make herself do it, she would have a much better weapon than the rungs from the broken chair.

Fearing she would change her mind if she thought about it too much, Skylie put her hands under the body, stooped down, and heaved. It took a couple of attempts, but she finally managed to roll the body over. It had taken a lot of effort, and for a moment, she felt dizzy. She thought about resting for a moment but decided that if she did, she might not have the courage to pull the knife out. So she forced herself to lean forward and search for the handle of the knife. When she touched it, she realized the knife had been driven in clear to the hilt.

The blood on the handle was dry, but when she forced her hand closer to the chest so she could get a good grip, blood oozed out of the wound. She felt her stomach churn. Resolutely, she gripped tightly and pulled with every ounce of strength she had left. For a moment, she didn't think the knife was going to move, but then it began to give way, and suddenly it came out.

She cleaned her hands on the victim's clothing and then did the same with the knife. The blade was sharp, about eight inches long, she estimated. The tip was slightly dulled from when she had turned the body over and the tip had struck the cement floor. She crawled away from the body and worked at sharpening the point of the knife by whetting the tip on the cement floor.

She liked the feel of the knife in her hand. She slipped it from hand to hand and then crawled toward the door. She finally got to her feet and stood near the door like she had just before the body had been thrown in. She held the knife high, imagined herself bringing it down and into the back of the next person to step through that doorway.

What if no one comes back?

That was the second time that thought had entered her mind. Would she die in here with a corpse that would soon begin to rot and stink? The thought brought tears to her eyes, and she sunk to the floor and put her head between her knees. Sobs wracked her body.

* * *

Marama, who had lapsed into a coma, was being loaded into the medical helicopter to be transported to Wellington. Kiana and I watched, wishing we could have had one more opportunity to glean information from her about where she had seen Skylie—*if she really had.*

Kiana had been loaned a police car at Inspector Keller's request. He agreed that the odds were now in favor of Skylie being held in Christchurch and had given us permission, with the help of some of the local officers, to search residences and businesses around where Marama had been found.

A pair of officers, in plain clothes, was stationed at the hospital, ordered to watch for Antony Bahr and arrest him if he showed up there again. Kiana and I were taken to the intersection where Marama had been found. We were exhausted, but we kept at it hour after hour, canvassing the area, checking block by block. We began with those blocks closest to our beginning point with the plan that we, along with the four officers who joined us, would gradually work our way out in all directions.

Each of us worked all the way around a block alone, and then we'd come together, compare notes, and start again. We were talking to everyone we found, asking if anyone had seen someone of Skylie's or Marama's description in the area. We also were asking people if they had seen anyone going into any of the buildings that had been condemned and wouldn't normally have anyone entering them. And finally, we entered every structure that seemed to be abandoned and searched every room for signs of Skylie or even evidence that she might have been held there.

Some of the structures were locked tight, and those we noted for a closer inspection with warrants later on if we failed to find Skylie. We worked until darkness encroached upon us. Only then did we look for a place to spend the night. Over dinner, Kiana and I discussed what we had learned so far. "This is one of the areas damaged the most by the earthquake," Kiana said, repeating what one of the local officers had told her.

"Which is why there are so many damaged, vacant buildings." I nodded.

"After going into so many of those empty buildings, I shudder to think what it would be like to be locked up or tied up in one of them," Kiana said.

"I can't help but think it's the kind of place whoever took Skylie might use," I reasoned.

"I suspect Marama walked quite a ways before she collapsed," Kiana said a few minutes later, as our meal was served. "So maybe as we get farther out, our odds of finding someone who saw something will increase."

"I hope so," I said, toying with a forkful of potatoes, thinking about what Skylie must be going through, hoping she was going through *something* because that would mean she was still alive. I wanted more than anything to hold her again, to feel her head against my chest, and to feel the sweetness of her lips on mine.

We agreed to resume the search at daybreak and went to our rooms for the night.

I had just stepped out of the shower when I got a call from Inspector Keller. "They found the murdered constable on a stretch of beach near Auckland," he said when I answered. "He'd been stabbed numerous times."

I groaned as sadness enveloped me. "I'm sorry."

"We all are," he agreed. "A typewritten note was found with his body, warning that you would be next. It was unsigned."

Despite my best effort, a bolt of fear shot through me.

"It was a warning of sorts, I suppose. So be warned. Be doubly careful."

I promised I would and brought him up to date on our activities in Christchurch.

Then he said, "Get some sleep, Mike." A moment later he disconnected.

I felt a little cleaner after my shower but had to put on the same clothes I had been wearing, since they were all I had. I was both physically and mentally worn out. I plopped down on the bed and fell asleep almost instantly.

I was awakened from a dreamless sleep by the ringing of a phone. It was an unfamiliar ring, and it took me a moment to shake the cobwebs from my head and realize what that meant. It was the cheap phone with the number I had written on the note I had taped to Antony Bahr's front door.

The phone was on the bedside stand next to my iPhone. I turned on the lamp first and then answered the phone with a simple, "Hello."

"Mike, you're an idiot," the despicable voice on the other end said. "Your life is as good as over. You have no idea how many people are looking for you, and when they find you, they will kill you."

"Actually, Cal, I think you're the one in over your head, but I think I can help you if we can get together somewhere, just the two of us," I told him.

"It ain't going to happen," Cal growled. "I'm not as stupid as you are. I only called to let you know you're wasting your time. You should get out of this country before somebody kills you."

"Somebody like you?" I asked. "I know what you tried in LA. You set me up to be killed," I said bitterly. "But that's not the reason I want to meet. I don't really care, quite honestly, if you get out of the hole you've dug yourself into or not. What I really want is to find someone that some of your buddies kidnapped."

"I have no idea what you're talking about, Mike," he said.

"Her name is Skylie Yates. Ask around and call me back," I said. "If you help me find her, I'll see what I can do to help you stay alive."

"My life isn't in danger," he said. "Yours is. And as for your little girlfriend, I wouldn't help even if I could."

"That's something I believe. But quit playing games with me. I know you know something about Skylie. After all, you sprung Antony Bahr from jail in Honolulu, and Antony was after her. I saw him this morning. Think about it, and then call me back; we'll work something out."

"I don't know any Antony Bahr, Mike. So it appears you don't know what you're talking about. Don't bother me again," he said. Before I could say more, the phone call was cut off.

I sat there looking at the cell phone in my hand. I felt the urge to slam it into the wall, but I gritted my teeth, got to my feet, and paced the small room for a minute. I gradually calmed down. He might call back; he might think it over and decide to help. But deep down I was quite certain that would never happen.

I put the phone back on the bedside table and then wondered what to do next. I had promised to call Inspector Keller when Cal called me and also to call Josh. But with nothing arranged, I decided that the calls could wait until morning. That decided, I went back to bed.

* * *

Cal Granberg stared across the table in the small bar on the outskirts of Auckland. Sergeant Sam Hart looked back at him. "I take it you aren't going to meet with him."

Cal chuckled mirthlessly. "Not on his terms, that's for sure. I've got his phone number. I'll wait a day or two and call again. Antony wants the meddling fool out of the way. I tried once to get rid of him, but Wilson missed. We won't miss again."

"I didn't miss." Wilson grunted from his seat on the other side of Cal. "I hit him right in the head, but he ducked. It looked like he was dead, though, so we left."

Sam stared at the two men, trying to make sense of what they were saying. It gradually dawned on him, and he felt a terrible, painful stirring in his gut. He remembered that day well, but he hadn't known until this very minute that they had tried to kill Mike. He fought the urge to wretch. His hands were trembling, and he set his drink down before he spilled it.

His companions were both staring at him. "You mean, she didn't tell you?" Cal asked with a chuckle.

"Who didn't tell me what?" Sam asked, trying to act like nothing was wrong even though he was as shocked as he'd ever been in his life.

"Your wife, you idiot," Wilson said, his eyes narrowed. "Jeanette was the other half of the staged domestic dispute, although she didn't have to do much. She just wailed a little and screamed a couple of times."

Sam nearly doubled over. "Did she know what you were doing?"

"Of course she did. And she told us you knew too," Cal said coldly. "She's in it up to her pretty eyebrows, Sam."

"Hey, all I did was help you get a few guns out of the country," Sam said, his short, thin body, shaking. "Why would she do that?"

"She wanted to. She said something about how much she despised Mike," Cal said. "She wanted him dead. She should have told you. She said you felt the same way about Mike for the same reason."

"I don't like Mike, but I didn't want him dead," Sam said, slamming his fist on the counter. "I don't know why she would either."

"It was something about her nephew, some guy she says the two of you were real close to. Reece something," Cal said.

"Reece Nesbitt," Sam said softly. "Her dead sister's son. Frankly, I despise the guy, but I have no idea why he would have hated Mike. Makes no sense to me."

Cal leaned toward Sam. "I take it there's a lot you and Jeanette didn't talk about. Now I'm wondering if she told you about her part in getting Antony out of jail."

The shock on Sam's already sick face was all the answer Cal needed. "She handled the phone call from the jail, acting quite well the part of a superior court clerk. She told me you knew what she was doing."

Sam pushed back from the table, his hands shaking so badly that he caused his glass of liquor to fall over, spilling the contents. Cal shoved his chair back before his lap got wet. "Where are you going?" Cal demanded.

"To the hotel and to bed," Sam said.

"Don't leave yet, Sam. Me and Wilson . . . and you, we gotta figure out how we're going to find Mike and finish what we—and your actress wife—started back at that *fake* domestic dispute."

"Sorry, guys," Sam said, backing away from his partners. "You're on your own on that one."

"Nope, you're part of it. We go down, you go down," Wilson growled. He'd had one hand under the table the entire time they'd been talking. He pulled it out and stood up. The hand was wrapped in a large, soiled bandage. When he stepped in Sam's direction, he favored one leg, limping badly. "Don't kid yourself that you won't. But we don't intend to go down."

Sam shook his head and continued to back away. "I mean it, guys. This is your deal. I'm only helping move the guns."

Wilson's face darkened. "Afraid not, Sam. The three of us—the *four* of us—are in this together. We have your wife on tape saying she told you all about it. There's nothing you can do to change that."

Sam shook his head. "I've got to sleep on it."

"You do that, Sam," Wilson said. "We'll get with you in the morning. We'll be going to Christchurch to join Antony—all three of us."

Sam backed a couple of more steps. "What happened to your hand, Wilson?"

"Nothing," he said with an angry scowl. Sam didn't pursue the lie and said nothing more. He left the bar and hurried back to his room. Once he got there he retched into the toilet, wiped his face with a towel, and retched again.

* * *

I had finally managed to get back to sleep. But I guess it wasn't meant to be. That cheap phone went off again. I turned on the light, picked up the phone, and clicked the button. "Change your mind, Cal?" I asked.

"It's not Cal, Mike. It's Sam Hart."

"What are you doing on Cal's phone?"

"I'm not on Cal's phone. I'm on mine," Sam said. "Cal borrowed it to call you."

His voice was not that of the confident, self-centered sergeant I had worked for. It sounded like someone had shoved a fistful of cotton balls down his throat. "What's the matter, Sam?" I asked.

He cleared his throat, getting enough of that cotton out to speak more clearly. "We need to get together," he said.

"If you bring Cal, I'm all for it," I agreed.

"No, not with Cal or Wilson," Sam said, desperation evident in his voice. "I need your help, Mike." I'd swear I heard him sob.

"What do you need my help for?" I asked coldly. "And why would I *want* to help you? I nearly died because of you and your buddies."

"You got it all wrong, Mike. I didn't have anything to do with that. And I didn't know Jeanette did until a few minutes ago." He paused, and I listened as he blew his nose. Finally he came back on again. "I had no idea my wife was there when you got shot. In fact, I had no idea that Wilson and Cal set that up. You've got to believe me, Mike. And you've got to help me. I'll testify against those two. If they don't go to jail, I'm dead. They expect me to help kill you. They know you're in Christchurch. They're flying there to meet Antony Bahr and then to try to find you."

The more he talked, the stronger his voice became. I wasn't sure whether to believe him or not. He sounded like he was honestly in fear for his life, but his wife was a good actress. Maybe she'd given him a few pointers.

"Please, Mike. I'm begging," my former sergeant wailed.

I decided to play along. "Okay, I'm listening, Sam, but first, tell me where your wife is."

"She's in New York visiting a friend."

"She's not here in New Zealand?"

"No, she didn't want to come. But she helped Cal and Wilson try to murder you. That's too much. I don't owe her anything," he said. "I'm through with that woman."

"Okay. What do you need me to do?"

"You know some of the cops here, don't you?"

"You know I do."

"I need to turn myself in, have them protect me. You're the only one who can help me do that."

"When?" I asked.

"Now."

"Where?"

"You tell me."

"Give me the address of your hotel and the room number you're in. I assume you're in a hotel?"

"I am. Do you think they can come here and get me?" he asked with a trembling voice that was nothing like I'd ever heard from him.

"I'll see what I can do. I'll let you know what's happening as soon as I know."

"Hurry, Detective. That cousin of Cal's is a dangerous man," he cried.

"And Granberg isn't?" I said in disgust.

NINETEEN

"WHY IS IT YOU ALWAYS seem to call in the middle of the night?" Inspector Keller asked grumpily after he'd answered the phone and I had identified myself.

"I was going to wait until morning to tell you that Cal Granberg called me," I began.

"No, you're right, Detective. I told you to call as soon as you heard from him," the inspector said, not so grumpy now but still sounding . . . tired.

"Cal refused to meet with me. He said I was setting a trap for him and that he wasn't falling for it," I explained.

"That could have waited until morning," Inspector Keller said, sounding grumpy again.

"That's what I thought, but the next call I got was more urgent," I said, hurrying on. "Sam Hart, my former sergeant, is asking for protection from Cal and his cousin Wilson Blanco."

"Okay, now we're getting somewhere," the inspector said. "If he'll cooperate with us, that is."

"I think he will. Unless I read him wrong, Sam is one terrified guy right now. That's not like him," I explained. "He's usually pretty cocky, but right now, he's not that at all. He's either frightened out of his wits, or he's an awfully good actor."

"Do you know where he is?" Keller asked.

"I do," I said. I gave him the name and address of the hotel along with Sam's room number.

"Should I have some officers pick him up there?" he asked.

"That's what he wants, but make sure that whoever goes knows it could be a setup of some kind," I warned. "I don't think it is, but I don't want to take a chance on anyone getting hurt."

"Okay, Detective. I'll pass that along when I set it up."

"Thanks, Inspector. After they get him, I'd like a chance to meet with him," I said. "Soon, hopefully."

"I'll see that it happens," Inspector Keller promised. "I'll get back with you. Now you need to try to get some sleep, mate."

The inspector was right about that. I dropped onto the bed, hoping to fall right back to sleep. But it wasn't to be. Images of Skylie's beautiful face and sweet smile kept slipping behind my eyelids and haunting me. And then, to add to my misery, thoughts of my precious son joined her there. The last time I looked, it was three o'clock. I suppose I must have drifted to sleep sometime soon after that because at about four thirty, my iPhone rang, waking me up.

I was so tired I wanted to cry, but I forced myself to sit up, swing my legs over the side of the bed, and pick my phone up. The call was from the United States, a California number. I didn't recognize it, and for a moment I thought about ignoring it, but I decided I better not.

"Hello," I said, trying to keep my voice from sounding like a frog.

"Mike, I've been trying to call your house. I finally found where I'd written down your cell phone number," my ex-wife said. She sounded stressed, but I didn't think she could possibly be as stressed as me.

"Macy!" I said, unable to mask my flaring anger. "What are you calling me for? Especially at four thirty in the morning."

"It's not four thirty. It's seven thirty," she said, sounding less stressed and snottier.

"Not where I am," I said. "Anyway, you and I have nothing to talk about."

"Mike, don't be mean," she said, the snotty gone and something else in her voice—could it be fear?

I rubbed my throbbing forehead and then got to my feet. "If you need something, call your new boyfriend."

"He's not my boyfriend," Macy cried.

"You mean the marriage is off?" I asked, thinking I'd have to continue alimony payments after all. I'd so looked forward to those ending in January.

"No, he's my husband," she said.

"But I thought the wedding was set for January," I said in surprise. Now I wondered if I'd been paying alimony when I didn't even owe it.

"Macy, how long have you been married?" I asked, suspicious that she'd tried to hide it from me.

"Only a few days," she said. "I was tired of just living with him. I talked him into getting married sooner. I was going to let you know."

I made a mental note in my foggy brain to follow up on that when I had a little time. I didn't know if I should believe her or not. "Then call your new husband," I suggested, trying to remain calm and keep my voice soft. I wanted to shout at her, but I knew Macy, and shouting wouldn't help.

"Mike, I can't," she wailed.

I took a deep breath, trying to keep my anger in check. She sounded like she was losing it. "Okay, Macy, what's the matter? What do you need?"

"I need you to come get me. I'm afraid of him."

That rattled me. She might actually be in trouble. "Macy, that's impossible. I'm half a world away."

"Mike, you can't be. I need you," she begged.

"Sorry, but I am. I'm in New Zealand," I said, thinking how a few months ago it would have been wonderful to hear her say she needed me. She was too late now. Skylie needed me, and I wanted only Skylie.

"What are you doing in New Zealand? Who told you that you could go to New Zealand? I need you here!" she cried hysterically, and I could tell there were tears gushing from her pretty eyes all those thousands of miles away.

Typical Macy. She thought only of herself, and yet, maybe she had good cause. I had to find out. "Macy," I said. "You've got to calm down. Take a couple of deep breaths, and then tell me what's happening."

For once, she seemed to be taking my advice, not something that had happened in those last months of our failed marriage. I listened as she gulped in a great lungful of air, releasing it slowly. She repeated that a couple of times. Finally, sounding calmer, she said, "He beat me up and left a little while ago."

"Your new husband?" I asked. "He beat you up?"

"Yes, and he said he'd kill me if I told anyone, so I called you."

I guess that meant I was *nobody*. That wasn't news. I'd been nobody to her for a long time. "Macy, I'm seriously in New Zealand," I said. "There's nothing I can do for you from here. If you want help, you need to call the cops in LA."

"But Reece said he'd kill me," she said, the hysteria building again.

That was the last thing I wanted for Macy. Despite all that had happened, she still occupied a little place in my heart. We were bound by the memory of our son. "Is that your husband's name?" I asked.

"Yes, Reece Nesbitt."

"If he's not there, then the cops can get you somewhere safe before he comes back."

"I don't dare, Mike. You don't know Reece. He can be really mean."

"It sounds like you didn't know him very well either," I said. "I can call the cops for you, but that's all I can do from here."

"I don't know. He's a terrible man, Mike. I should never have married him."

I couldn't argue with that. "Would you like me to call someone to help you? Or why don't you call your mother? She'll come get you."

"My parents are on vacation. They're out of state with Reece's aunt," she said. "They've become friends since Reece and I got together."

I got the strangest feeling just then, accompanied by a far-fetched thought. I didn't know anything about who Macy had married other than his name, which I had just learned from her. She'd told me in an e-mail a few weeks ago that she was getting married in January. It was impersonal, and there was no mention of who the *unlucky* guy was. So I asked her, "Where did you meet this Reece guy, Macy? Surely you dated him long enough to know he was mean, as you say. "

"I met him at a Christmas party you took me to the Christmas before Mike Jr. was born," she said. "He was there with his uncle and aunt."

My insides began to roil. "You mean to tell me you had a boyfriend even before we were divorced? Even before our son was born?"

"He was nice to me."

So was I, I thought, but that apparently didn't matter. The far-fetched thought didn't seem quite so far-fetched now. "Who are his uncle and aunt?"

"Sam and Jeanette Hart," she told me. My far-fetched thought proved to be true.

My sergeant and his actress wife. Reece Nesbit was a relative of theirs. What was that all about? But I had a sneaking suspicion that I knew. She and her nephew probably wanted me out of the way so he could marry Macy. I pushed that thought aside for now. I could come back to it later. "Can you get in your car and drive somewhere? Just tell me where, and I'll have some cops meet you there."

"I can't. He took my car keys," she said. "And he took all my money and credit cards. I can't even call a cab." She sniffled.

I was beginning to see that my ex-wife, a girl I had once loved, had left me to marry a monster. "Macy, give me your address. You stay right there. I'll get someone to you as quickly as I can."

She hesitated, sniffled a little more, and finally said, "Okay, but they need to hurry. He might come back."

"I'll call you back as soon as I get someone on the way," I promised and ended the call. I dialed another number.

"Detective, what's happening this morning?" Captain Bertrand asked. "Good grief, it must be awfully early there."

"That's for sure. I need a huge favor that has nothing to do with what I'm doing down here. At least I don't think it does," I said as I began to wonder if Reece Nesbitt could have anything to do with Cal, Wilson, Sam, and the gun theft thing.

"What do you need?" he asked.

I told him, and he said, "I'll get some officers to give me a hand. That address isn't too far away. I'll call you back once she's safe."

"Thanks, Captain. And when you call back, I'll fill you in on what's happening down here. You won't believe it."

We ended the call so he could go get Macy.

I made a short call to Macy to tell her what I'd done, and then I settled back down on the bed. I hoped that Captain Bertrand got to Macy before Reece got home. I had done all I could for her. Now if I could just fall asleep again. But this time, not only Skylie's face appeared behind my eyelids, so did Macy's—though not for the same reasons.

I groaned as my phone rang again.

"Detective, we picked up Sam Hart," Inspector Keller said. "I think he's going to be a great help to us, but he wants you to be present before he tells us anything. My colleagues are going to fly him down here from Auckland, and then I will fly with them on down to Christchurch. I'll see you there in a few hours. I'll call you when I'm close."

"I hope Sam can help us find Skylie," I said, knowing that was a long shot but possibly a better one than the search we planned to resume in a few hours.

We didn't talk much longer, and I once more took advantage of the soft bed. For all the good it did. Captain Bertrand called me back. "Macy's with us now, Detective," he said. "She's scared to death of her husband and for good cause. She's in pretty bad shape. We're taking her to the hospital to be checked out, and then if they don't need to keep her there, we'll get her to a safe house."

My blood boiled. I despised men who beat their wives. "Will you get a warrant for her husband?" I asked.

"I've got an officer working on that right now. Do you know *exactly* who her husband is?"

"Reece Nesbitt, Jeanette and Sam Hart's nephew," I said. "She told me when she called. I didn't know before."

"I ran a records check on him," Captain Bertrand told me. "He's not a clean one, that's for sure. He has a lengthy criminal record. I know you and Macy are divorced and that she's not your responsibility, but—"

"Keep me informed," I broke in. "And tell her to stay in touch as well, at least until we're sure he can't hurt her again."

He agreed, and that call ended. I was so tired my eyes were blurred. I rubbed them and then looked at my watch. It was six o'clock already. I decided to try once more to get some sleep.

I fell asleep quite easily that time, but I was jolted awake when someone pounded on my door. I rolled out of bed and stumbled to the door, looked through the peephole, and then looked again at my watch. I'd slept for an hour, *only an hour*.

I opened the door, and Kiana said, "You don't look like you're ready to go yet." Her smile faded as she looked me over,

"I'm tired," I moaned.

"You look it," she agreed. "But at least you're up and dressed. Didn't you sleep well? I did, for a change."

"I wore these clothes all night. And no, I didn't sleep. I don't even have a toothbrush," I complained.

Kiana grinned. "I bought one downstairs along with a small tube of toothpaste. I'll go get you one while you do whatever you need to before we start searching again."

I shook my head. "There's nothing I can do here. I feel grungy, but without a change of clothes, I guess I'll just have to live with it. I am hungry though. Let's go get something to eat. I've had a busy night, and I don't mean a busy night sleeping. I'll tell you over breakfast."

Thirty minutes later, I had brought Kiana up to date on Sam Hart's activities. I'd also told her I'd been on the phone several times over some problems in Los Angeles. I didn't mention my ex-wife, but I did tell her that the trouble there had to do with the nephew of my former sergeant and his wife. Even as I told her about Reece, I wondered again if he could possibly have any connection to the illegal, corrupt activities of Cal and Sam.

We once again met officers from Christchurch and began our seemingly impossible search for Skylie beneath dark, threatening skies. I had a feeling I was going to get wet again.

* * *

Skylie had slept for several hours on the floor beside the door. She had wanted to stay awake in case someone came again, but she didn't want to be clear across the room. Even now, awake and chewing on a tiny bit of the single remaining sandwich, she sat near the door, her ear tuned to what might happen beyond it.

A terrible, recurring thought struck her yet again, the thought even worse than her captor coming back—that he *wouldn't* come back, leaving her here alone with a corpse that would soon start stinking. And eventually, she would become a corpse. She shuddered at the thought, took a sip of her water, and began to consider her options.

There weren't many. She could finish her food and water then sit down and wait for death to overtake her. But as discouraged as she was, she wasn't willing to give up. She picked up the knife and thought about it for a moment. There was a second option, she thought as a little bit of hope coursed through her. The door was wood, and the knife was sharp. She'd read stories of men who'd broken out of jail by scraping the mortar between the bricks with a spoon. She had an advantage over them. She had a knife and only wood to go through. She went to work, chipping away on the door frame, thinking that the easiest way to get the door open was to free the latch. She could do it. *She would do it.* She berated herself for not thinking of it earlier.

TWENTY

I WAS GLAD TO GET a break from the search, both because I felt like we were accomplishing nothing and also because I was soaking wet. It had started storming an hour after we had begun, and it hadn't let up. Kiana and I were both wet, but at least we were inside now, in a warm room in a police station not too far from where we'd been searching.

Sam Hart was not the same man I had known. He kept his eyes on his hands, which were clasped on the table in front of him. His short brown hair was showing flecks of gray, something I didn't remember noticing before. His skin had a sickly, gray pallor, and he seemed to have more wrinkles around his eyes than he used to. When he spoke, there was a tremor in his voice. I was in the presence of a broken man. I just prayed that he was not so broken he couldn't help in the search for Skylie.

"Sergeant," I began, out of force of habit not respect, "there are a lot of things we need to discuss. Everything is being recorded. Do you understand that?"

He nodded as I looked around the room at Inspector Keller, Constable Lever, and Constable Portill. Portill had flown with Keller when he brought Hart to Christchurch a little earlier. I mentioned each officer by name for the sake of the recording then said, "The most pressing matter we're dealing with is something I hope you can help us with. A young woman by the name of Skylie Yates was kidnapped a few days ago. Have you heard anything from any of the people you've associated with since arriving in New Zealand that might help us locate her?"

"I've heard the name," he admitted, "but I don't know where she is."

That was not what I'd hoped to hear, and I felt a heavy weight press down on my shoulders. "Surely, someone at least hinted to where she was being held."

Sam looked up and into my eyes. He shook his head. "Sorry, Detective, but all I heard was that she was missing. Well—this probably won't help, but I know that Antony Bahr is in Christchurch. Maybe that means she's here somewhere. I'm sorry I can't help more than that. What I can do is tell you all I know about what Cal and Wilson have done—in exchange for protection and immunity from prosecution, of course."

"We'll get to that in a moment," I said, not sure how I would deal with the immunity request. He hadn't mentioned *that* during his call in the middle of the night. "First, we need the names of everyone involved with Cal, every name you've heard, whether you met the individuals or not."

"I'll try," he promised, "but you've got to understand that I was never really in favor of what Cal was doing."

"Then why did you help him?" I asked.

He started to sweat, his forehead beading with moisture. He looked at me, and I saw fear in his somber green eyes. He was afraid of someone or something. I waited for him to answer, something I had observed him do in interrogations. Sam was an excellent interrogator, and I had learned a lot from him. As angry as I had become, I couldn't help but feel sorry for him. I'm sure he'd never expected to be on the wrong side of an interrogation like he was now. He blinked rapidly, and then he finally said, "It was because of Jeanette's nephew. You might have met him. His name's Reece Nesbitt. He's about ten years younger than her, but he and Jeanette are very close. His mother was Jeanette's oldest sister. She passed away when Reece was in his early teens, and he lived with us for several years after that. He and his father didn't get along, so Jeanette took him in—over my objections."

I knew the Harts had no children of their own, which would explain the close relationship between Jeanette and her nephew. I took a deep breath and then slowly exhaled. "Reece is the man who stole my wife," I said, unable to keep the bitterness from my voice.

"You knew about that?" he asked.

"I barely learned it, but yes, I know now that he's a major reason Macy left me," I said. "Why do you blame Reece for what you did?"

Sam rubbed his hands over the stubble on his face. "My wife would do anything for Reece. They had a strong bond even before he came to live with us. She's always wanted him to have whatever his selfish heart desired."

"And she forced you to help?" I guessed.

"I suppose you could say that, but Mike, I didn't know about everything she did for him. I only knew about those things she forced me to help with."

"How did she *force* you to do things?"

"You don't really know my wife very well, do you?"

"No, I can't say I do, Sergeant."

"She's a strong-willed woman," he said.

"A lot of men are married to strong-willed women, Sergeant," I told him, holding his eyes with mine. "But that doesn't mean those men can be forced into doing things that are against the law—things that could land a man in prison."

Sam lowered his eyes and mumbled, "She said she'd leave me if I didn't do what Reece wanted."

"Then you should have let her leave you," I said, thumping my fist angrily on the table.

"I couldn't do that," he said, his eyes downcast.

"Why not?" I asked.

"Because I loved her, Mike. She's all I have. We never had children. I needed her."

There really wasn't anything I could say to that. Men throughout history have done terrible things in the name of love. "You got involved with Cal," I said, steering away from the discussion about his wife. "Was that because of Reece?"

"Yes, it was." He nodded.

"Would you like to tell us how it happened?"

Sam pressed on his eyes with his fingers for a moment. Then he said, "I need a promise of protection and a guarantee that I won't be prosecuted."

"Sergeant, you've been a cop for a long time. You know how it works. The only one who can guarantee you won't be prosecuted is the district attorney and the US attorney, depending on what laws have been broken," I reminded him. "We, the police here and in LA, can protect you, but all we can promise is to put in a good word for you when it comes to prosecution."

Inspector Keller broke in at that point and said, "I'll give you my promise in writing to not only provide every level of protection I can but also to give a positive recommendation to any prosecutor you may have to deal with. Of course, that depends on whether or not your information is any good."

"And I'll do the same," I added.

Sam looked at me, then at Inspector Keller, and then back at me. "I know you're a man of your word, Mike, but I'd prefer a hard-and-fast guarantee," he said.

"Sam, you know we can't do that," I said. "We are offering you the very most we can and, frankly, more than I think you deserve."

He rubbed his eyes again, wiped the sweat from his face, and said, "You're an honest cop, Mike. I'm sorry for the trouble my wife and nephew have caused you." He paused, looking down at the table.

"Does that mean you're not sorry for the problems *you* created for me?"

He shook his head vigorously. "Oh no, I didn't mean that, Mike. I am sorry. But what Jeanette and Reece did to you was something I knew nothing about until Cal and Wilson told me last night. That's why I called you and why I'm sitting here right now."

"Very well," I said. "Let's get some things written down, and then you can tell us what you know about Cal, Wilson, and their activities, both here and in the States."

"Constable Lever, would you see if you can get us a couple of sheets of paper?" the inspector asked.

She nodded and left the room. When she came back, Inspector Keller and I both proceeded to write. When we were done, Sam read the documents, nodded, and handed them back. We signed and gave them to Kiana to get copies made, and then we began the serious business of finding out exactly what he knew that would help us in the gun smuggling case.

Two tedious hours later my clothes had dried and the recorder was still going. Inspector Keller and I each had several pages of notes. We also now had a clear picture of how the guns were stolen from various places in and around California and then turned over to Cal and Sam, who arranged to have them smuggled across the border to Mexico. From there, they were taken by private ships to Samoa, where a cousin of Hemana's personally took them to New Zealand, avoiding major ports and unloading at a dock where slipping a few hundred dollars into the right hands got them into the country.

Sam couldn't name the border agents who were on Hemana's payroll, but Inspector Keller felt he had enough information that the New Zealand Police could figure out who they were. I also had enough information that I was quite certain a call to Captain Bertrand—with the names of individuals, approximate dates, and rough descriptions of the weapons involved—would allow him to move forward rapidly and make some arrests in the next few days. In addition, Sam had told me where LAPD investigators could go to find evidence of the stolen car ring operated by Wilson Blanco. Sam even admitted that he'd taken kickbacks from Wilson to look the other way, but he was quick to point out that the dirty money he had received was only a fraction of that which Blanco paid Cal—as if that excused his behavior.

As we talked, Sam's face had grimaced every time he had to mention the name Reece Nesbitt. Reece was one of a handful of men who actually stole the weapons that had been sent on to Hemana in New Zealand. In telling us this, Sam had made it clear that he detested Reece and would love to see him go to prison. In his mind, it was Reece who had corrupted his wife and had, by association, caused him to do what he had done. Sam had mentioned that Wilson Blanco had been injured somehow and described the way one hand was heavily bandaged and the limp he walked with. "Did you ask him what happened to him?" I asked. He told me Wilson had refused to tell him.

"Sergeant," I said at the end of the two-hour marathon, "you know Reece isn't the only one who could go to prison for the things he did, don't you?"

His chin quivered, and his voice broke as he said, "I loved Jeanette, and I risked too much for her; I know that. But I would never have said a word had she not crossed a line that I simply cannot overlook, despite knowing that it will end our marriage."

"And that line was?" I prompted him.

"Conspiring to have you murdered," he said.

"Sam," I urged, "I would appreciate it if you would tell us exactly what you know about that."

He rubbed his eyes, and then he looked at me, his face a portrait of misery. He proceeded to tell us what Cal and Wilson had told him at the bar the previous night. "I swear to you, Detective, I knew nothing about that, or I would have put a stop to it before you got hurt."

I believed him, but there was one more thing I wanted to know. "Did you know that the gun used by Wilson Blanco that day, the .38 caliber Smith and Wesson revolver, was illegally removed from the evidence room and sent in one of the shipments to New Zealand?"

"I knew that was what was intended for it," he said. "Cal personally removed it. He told me he had and that it would be shipped. I don't know if that ever happened or not."

"Oh, it happened all right," I said sharply. "A man who went by the nickname of Snake, a man who was murdered a few days ago at a place called TopHouse, had it hidden in his apartment in Wellington. It's been positively confirmed that it is the same gun."

"I'm not surprised," Sam said.

"Now, Sam, I want you to think about your nephew, Reece," I began.

"Not my nephew, Jeanette's," he corrected me with a snarl. "I don't claim the guy."

"Whatever," I said. "Think about him, and then tell me if there's anything else you know about him that you would like to tell us."

"Like what?" he asked.

"Has he been married before? If so, what happened to his wife? Does he have children anywhere? Are there other major crimes he was never prosecuted for?"

Sam did think, and he finally said, "Two previous wives. There were no children in either marriage. They both left him. He physically abused them both, but my wife paid them not to press charges."

I cringed. "Anything else?"

"Not that I can think of right now, but I might remember something else after I've had a chance to think about things for a while," he said.

"Just one more thing," I said. "Did Reece want me dead so he could marry Macy without her having to go through a divorce?"

"I can't be sure, but I think that's possible," he said.

I stood and attempted to stretch the kinks out of my legs, back, and shoulders. The others did much the same—all but Sam Hart. He remained seated, his eyes down, his thin body trembling. "What happens now, Inspector?" he asked.

"We take you to a safe place where you can try to think of anything else. In the meantime, we will go to work on what you've told us," Keller said. "And I suspect Detective Denton will call his captain and get the investigation started in Los Angeles. Is that right, Detective?"

"That's right. Then I need to get back on the search for Skylie Yates. Every hour she's missing makes the odds of her being found alive a whole lot slimmer." I turned to Kiana. "Are you ready to get wet again?"

"When I stepped out to make copies, I looked outside. The sun's shining now," she said.

Somehow that was encouraging to me. "Great," I said. "Then, as soon as I've spoken with Captain Bertrand, we'll get back at it."

Before we left the police station, I placed a call to Macy. "Hi," she said. "Thanks for helping me this morning."

"You're welcome," I said.

"Mike, I'm sorry for all I've put you through," she said. "I was stupid for letting Reece make me think he could provide a better life for me than you could. I wish I'd never met him."

"I wish that too, Macy. But you did, and you chose him over me. But that's all history now."

"I'm so sorry," she said again.

"Anyway, he'll be arrested for assaulting you," I told her, more or less ignoring the apology. "And he'll be ordered to make no contact with you."

"As if he'd obey something like a flimsy piece of paper," she said with a hollow laugh.

"I know, but you're safe now and will be protected until he's behind bars. And if he bails out, the protection will continue. Captain Bertrand has given me his word."

We talked for a minute more, and then she said, "Mike, I still love you. Can we start over? I should never have left you, and I promise I'll be a good wife to you if you'll just give me another chance."

That rocked me. I was so surprised that it took me a moment to respond. I finally said, "Macy, I hope you can find someone decent the next time you get married. I'm sorry, but it's over, and it will stay over."

"Please, Mike. At least think about it," she begged. "I love you."

"No, I will not do that," I said firmly. "But I will call again when I learn more about Reece." There was one other question I had wanted to ask her, but I decided that Captain Bertrand or one of his detectives would be more likely to get the truth out of her. So I let it go.

TWENTY-ONE

NEXT, I CALLED CAPTAIN BERTRAND. "Mike, I was just about to call you," he said. "Macy's safe now."

"Has Reece been arrested?" I asked.

"No. Reece is dead," he said. "He tried to shoot it out with the officers that were waiting for him at his house. They're fine, but he didn't make it."

"I know I shouldn't say this, Captain, but I'm glad."

"I'm not exactly brokenhearted myself," Captain Bertrand said, "but I'd have liked to have had a chance to interrogate him. He might have been the source of a lot of helpful information. Would you like to tell Macy he's dead, or do want me to?" he asked.

"Go ahead," I told him. "And when you do, there's something I'd like you to ask her."

"Certainly."

"I want you to ask if she knew that Reece was part of the plot to have me killed, to get me out of the way so she would be free to marry him."

"O . . . kay," he said, drawing the word out. "I can do that. I suppose that means you have something to report about Sam Hart."

"Lots," I told him. "I can give you a thumbnail sketch right now, but I think it would be best if I e-mail you a copy of the recording we made of our interview, over two hours' worth."

He agreed. After giving him a quick version, I worked with the staff at the police station to help me prepare the recording and then e-mail it to the captain. Once that was done, Kiana and I got into her loaner car and proceeded back to the area we'd been searching.

Other than the lingering areas of destruction, the neighborhood was sparkling and green, the yards filled with the sweet scent of colorful flowers and shrubs. The people I talked to were wonderful, friendly people, and many expressed the desire to assist me but simply didn't know anything that was of help. I left my cell phone number with any who would take it.

I was speaking with one particularly friendly lady who was telling me that she'd seen someone in the middle of the night a couple of days previous, when my iPhone rang.

"Sorry," I said to her. "I need to take this. Can you give me just a moment? I very much want to hear what you have to say."

"Detective," a familiar voice said, "this is Josh Infelt."

My heartbeat accelerated. "Have you got something for me, Constable?"

"Yes. I need to meet you as soon as possible," he said.

"Is this about Skylie?" I asked hopefully.

"Sort of," was his vague answer. "Listen, this is important, but I need to join you in Christchurch as soon as I can fly down there. It appears that my cover's blown. My supervisor has ordered me to drop my undercover assignment and get away from here. As a precaution, my family is in hiding."

"Where do you want to meet?" I asked.

"Let's meet at the police station where you met with Sam Hart. Inspector Keller knows what's happened here and promised to pick me up in his plane as soon as he has Hart someplace safe. We'll fly down together."

"All right, just let me know when you need me," I said. "But can you tell me anything right now?"

"I think there's been some sort of a double cross within the gang," Josh said. "I bought a gun directly from your former partner, Cal Granberg. Apparently, that was in direct opposition to Hemana's orders. Cal has disappeared, along with his cousin. There is, as I said, a good chance my cover's blown."

"So you don't have contact with any of the gang now?" I asked.

"Well, there is one gang member I've gotten quite close to who I think I can trust if I need to. But that's something we'll play by ear. For now, my assignment is finished."

"One more thing, Josh," I said as the unpleasant odor of my soiled clothing wafted up to my nose. "Would you and the inspector mind getting Kiana and me a change of clothes? The inspector knows where I'm staying in Wellington, and he could have the folks at the hotel let him into my room to get my suitcase. For Kiana, I think he could go to her home and see if her parents would fix her up a bag."

"I'll see that it's done," Josh promised.

I walked back up the sidewalk to meet with the old lady, who seemed so anxious to tell me something. Her name was Jane Somers, and she looked like she must be in her late sixties. She was as tall as me, slender, and had a distinct stoop. Her hair was long, gray, and stringy. She spoke with a raspy voice, made that way, I supposed, from a lifetime of cigarette smoking. She was smoking one she'd lit when I was on the phone.

"You may have seen someone suspicious," I prompted her after she had invited me to sit across from her on her small deck in a green wicker chair. "Would you like to tell me more about it?"

She put her cigarette out in an overflowing ashtray on a small table and smiled at me. Her eyes, light gray in color, held a degree of warmth and kindness that contrasted with the yellow of her tobacco-stained teeth. Her dog, a huge black creature of a breed I didn't recognize, lay at her feet.

"Sometimes I don't sleep so well," she began. "When I'm awake in the middle of the night, I like to take walks. I love the sweet smell of the flower blossoms and the peacefulness of the night. I always take my dog, Bambino, with me on a leash. That night—I think it was two nights ago, but I could be wrong—it was not so peaceful." She scrunched her eyes in thought. "The days and nights run together for me, Constable. It was recent, though. Of that I'm sure. Anyway, I was walking west along the street there," she said, pointing to the street that passed directly in front of her fenced front yard. "An old lady scrambled by on the far side of the street."

"Can you describe this old lady?" I asked with sudden excitement. "And can you tell me what direction she was coming from?"

The smile crossed Jane's face again. "I know you think I'm an old lady, and I am. This woman was probably about my age. I think she was Māori, much shorter than me and quite heavy. She was breathing hard, like she'd been running. But when I saw her pass beneath the street light on the far side of the street, she wasn't going very fast. She was trying to, but it looked more like a *scramble* to me. Could that have been the woman you asked me about?"

"Yes, that could be her," I said with rising hope. "Which way was she coming from?"

"West, that way," Jane said, pointing the opposite direction from which she had indicated she and her dog had been walking.

"Did you talk to her?" I asked.

"No, I don't think she even saw me. And Bambino was pulling me that way," she said, pointing east. "Bambino seemed upset about something. He was pulling so hard I had to struggle to keep hold of his leash. The lady's head was down, and she was, as I said, breathing heavily. I could hear her gasps even from across the street."

"Did you see where she went?" I asked.

"Come, I'll show you," she said, and I followed her to the street. Her house and yard were surrounded by a tall, white, wooden fence. The gate we went through was solid and also tall. She shut the gate on her large dog, instructing him to stay, and then said to me, "She turned north there." She pointed to an intersection a few houses to the west.

"Did you think about calling the police?" I asked.

"I thought about it, but then I met an angry man. He was coming straight toward me on my side of the street. He frightened me."

"What did he do to frighten you?" I asked her.

"He held up his hand to stop me, but he didn't get too close because Bambino was growling at him. He asked if I'd seen a woman pass by."

"Did you tell him you had?" I asked, almost breathlessly.

She shook her head and looked at me, her gray eyes thoughtful. "No, I lied to him. I said that no one had come by here. I was afraid he intended to hurt her. She'd seemed so frantic, and he looked so angry and . . . and dangerous. He had blood on his face and his shirt. He stepped closer to me, and I had to hang on tight to Bambino. He didn't like the man. Bambino can sense evil in people. And I could see evil in the man's eyes, on his whole face. The old lady kept looking over her shoulder like she was watching for someone, someone she was afraid of."

"You were probably right," I said. "Can you describe the man?"

"Yes, I can," Jane said, shivering as she said it, although the sun was very warm. "He was taller than me, taller than you, over six feet tall. And he was very heavy. I wouldn't say fat, just very big. His hair was long, and even though it was so dark, I could tell it was dirty. Anyway, he had a beard, not too long but unkempt. And his face, that part that wasn't hidden by his beard, was covered with pockmarks, and blood. I could tell by his accent that he was an American. I wondered what an American was chasing after a Māori woman for. Does that mean anything to you?"

"I am afraid it does," I said as I ran the description of Wilson Blanco through my head. Could Wilson have been here and then returned to Auckland in time for his meeting in the bar with Cal and Sam? I looked at Ms. Somers as I pulled out my cell phone. "I have a picture in here," I said. "I'd like you to look at it."

"Is it of the bad man?" she asked.

"You tell me." I opened my messages and found the picture of Wilson that Captain Bertrand had sent. I showed her the picture.

She took my phone and studied it for a moment. "That's him, mate. I'd know that face anywhere."

"Thank you. So what happened after that, Jane?"

"He pointed his hand at me, and he shook it like this." She shook her hand toward me with her index finger extended. "He said, 'Are you sure?' I said, 'Yes, I'd know it if a woman walked by me this time of night.' And he said, 'I kill people who lie to me.'"

"What happened next?"

"He glared at me. Then he reached down and shook his hand at Bambino. I don't know why he did, but it was a mistake," she said. "Bambino lunged and bit his hand. The man bellowed like an angry bull. I jerked at Bambino, and the man tried to get his hand free. I told my dog to let go, and he did. The man stepped back, looking at his hand. It was badly torn and bleeding terribly. 'I should kill you both,' he said to me. It was all I could do to keep from fainting. Then, like he thought he could hurt my dog, he kicked at Bambino."

"Kicked at him?" I asked. "That's crazy. Bambino's a big dog."

"Yes, he kicked at him, but he missed. Bambino lunged to the side. I lost my grip on his leash, and he attacked the man. He bit him on the leg, but the man kicked him off. Then the man began to run. Bambino chased after him. They went out of sight down at the next intersection." She stopped, took a deep breath, and then went on. "I ran home."

"Without your dog?" I asked.

"Yes. I didn't know when he would come back."

"Why didn't you call the police?" I asked.

"I didn't dare," she said.

"Why not?"

"I was afraid the police would take Bambino and put him to sleep."

"Why did you think that?"

"Because my neighbors are afraid of him, mate. That's why I always keep him on a leash when I take him outside of my yard. They've warned me not to let him hurt anyone," she told me as she turned back toward her gate. "He is all I have in the world since my sister died."

Once we were back inside the yard, I said, "Your dog seems very friendly to me," as he came up and sniffed at my hand.

"That's because you're a good young man," she said. "Believe me, Bambino knows the difference."

I didn't argue, even though that seemed a little over the top. "How long was it before Bambino came home?"

"It was probably twenty or thirty minutes," she said.

"Did you see the man again after that?"

"No, but I haven't gone outside of the fence at night since then. And I keep a lock on the gate when it's dark."

I remembered seeing the lock hanging open on a hasp. "Had your dog been injured?"

"Not that I could see. He might have had some bruises, but he acted okay," she said. "But I think he might have hurt the man some more. Bambino had blood all over him, but it wasn't his blood. And I picked bits of cloth out of his teeth."

"Is there anything else you can think of, anything else the guy said or did?"

She shook her head and then said, "No, but I'm glad you came. I've been feeling guilty about not reporting the incident. I just hope they don't take my precious Bambino." She patted the dog affectionately on his large, broad head, and Bambino pressed tightly against her leg, his tail wagging vigorously.

"Jane, I will see that they don't," I promised her. "Your dog is a hero." I touched the scar on my head. "The man he bit tried to kill me a few months ago."

Her gray eyes grew wide. "Oh, my, but he is a bad man. I'm glad Bambino got him."

"So am I. Do you mind if I call the officers working with me and have them meet us here?" I asked. "We may have a few more questions for you."

"Of course you may," she said.

When Kiana answered the phone, I said, "I have a witness, Kiana. Bring the others here, and we'll decide where to go next. I know what direction we need to search."

"What's the address?" she asked.

I asked Jane for her address and then relayed it to Kiana. "You can't miss the place. It's surrounded by a tall white fence with beautiful trees, shrubbery and flowers growing right up against it."

Bambino stepped up to me, and as I knelt down to pet him, a shot rang out. Ms. Somers screamed and dropped beside me. We both asked the other if the shot had connected, but we were both okay. Together, we scrambled, along with Bambino, into some nearby shrubs. My heart was pounding.

"Are you sure you're okay?" I asked as we huddled in the bushes.

"I'm fine. That was a gunshot, wasn't it?" she asked, her voice quavering. "I've never been around guns."

"Yes, it was a gunshot," I responded as I punched a number into my cell phone. A moment later, Kiana answered.

"I was just shot at," I said. "So be careful as you approach, and watch for anyone suspicious driving away from here."

"Are you okay?" she asked.

"I'm fine." I disconnected and began to crawl out of the bushes.

Ms. Somers grabbed my arm. "You better stay here until your police officer friends come," she urged. "I don't know if the shot was for me or you, but either way, we better stay hidden."

"It was for me," I said, thinking of all the men who could be out there with a strong desire to kill me. "I'll be okay."

Besides Kiana and the constable she drove up with, four other officers appeared at the scene. The shot put a temporary halt to our search for Skylie, but I urged the others to get back to looking again. "Whoever shot at me must know we're getting close," I said. "We've got to keep searching."

The bullet was found embedded in Jane Somers's front door. It was a small caliber, but had it struck me, I could easily have been killed. I asked the other officers if they'd seen anyone leaving the area as they approached. One constable reported seeing a blue car; the driver had bushy black hair. "Keenan Chestain," I said to Kiana, who nodded in grim agreement. "I thought it was Antony Bahr." I shook my head. "But maybe not. Keenan is apparently more dangerous than I thought."

Trying to dismiss the attempt on my life, I explained to Kiana and the other constables what I had learned from Jane Somers. I emphasized that Jane hadn't reported the incident that night because she feared the dog would be taken away from her, and I extracted promises from each of them that they would make certain that didn't happen. After a short discussion, we left Jane with her hand resting on Bambino's back. Her face was white, but she was smiling. She wouldn't lose her dog.

After an unsuccessful attempt to reach Inspector Keller to ask him if Keenan was out of jail, we resumed our search. I was more hopeful now after speaking with Jane Somers. We worked blocks that stretched out to the west from Jane's home. We were also watching for the possible reappearance of the gunman. Whoever it was didn't want me to find Skylie, and that thought made me all the more determined to do so as soon as possible.

* * *

The odor in the room was becoming overpowering. Between the *bathroom* bucket Skylie kept in the farthest corner and the horrible smell that was already coming from the corpse, it was hard to keep focused. And yet, at the same time, the odor drove her to carve away at the door frame with her knife more frantically. But she found she could only work in short bursts since she was so weak.

She also had to do everything by feel because of the darkness. Her fingers and palms felt like they had blisters on them. Her wrists and ankles where the ropes had torn into the skin were a constant source of agony. Even though she still had a small amount of water and a few bites of sandwich left, the horrible stench had her stomach so upset that it was almost impossible to eat.

The hours dragged by. She wondered what time it was but had no way of knowing. She'd dozed for a few minutes, but she forced herself to her feet and once again began digging at the door frame with the knife. She worked for a few minutes, chipping only tiny slivers of wood out. But when she felt with her fingers, she was encouraged. She'd managed to make a fairly decent hole.

Skylie set the knife on the floor, grabbed the door handle, and pulled with all the strength she possessed. The door refused to budge. She sat down on the floor again, exhausted, promising herself that she wouldn't rest long. She had to get out of this terrible place soon, or she might not ever get out.

TWENTY-TWO

AFTER A SHORT BREAK FOR dinner that evening, Kiana and I resumed
the search. Two new constables replaced the ones we'd worked with all
day. We had proceeded several blocks west of Jane Somers's house. I was
getting worried that I hadn't heard from Josh Infelt and Inspector Keller;
we'd been unable to reach them on the phone. I had expected them to
be here before now. Despite that, I kept searching and talking to anyone
I could find, desperately hoping to learn more about where Skylie was
being held. I was still on the lookout for Keenan or any of the other men
who might have tried to kill me. It made the search more difficult and
was terribly nerve wracking. As I was trudging tiredly past a vacant lot,
one where a damaged house must have been removed, my iPhone began
to ring.

"I asked Macy your question," Captain Bertrand said the moment I
answered.

"And?"

"She looked horrified that I would ask such a thing. She said, and
these are her words, 'I love Mike. I never quit loving him. I don't know
why I let Reece lead me away like he did.'"

"Her exact words?" I asked.

"Well, pretty close," he said. "She said she had no idea he wanted to
have you murdered. She said she was just having a *fling*—that was her
word—and that at that time she had no idea Reece wanted to marry her."

"Thanks for asking, Captain. How did she act when you told her
Reece had been killed?"

"She cried, but mostly in relief. She wants to talk to you again."

"Where is she now?"

"She's at her house. She didn't want to go there, but it's really the only place she has, and I couldn't justify keeping her in the safe house anymore. She'd have gone to her parents' home, but the place is locked up tight."

"Did you get a chance to listen to the interview with Sam Hart yet?" I asked.

"Yes, and it's immensely helpful, Detective. He'll face charges if we can get him back here, but if everything he told you pans out, I'll do all I can to get the prosecutors to go easy on him," he answered. "I have officers following up on some of those leads now. We even got a search warrant for Blanco's shop, which is being searched as we speak. A couple of his employees are already in custody and want to talk. I suspect that when they do, we'll learn a lot more about both his and Cal's involvement."

A few minutes after my conversation with Captain Bertrand, Inspector Keller called me. "I see you and Constable Lever have been trying to call. Constable Infelt and I ended up helping on a multiple car accident and couldn't even get free to answer our phones. Anyway, before you tell me what you were calling about, I have some information for you. Marama Parata is awake, and she remembers a little bit," he told me, "but it's fragmented. She says she was with Skylie in a dark place. She keeps asking if Skylie is okay now."

"Does she remember where that place is?" I asked as hope surged in me.

"No, I'm afraid not," he said. "There seem to be some things she remembers and some she doesn't. I asked her how she got away, and she said a big man was chasing her. But when I asked her where Skylie was at that point, she got a blank look on her face and didn't seem to know. I'm hopeful that with a little time she'll remember more."

"I know who the man chasing her was," I told the inspector.

"You do? How?"

"It was Wilson Blanco," I said. "I found a witness who talked to him." I explained about Jane Somers, her dog, and their encounter with Wilson Blanco. "It was him. Ms. Somers's description was accurate, and she also identified him from the picture of him on my iPhone. And she told me her dog bit him. Sam mentioned that Wilson had one hand wrapped in a bandage and that he was limping, like his leg had been injured. Now we know how that happened."

"Yes, I'd say so. Is that what you were calling about?" he asked.

"Well, partly," I said, and then I told him about being shot at and the fact that someone meeting the general description of Keenan Chestain was seen leaving the area. "Is he still in custody?" I asked.

"I'm afraid not, Detective," he said. "We had to release him. We didn't have enough to hold him on. We had an officer assigned to follow him, but apparently Keenan spotted him, because he did some crazy driving and got away from the constable. I'm sorry about that. Later, shortly before I got the call to help with the accident, I received a call from one of Keenan's neighbors, who said they saw him coming out of Rongo's house. The officer who was supposed to be following him checked it out. He'd broken the lock on the door, but he was long gone. I joined my man there and found a note on Skylie's bed."

"What did it say?" I asked.

"It was written to Rongo. It said that it would have been best if Skylie had never looked at another man. That's all it said, but it sounds like a threat. It made me wonder if we should look closer for other threats, older ones. I searched Skylie's room and found a letter from him dated the day you and Skylie flew in from the States. It was on her bed stand." Before I could ask, Keller told me what it said. "It was similar to the other one. He wrote that it would be in her best interest to not even think about marrying anyone but him, that he was the only one who could make her truly happy."

My blood ran cold. "How did it get there?" I asked. "It wasn't there before we went to the TopHouse."

"He was in there sometime before Skylie was kidnapped. Maybe it was after Snake had been there. I guess he expected her to come back and find it."

"But then, for some reason, he might have gone to the TopHouse," I reasoned. "Inspector, he could be the one who has her."

"That's what I was thinking. I wanted to arrest him again, but we couldn't find him. Now I know why. It sounds like he's in Christchurch. I'm sorry I was delayed, but Josh and I are driving to the airport now, so we will be in Christchurch before too long. Would you and Kiana meet us at the airport in about an hour?" he asked.

I renewed my search with more urgency after that call. I couldn't get Keenan off my mind. Knowing he wasn't in jail made it very likely he was the shooter, that he had tried to kill me. I finished the canvass of the block I was on and then called Kiana. "Inspector Keller wants us to meet him at the airport. Constable Infelt is with him, and they should be there pretty soon."

She told me where she was, and I hustled to meet her there. While I helped her complete the block she was on, I told her about Keenan's release from jail and his threats. We contacted the constables who were helping us and told them we had to go to the airport. They said they'd keep looking.

We arrived just as the inspector's plane landed and began taxiing toward us. Josh's appearance had changed remarkably from when I had seen him at the Ruakuri Bush Walk. His brown hair was shorter, he was dressed neatly, and his face was clean-shaven. I watched him as he walked toward the car. Something was bothering him—a lot. After a short greeting, we piled into the car, with Kiana driving, and headed for the police station. Very little was said. Both the inspector and Josh seemed withdrawn. Their demeanors worried me.

We were soon in the same room where we had, hours ago, interviewed Sam Hart. Josh explained what had happened and how he was afraid his cover had been compromised after he had bought a gun directly from Cal. I supposed that was what had him so clearly upset.

"So could Hemana know who you are?" I asked.

"Probably not," Josh said. "If he suspects anything, like I fear, he would only know who I'm *not*. The same is true of Cal. He has no idea who I am, but from something he said to the one man who I still trust, he suspects I might be a cop. That alone makes it too dangerous for me to continue undercover. So now my role is back to being an investigator from outside."

I asked, "Are you safe?"

"Probably not," he said. "That's why I had to get out. I've got my family tucked away in a safe place until we can get the gang rounded up. And while I am here in Christchurch, I'll have my parents leave their home for a few days. This is where I'm from, and they could be in danger as well."

"You told me on the phone that Cal and Wilson were missing," I said. "Do you think they're trying to keep out of Hemana's sight after my conversation with Cal?"

"Hemana doesn't know where they are, and he's not happy about that," Josh explained. "So yes, I think they're carefully avoiding him."

"But they know Antony's in Christchurch. Does Hemana know that?"

Josh shook his head. "I sort of don't think so, but I don't know for sure. I don't think Hemana has as much control over some of his people as he thinks he does."

"Have you heard anything that might help us find Skylie?" I finally asked, hoping beyond hope that he had.

Josh's face fell, and his eyes looked pained. "I'm sorry, Detective," he said as his voice choked up. "I hate to have to tell you this." He paused, rubbed his eyes, and I waited. Finally he continued. "I'm afraid my sister is lost to both of us."

My heart nearly stopped. I felt beads of sweat the size of popcorn kernels break out on my brow. I wiped them away, took several deep breaths to calm my heart, and asked, "Why do you say that?"

"You were right about Wilson Blanco seeing her. According to my contact, one of the last things Blanco told Hemana before . . . vanishing was that the girl was dead, that he'd killed her. I know nothing more than that. I can only hope it's a different girl, but that seems very unlikely."

"We can't stop searching," I said as my heart filled with ice.

"You're right, and we won't. She's my sister, even though I never met her or knew she even existed until a few days ago."

"You would have loved her," I said with a choked voice. "She was beautiful and sweet." I couldn't go on.

"If she's alive, we'll find her," Josh said. I nodded in agreement. "I won't rest until we have. I also won't rest until I find Wilson Blanco and—"

A sharp look from Inspector Keller caused Josh to leave the sentence hanging. Then the inspector said, "He will be found, and he will be brought to justice, Constable. But it will be done according to law."

I knew it had to be that way, but I could feel what Josh was feeling. I wanted, in my anger and my anguish, to see that Blanco suffered for what he had done. I wasn't sure that would happen if he just went to prison. But I kept my thoughts to myself. I knew the inspector was right.

"You found someone who spoke to Blanco?" Josh asked after the tension in the room had dissipated a little and our emotions were in check.

"I did," I said. "And because of that we've narrowed our search to a smaller area, but it's still not exactly *small*."

"I'll help search now," Josh said firmly. "I'll make sure my parents are safe, and then I'll work with these officers."

Inspector Keller rose to his feet. "I would expect nothing less. I'll need a ride back to meet my pilot, and I'll return to Wellington. I have much to do there."

Kiana and I took him to the airport while Josh, in a borrowed police car, left to warn his parents. As Kiana and I were driving back to the search area, I was surprised when my second phone rang, the one that first Cal and then Sam had called me on.

Kiana looked over at me. "Is that your cheap phone?"

"It is," I said. I dug it out of my pocket, punched the proper button, and said, "Hello. This is Mike."

"Mike, Cal here. I have some information that will help you find Skylie Yates," he said. Despite the terrible news Josh had delivered, I felt a stirring of hope in my heart that she was alive.

"Thanks for calling, Cal," I said. "What can you tell me?"

"She is being held in Picton," he said. "I have it from a good source. The address has been fastened to the door of her home in Wellington. Go to the Paratas' house, find the note, and then you can go to Picton and rescue her."

"Cal," I said, "I heard that she was killed. Someone overheard Wilson Blanco brag that he had killed her."

For a moment, all I could hear was Cal's heavy breathing. "How did you hear that?" he finally asked, suspicion in his voice.

"I can't tell you that," I shot back.

"It's not true. Blanco hasn't seen her. He couldn't have seen her. And he certainly didn't kill her. That's ridiculous. Wilson isn't a killer," he said. "Anyway, he's been with me in Auckland."

"Are you sure, Cal?"

"Of course I'm sure. But she might be getting very hungry and dehydrated. You need to hurry if you're going to get to her in time to save her."

"Why don't you help me?" I suggested. "You could get the address from the Paratas' house and call me with it. I will head for Picton."

"You probably don't believe this, Mike, but I would help you if I could. Unfortunately, I'm in Auckland, and it would take me as long to get there as it would take you," he said.

Cal was right. I didn't believe him. I knew he was lying because I knew Blanco had been in Christchurch. And Sam believed Cal and Blanco were coming here now. I also was quite sure that Skylie was being held in Christchurch, if she was still alive, not in Picton. I suspected that any address I went to in Picton would be a setup, a potential ambush. But I said to Cal, "Okay, Cal. Thanks. I owe you for this. I'll go to Wellington right now."

"Good luck, Mike. I mean it. I'm sorry you and I haven't gotten along. You have the makings of a fine officer," Cal said. "Let me know when you find her. Take down this number, and call me when you do." He then recited a phone number, which I stored in my head, and then I ended the call.

"He's lying," I said to Kiana. "I can't believe he thinks I'm dumb enough to believe he's had a sudden change of heart."

"Call Josh," she said.

I did that and relayed the information to him. "My friend in the gang wasn't lying, Mike, I know that," Josh said. "Blanco told Hemana, in my friend's presence, that he had killed the girl."

"I understand," I said, even though in my heart I didn't want to believe it.

"My parents are leaving their home now," Josh said. "I'll take this car back to the station and then have someone take me to the search area and meet you there."

"You aren't really going to go to Picton, are you?" Kiana asked.

I put my phone on speaker so that all three of us could talk. "No, I won't go to Picton, but I'll see if Inspector Keller will send someone to Rongo's house and see if there's really a note. If there is an address, then he can decide what to do."

"Someone will have to go check out the address in Picton and be prepared to stop an ambush," Josh warned. "Whoever goes will have to be armed. We know Hemana's gang has guns, and it would be nuts for officers to go without weapons."

"I think it's nuts that you guys aren't allowed to carry guns regularly," I said, as much to myself as to my colleagues.

"I can't argue with that," Josh said. "But I can assure you they won't go to a potential ambush without them." He was thoughtful for a moment, and then he spoke again. "I think we should watch for Granberg and Blanco here in Christchurch."

"And Antony and Keenan," I added.

"Yes, that's right," he agreed.

"Do you think Granberg and Blanco will actually come back to this part of the city?" I asked.

"I don't know what to think," Josh said.

"We'll have to stay in the area all night, just in case they show up," Kiana said. "Mike, you need to go get some sleep. I know you didn't get any last night."

"I got some," I countered.

"Yes, an hour or two maybe."

"Better than none."

"We can take turns here while you sleep," she insisted. "I would suggest that you go do that now."

I would have argued further, but I had a feeling that if Cal or Wilson, or both of them were to come back, that it would be in the middle of the night. I could sleep now and be on watch here later—for them as well as for Keenan and Antony.

Kiana said, "I think I'll go back too, just long enough to shower and change clothes." The inspector had brought bags for us. "I'll head back to the search area as soon as I'm cleaned up."

"Why don't both of you get some rest?" Josh asked. "I'm good to go for hours yet. I'll go directly to the search area. The other officers and I can keep checking the area and watch for Antony, Keenan, Cal, and Wilson, just in case they do show up."

"Okay," she agreed. "But I don't need too much sleep."

"As long as I don't keep getting jarred out of my sleep, I'll be fine in four or five hours," I said.

I did get some sleep, but it wasn't as restful as I'd hoped for. My heart ached for Skylie. I had grown very fond of her, and the thought of losing her weighed heavily on my mind.

I awoke to the alarm on my iPhone. I looked at the time. It was two o'clock AM, time to get dressed and go. I was still tired, but the worst edge of my fatigue had been blunted. I'd be okay now.

I dressed and was ready to go when Kiana knocked on my door. We returned to the search area. Josh reported that there had been no sign of anyone suspicious in the area.

"Would you like to go get some sleep?" I asked.

"No, if you two don't mind, I'll just sit in the backseat while you drive around. For us to be walking now, with everyone in bed, is a waste of time, I'm afraid. And it's more dangerous if in fact someone is out there in the dark who might take a shot at you, Detective. If I get too tired, I can sleep a little in the car," he said.

We all climbed in the car, but before Kiana had started it, we heard a rumble, and then a moment later, the car began to rock.

"Earthquake!" Kiana cried out.

TWENTY-THREE

SKYLIE WAS AWAKENED BY THE shaking of the cement floor, where she lay curled on her side. She got to her feet, but the shaking knocked her right back to her knees. She knew what it was. She had felt the disastrous Christchurch earthquake of early 2011 even though she was clear up in Wellington on the North Island at the time. There had been hundreds of aftershocks in the many months and days since. Some, she had been told, had been quite pronounced. She prayed that this was one of those aftershocks and not something larger.

She stood again and leaned against the wall, her heart pounding loudly in her chest. Above, she could hear boards breaking and bricks falling. The shaking went on for what seemed like forever, but which she knew was probably only twenty or thirty seconds. When it quit, the house creaked and groaned for several minutes. She sat back down and hugged her knees, praying it was over. This was no small aftershock, she realized. It was something much more. She slumped against the wall, hoping the ceiling wouldn't fall in on her.

After a few minutes, she stood back up and moved over to the door. She forced herself to go to work again with the knife. She had sharpened it again on the concrete floor, and it bit into the wood a little easier than before. After a few minutes of work, she once more pulled on the door handle. To her amazement, the door only resisted for a moment before it gave way and swung open.

Skylie had never felt such exhilaration in her life. She was free! She stepped through the door and into the hallway that led to the base of the stairs. It was so dark that she had to feel her way along the wall with one hand while she held the knife in the other. Then she suddenly ran into something and tripped, falling to the floor. As she picked herself up again, she had a terrible thought. What if she was still trapped? What if the damage to the house was so severe that she couldn't force her way outside? And what if her captor was in the house?

For a minute or two, she stood, tears coursing down her cheeks. Then she whispered, "Skylie Yates, you are not dead. Don't give up now."

Hearing her own voice was reassuring, and she once again felt around with her hands, pushing fear from her mind and concentrating on escaping. She'd dropped the knife. She really needed it. She knelt down and felt around some more. The board she had tripped over was only one of many that lay scattered all about her. She couldn't find the knife in the rubble and finally forced herself to move on without it. If she needed a weapon, she'd have to use a board as a club. With that thought, she crawled ahead, making her way through the mess, carefully adjusting only the boards she had to in order to make room enough to keep moving forward.

She passed through the worst of it and found the stairs. She climbed up it carefully, on her feet now but moving very slowly, checking the space ahead of her with her hands before each step. She reached the top and moved cautiously into the room. But once again, she ran into trouble within a few feet. There were so many boards, bricks, and other material that she couldn't make her way through to the door she thought might be on the far side of the room.

Changing course, Skylie forced her way to the left and had better luck. She still ran into obstructions, but she was able to move through them without a lot of tugging and pulling. It seemed like an hour had passed before she found and moved through a doorway. She pressed on and soon realized that it wasn't quite as dark as it had been. She could see the obstructions as darker spots against a slight haze of gray. She was able to go around most of them, and before she knew it, she was at another door. It was shut. She turned the knob and shoved, and to her relief, it opened. She stepped out into the freshness of the outside world. For a couple of minutes, she took huge gulps of the clean, pure air, purging her lungs of the filth that had filled them in the basement prison she had left behind.

The backyard of the house was choked with vegetation. It smelled wonderful, but it was hard to force her way through. It wasn't as dark as it had been inside the house, and looking up, she could see stars shining brightly. She had no idea what time of night it was. The plants that blocked her way were shadowy, impossible to focus on. Her weakness made it even more difficult to move through the thick vegetation. She was unable to stand, but she was determined to keep going, to get away from the house, so she stayed on her knees, pushing her way forward. She had to rest from time to time, but she rested only long enough to get a little strength back before pushing through the thick vegetation again. She forced herself to keep at it, knowing she would soon be able to find help and be reunited with her loved ones—if Marama was okay. She had no way to know if her adoptive mother had escaped the big man or not. She had tried to make herself believe that Marama had gotten away since she had not been brought back, but Skylie really had no way of knowing.

She came to a fence. She pulled herself to her feet and explored it with her hands. It wasn't very high, not much over a meter, but it still took her a lot of effort and a long time to climb over it. When she finally made it, she collapsed in a heap on the ground and simply lay there, feeling relatively safe for the first time since the murder of her brother at the TopHouse.

She finally found the energy to get to her feet again and push through the shrubs and sweetly scented flowers that lined the fence. She reached grass, short and soft. This yard was obviously taken care of and belonged to a house where someone still resided. She became aware of the muted sound of voices. Light shone through one of the windows only twenty meters or so away. The light was bobbing around, and it took her a moment to realize that the quake had probably knocked the power out and that whoever was in that house was using a flashlight. She felt the urge to hurry and picked up her speed. Help was close.

Suddenly, her right foot was over—nothing. Her hands flailed, but she couldn't keep from plunging forward. She felt her body drop, and then there was a sharp pain in her head. Blackness enfolded her.

* * *

The sun had just risen when Kiana, Josh, and I reluctantly headed for our car to leave the search area and participate in a search of Sage Decorte's apartment at the request of Inspector Keller. "I know you want to continue there, but they need every officer they can muster in Christchurch to deal with the problems the quake has caused," he said to me on the phone. "The three of you will be working with Inspector Edward Watson, the only officer they can spare to conduct the search. This is important. Snake's girlfriend could be a key in the investigation. That's why I need you there."

"Okay, we'll go," I said. "But will any officers be able to stay in this area and keep looking?" I asked. "Someone needs to keep watching for

Bahr, Chestain, Granberg, and Blanco, on the off chance that any of them show up."

"They say they can't spare anyone," the inspector said. "But I can't imagine any of our suspects showing up there in broad daylight."

"Unless they think the earthquake is enough of a distraction that no one would notice them," I suggested.

"That's a good point, Detective. I'll have Josh stay there and keep watch while you and Kiana assist Inspector Watson. I know it will leave Josh on foot, but there's nothing we can do about that," Inspector Keller said. "I'm sorry about this, but as soon as you finish at Miss Decorte's apartment, you and Constable Lever may return to the area."

"All right," I said. "We're heading there now. What is the address?"

The inspector gave me the address and then said, "There was a note on the door of the Paratas' house. I'm flying back to the South Island to see what we can find at the address the note gives."

"Be careful, Inspector," I said. "I think it's a setup. I'm quite sure that Skylie, if she's alive, is in Christchurch."

"We'll be armed and alert, Mike. Call me when the search at Miss Decorte's place is over," the inspector instructed before he ended the call.

"So Keller wants me to stay here?" Josh asked.

"That's right," I said. "Sorry."

"Don't be. It's my sister we're looking for. We've got to have faith, Detective, even though . . . Anyway, I'll stay, and if I need a car, I'll persuade some good citizen to lend me one," Josh said. "So you guys go. I'll be fine here alone."

Kiana and I began the drive to the far side of the city. The quake, though apparently not as strong as the one in 2011, had caused a lot of damage. Some streets were impassable due to downed trees and power lines; others had broken pavement and large potholes. Residents were out on the streets, seemingly fearful to go back into their houses in case another quake struck. We had to backtrack several times, but we finally arrived at the apartment complex where Sage was purported to live.

We parked the car and were greeted by a tall, thin man with a thick head of black hair and a ready smile. "I'm Inspector Edward Watson," he said. "And you must be Detective Denton and Constable Lever."

We shook hands. "Do you know yet whether Miss Decorte is at home or not?" I asked.

"No, I didn't want to approach the door until you two got here. She could be milling about with these other people." He waved toward where several groups of people were walking about in front of the apartment complex. "I wasn't sure how long you two would be. I expect it was a bit hairy driving across the city," he said.

Kiana nodded her head. "It was awful. These poor people here in Christchurch."

Inspector Watson shook his head and chuckled. "We people of Christchurch can handle it. After all, we Kiwis live on top of a hotbed of potential trouble. Earthquakes and even volcanos shouldn't surprise us too much." Without waiting for further comment, he held out the search warrant. "This is the warrant," he said. "The damage here seems to be light. These apartments were built after the last quake, so they were constructed to higher standards. Should we go see if the young lady is home?"

Even though the apartment complex was not noticeably damaged, many residents were, as Inspector Watson pointed out earlier, milling in groups in front of the complex. We searched for the woman with red hair and a kiwi tattoo on her neck but didn't spot her. No one answered the door of her apartment either.

After a five-minute search, the inspector found the manager, and we were admitted into Sage's apartment. We conducted a quick, cursory search just to make sure no one was home. Sage wasn't there, but it appeared that she had been fairly recently. Mail from the past two or three days was in a pile on the floor behind the mail slot in the door. Bills and a checkbook were sitting on the kitchen table. The last check had been written three days previous. Most of the food in the refrigerator was still good, although there was some lettuce that was wilted. The milk smelled fine. In the bedroom, the bed was neatly made up, and there were no clothes strung about. She seemed to be a good housekeeper.

"She's been gone for a while but not too long," Inspector Watson said, summing up what we had all concluded.

We began to systematically examine the apartment room by room. Kiana found a stash of marijuana in a dresser along with a baggie containing a white powdery substance we suspected was cocaine. There were ashes in an ashtray that weren't tobacco ashes. I sniffed at them. "Marijuana," I said.

After an hour, I was getting discouraged. We hadn't found anything that gave us a clue about the murder. I had hoped to find some kind of correspondence, either in writing or on her computer, that could give us an idea who might have wanted Snake dead. So far we had found nothing in that regard.

We left the kitchen for last. Sage had a small file cabinet near her kitchen table where we found what appeared to be her important papers. There was correspondence, paid bills, stamps, and some loose change in one of the drawers. I thumbed through the correspondence. One envelope grabbed my attention. It was addressed to Sage, but what caught my eye was the return address.

According to the date on the front of the envelope, it had been mailed in Los Angeles about six weeks previous, near end of October, by Wilson Blanco. I started to carefully remove the letter from the open envelope when my cell phone rang. I set the letter down on the kitchen table where I'd been working and answered the call.

It was Inspector Keller. "You were right, Detective," he said in a very calm, matter-of-fact voice. "It was a setup, an ambush, but we were ready for it. Shootouts in New Zealand are almost unheard of since we have so few guns in the country, but I'm afraid we had a shootout today, a right nasty one. None of our officers were killed, although one constable took a bullet in his right shoulder. Three ambushers are dead, and one more is critically injured. As far as we know, there were only those four involved."

"Were they part of the gang from Auckland?" I asked.

"We believe so," the inspector said. "Two of the dead were either Samoan or Tongan, as is the one survivor. The fourth was Tristan Bahr. He was still alive when we found him, and he made a confession just before he died. He admitted he was the one who'd taken the loot from the robbery."

"You've got to be kidding me! Did he also kill Snake, then?"

"He didn't admit to that, so I don't think so, but he did admit to killing the constable who was staking out his house. Since he had the stolen money, Tristan said the officer made him nervous. I also asked him about Skylie. I don't think he had any idea where she was being held, although he did know she had been kidnapped."

"I guess he wouldn't have been very forthcoming with Hemana or his people about Skylie since he couldn't exactly confess that he was the one who had taken all the loot," I said bitterly.

"That's right. Of all the people in Hemana's gang that were looking for the money and suspecting Snake of having taken it, he was the one who wouldn't have had a reason to kill Snake or kidnap Skylie. Anyway, we now know Tristan had the money all along."

I thought about it for a moment. Finally I said, "Maybe Tristan did it just to deflect any suspicion from himself—none of the gang would suspect him if he was the killer."

"That's a great point, Detective, but again, he didn't admit it before he died, and what he did tell us is quite believable," the inspector reminded me.

I thought again and then said, "I take it his brother doesn't know he stole the money."

"If what Tristan said to me is true, and as you know, the confession of a dying man is considered to be quite reliable, Antony didn't know," Inspector Keller said.

"Wow! The guy must have been pretty brazen. Where is it hidden?" I asked. "Did he tell you?"

"I'm afraid he didn't, so we still don't know where it is," he said. "I tried to get him to tell me, but he died before he got it out. We have some work to do, I guess. Two of Hemana's men were dead before we got to them. The other one, we hope, will regain consciousness and tell us something at some point. But I don't expect him to know anything about the money. That was Tristan's secret."

"So Snake died for something he didn't do. And, of course, Skylie knew nothing of the money or where it was. She didn't even know Snake existed until a few days ago," I said. "That makes all this that much worse."

"Yes, it does. There is one other thing Tristan told me, another reason I don't believe he is the killer. He said he was helping keep Snake hidden from Antony and Hemana. He said he and Snake were good friends and that he wasn't going to let his brother do something to Snake. If that was true, then he had no motive. That also confirms, I think, that it was Tristan who was with Sage and Snake that day at Rongo's house."

"Did he tell Snake that he had the money?" I asked.

"He said he didn't, and I'm inclined to believe him. Even though they were friends, I don't think he'd have risked it."

"I don't suppose you know whether or not Keenan has been found."

"That was the other thing I was about to tell you. I got a call from my counterpart in Christchurch. He said one of his officers was in the process of pulling Keenan over when the earthquake struck. At least he thinks it was Keenan. But when the ground started to shake, the man drove away. The constable would have chased him, but a woman screamed for help; her husband was pinned beneath the car he'd been working on in their driveway."

"Where was that?" I asked. The inspector relayed the address, and I groaned. "That's only a few blocks from where we've been searching." I sighed. "I guess I should tell you about the search at Sage's apartment."

"Did you find her?" the inspector asked.

"No. Snake's girlfriend isn't here, but I found something that will interest you. I have an envelope here addressed to Sage, mailed by Wilson Blanco from Los Angeles."

"Are you telling me those two knew each other?" he asked, sounding surprised.

"She got a letter from him," I replied, "so I guess they did."

"What does the letter say?"

"I don't know. I was just getting it out of the envelope when you called me."

Kiana was leaning over my right shoulder, and Inspector Watson had pulled a chair up and was now seated to my left.

"I want to hear what it says," Inspector Keller said. "Read it to me over the phone."

"Okay, let me see," I said. I fumbled with the envelope and pulled the letter out. It was short and addressed to Sage as *Miss Decorte*. I read it word for word. "*I am writing in receipt of your prepayment for the pistol you're buying for your friend. You can expect it to arrive in Auckland before the end of November. You will be contacted by someone there who will arrange to meet you and deliver the gun. It's a .38 caliber Smith and Wesson revolver, commonly known as a Chief. It's in excellent shape. The serial number has been sanded off, making it untraceable. Thanks for your business.* It is signed, Wilson Blanco."

"That's the pistol you found in Snake's apartment," the inspector said.

"The one I was shot with in Los Angeles," I added. "What does this mean?"

"I have no idea," Inspector Keller said. "But when we catch up with Blanco and Granberg, I hope we can find out."

"And Sage Decorte," I added. "She could tell us all about it."

"Yes, her too," he agreed. "Let me speak to Inspector Watson."

We didn't find anything further, but what we had found was, at least to me, as earthshaking as the quake we'd experienced a few hours earlier.

As we prepared to drive back across the city, Inspector Watson told Kiana and me, "I'll get charges drawn up against Sage Decorte for the drugs and whatever I can for conspiring to obtain an illegal weapon. As soon as we find her, I'll let you know, as I'm sure you'll want to talk to her."

"You're right about that," I said.

A small aftershock, the third we'd felt, shook the sidewalk under our feet. The people still wandering about were quite calm now, and the aftershocks didn't seem to upset anyone too badly. They were used to aftershocks, having experienced hundreds of them since the powerful 2011 earthquake.

The trip back across the city was as slow as the earlier one. Josh reported that he had found nothing more. We went back to work, but it felt like we were spinning our wheels. Despite what I'd heard about Wilson bragging that he had killed *the girl*, I tried to hold out hope that he was lying. But that was all I had—hope.

TWENTY-FOUR

RAYMOND AND LAYLA FARNDELL WERE a retired couple who didn't get out much. Mostly, they spent their time caring for their yard and house. As a result they had a picture-perfect yard. The well-kept lawn was surrounded with flowering shrubs, all kept neatly trimmed, and tall trees grew the full length of the fence. Flowers grew against the house and in several neat beds throughout the yard. Toward the back of the yard was a grove of several large trees that provided a cool, shady spot in the hot days of summer. There was also a picnic table and a small brick fireplace that they used for cooking when the weather was just right.

The Farndells' home had received very little damage from the earthquake of 2011, while their neighbor's house had been condemned. The trees and shrubs lining the other side of the fence were unruly and thick. It was almost impossible to see the condemned house from their yard, but the couple liked their privacy, so they paid it little attention.

The morning had worn on, and when the power hadn't been restored by noon, Layla said, "It's nice out today. I guess we could eat in the yard, Raymond. If you'll go out and build a fire, I'll make some hamburger patties. We need to use the meat before it goes bad. The refrigerator will be getting warm by now."

"I think the power will be back on before too long, but it would be nice to eat out there anyway," Raymond said.

He went out the backdoor, stopped, and gaped. A hole had opened up in the yard about ten meters from the house. There had been a slight depression there after the big quake, but this was much more than a depression. He stepped over to it and was shocked to see the body of a woman. It wasn't a deep hole, only about two feet, but it was big enough around that the girl's entire body was in it. He turned and ran to the house and shouted, "Layla, call for an ambulance. There is a woman in a hole in the backyard."

"A hole?" she asked. "What do you mean, a hole?"

"From the quake, just get an ambulance on its way. This woman looks like she's hurt badly—if she's even alive. She's not moving at all."

Raymond ran back outside. Lowering himself carefully into the hole, he reached beneath the girl's neck. When he found a pulse, he heaved a sigh of relief. He tried speaking to her, but there was no response. A moment later, his wife came over to the hole. "The phones are down. I knew we should have got one of them cell phone things."

"Probably should have," he said, "although we probably couldn't have gotten an ambulance anyway. They're probably all busy."

"What should we do? Can you tell if she's alive?" Layla was wringing her hands and bobbing her head.

"Yes, she's alive. We'll have to take her in our car," Raymond said decisively. "She's not very big. I can lift her out and carry her around to the car. You open the gate and then the car door."

Raymond Farndell was not a young man, but he was in good shape. At seventy, he was a lot stronger than most men his age and many more who were much younger. He knelt beside the girl and spoke gently, even though he knew she couldn't hear him. "Okay, young lady, I'm going to roll you over on your back so I can pick you up. I'll be as gentle as I can."

When she was on her back, he took a closer look. "You've been hurt, starved," he said in shock as he realized that her thin, pale face was not normal. "Okay, I'm going to lift you out now and lay you on the grass at the edge of this hole."

When he had completed that task, he climbed out of the hole. "Now I'll just pick you up and carry you to the car. We'll get you to a hospital as soon as we can."

Layla sat in the backseat and held the girl while Raymond drove. They passed a number of people, but Raymond just methodically worked his way through the streets to the hospital. It took him close to a half hour to make the journey. When he got there, he left Layla and the girl and rushed inside.

When he explained that he had an injured woman in his car, he was told he would have to wait his turn, that the emergency room was full of injured people, but when he told the nurse that the woman was unconscious and near death, he got some action.

Once she was inside, the girl was given priority. A doctor, who introduced himself as Dr. Fletcher, said, "Is this your daughter?"

"No, we don't know who she is," Raymond said.

"Where did you find her?" Dr. Fletcher asked, gently examining her.

"She was in a small sinkhole in our backyard, one caused by the quake. I don't know how she got there," he answered.

"She's in bad shape," Dr. Fletcher said. "She's very dirty, as you can see. Her fingers are bloody." He peered closer. "Look at these wrists. They're chafed and raw. There's infection there. This girl has been held against her will somewhere or I miss my guess."

"I don't know where she came from," Raymond said, wringing his hands now just like Layla was doing.

"She's lucky you found her. You saved her life," the doctor said. "Well, I guess I should say you gave her a chance. She's pretty bad right now. I'll need you folks to step out so we can do a thorough examination. You'll need to stay here at the hospital for now. Also, you'll need to give the nurse your names and address. She'll show you to a waiting room."

An officer entered the waiting room a little later. "I'm Constable Mench," he said. "Are you the people who found the woman that had fallen into a hole?"

"Yes. Raymond and Layla Farndell," Raymond said as he rose to his feet, towering over the young constable. "We have no idea who she is or how she got into our yard."

"Dr. Fletcher tells me you saved her life, mate," the officer said. He was a rotund young man who appeared to be in his late twenties. He was at least eight inches shorter than Raymond but couldn't have weighed much less. "The doctor called me because he said that the young woman had been abused. She has had ropes on both her ankles and her wrists, and her fingers are raw and bleeding. She also has numerous bruises, and she's malnourished and dehydrated."

Raymond ran a hand across his short gray hair. "Is she going to make it?"

"She's unconscious, but they believe they can save her. When she'll wake up is anybody's guess though. But if she'd been in that hole much longer, well, she'd have soon been dead," Constable Mench said. "I would like to see where you found her."

"Certainly," Raymond said. "Why don't we take our car, and you can follow us."

"Raymond, I think I'll stay here," Layla said. "If the girl wakes up, I want her to know there's someone here to support her. Anyway, the doctor wanted us to wait."

Raymond smiled at his wife of fifty years. She had a soft spot in her heart; that was one of the things he loved most about her. She was standing a few feet from him. A few gray hairs had come loose from the bun she always wore her hair in, and her face was pale with worry.

"Is that all right, Constable?" he asked.

"Of course it is. In fact, why don't you and I go in my patrol car, and we can save some time getting to your house. When we're finished there, I'll bring you back."

Twenty minutes later, Raymond and Constable Mench were gazing into the hole. They were both shaking their heads when the constable said, "This is really strange. She must have been fleeing from somewhere."

"Probably while it was still dark but after the earthquake. There's a house over there," Raymond said, pointing. "You can't see it from here because of the trees and bushes. It was condemned after the big earthquake. I wonder if she might have come from there."

The officer walked in that direction, and Raymond followed. When they reached the fence, they both studied it. Raymond leaned over it and said, "There are broken flower stems, and the shrubs have been disturbed on both sides. It looks like someone crawled through them to the fence, climbed over, and then walked through the shrubs and flowers to my lawn," he said as he continued to look around.

"Let's go have a look over there," Constable Mench suggested. They crossed the fence. "I'll take the lead. You're right. It looks like she might have come through here. It must have been difficult for her; I think she was crawling," the officer said, moving branches away from his face and working his way through the heavy growth.

It was difficult, but soon the two men had pushed their way across the yard. At the back door, they studied the house for a moment. "This place has sustained a lot more damage today," Raymond said. "If that girl was in there, she was lucky to get out."

"I think I'll see if I can get some more help here," Constable Mench said. "Then we'll go inside."

* * *

"Mike, come here," Kiana called through the open car window as she and Josh drove up beside him.

"Did you find something?" I asked, my heart racing.

"No, but there's a Constable Mench who called his office asking for assistance right away. I don't know what the problem is, but I told the dispatcher that the three of us would help. It's only three or four blocks from here," she said. I was already climbing in, and as soon as I got the door shut, she took off.

A tall, elderly man and a short, rotund constable were waiting for us on the sidewalk in front of a badly damaged house surrounded by a forest of unruly shrubs, trees, and weeds. We got out and introduced ourselves.

Kiana got down to business. "What have you got here?"

"We want to look inside this house," the chunky constable said. "We think someone may have been held captive here." He turned to the older man and said, "You stay out here, please. This could be dangerous."

"What makes you think—" I began, as my heart accelerated.

"I'll fill you in later," Constable Mench said sharply. "Let's just get inside. Follow me."

"But—" I cut my protest short when Kiana shook her head.

The house was a mess and quite dangerous to move through. We had to pick our way carefully through broken boards, busted wallboard, loose bricks, and shattered glass. We examined the main floor but couldn't see much but the debris.

"There's a stairwell here," Kiana suddenly called out. "I think we can get down it."

We moved toward her and started down the stairs. With the four of us, it didn't take long to move the debris out of the way and start down. Kiana had a flashlight from the borrowed patrol car. Constable Mench also had one. Josh and I had only the lights on our iPhones, although that was better than nothing. We slowly picked our way through the rubble. Josh was now in the lead, and he suddenly leaned down. "I just found a knife," he said.

"Leave it for now," I said, thinking that if this turned out to be a crime scene, we didn't want to disturb any potential evidence. We all shined our lights on the knife and then stepped over it to a door hanging partially open just a few feet in front of us.

"Oh my, this smells awful," Kiana said, choking.

"I'll say," I agreed.

Kiana stepped past Josh and was the first one through the door. She let out a gasp and rapidly backed out. "Mike, don't go in there!" she cried.

"What is it?" I asked, pushing forward, but Constable Mench held me back.

"The constable said for you to stay back," he said fiercely.

"Please, Mike," she said as I attempted to push Mench aside. "You don't need to see what's in there."

Josh stepped past the three of us, and Kiana said, "No, don't you go in either Josh. Let's go back upstairs and call for more help."

"Kiana, what is it?" I asked again, shining my light so I could see her face. There were tears in her eyes, and she was trembling. She stumbled over and grabbed onto me like she was offering support.

I held Kiana, but my eyes followed Josh as he moved into the room, followed by a stuttering Constable Mench, who was still trying to enforce Kiana's request. But the second he passed through the door, his protest stopped. "There's a . . . a . . . dead woman in here," he blurted.

"I'm going in," I said, my heart filled with dread. Kiana followed me. A moment later, four lights were shining on the woman, who was lying face up on the concrete floor. Her chest was covered in dry blood, as was the floor around her. Josh bent over and took a closer look, but all I could do was stand where I was and stare. Was it Skylie? It was still too dark to tell. I had to fight to keep from retching.

Constable Mench finally said, "This is a murder scene. This woman is dead, so there's nothing more we can do here. I'll get some investigators on the way."

No one said anything else until we were outside on the sidewalk in front of the house. Then Josh spoke, anger in his voice. "That must be my sister. Wilson Blanco stabbed her to death."

"I don't know for sure," I said, having a hard time keeping my voice level. Having had a few minutes to think about it, I had found a glimmer of hope. The hair hadn't looked right to me, and her face was smashed, discolored, and bloated. I desperately wanted it not to be Skylie, and yet who else could it be? I wondered as I felt acid stir violently in my stomach.

Constable Mench said, "I'm not sure who you guys are talking about, but there was a—"

Kiana cut him off. "Mike, look! Is that the Blanco guy?"

I looked at the car that was slowly approaching. Suddenly, the driver gunned it and flew by. I caught a fleeting glimpse of the passenger and assumed it could be Blanco, but the driver I knew without hesitation. It was Cal Granberg.

"Don't let them get away!" I shouted.

"It's Blanco and Granberg, all right," Josh confirmed as we dashed for Kiana's car. Constable Mench jumped in his car as well. He followed as we began a chase through the dangerous streets of Christchurch. I gripped the dashboard so tight I was sure my fingers would leave permanent indents. Josh was leaning over the seat with his head between me and Kiana.

The chase reached speeds of well over 100 kilometers per hour. Kiana drove like a pro, but the car ahead of us, driven by a desperate man not used to driving on the left side of the road, was having a lot of trouble. The chase ended after about ten blocks, when Cal lost control on a curve and smashed head-on into a huge tree. By the time we got to the car, Blanco was dead. I felt no loss. The driver was moaning. "Cal's alive," I said. Despite our history, I did everything I could to help him. Maybe I just wanted him to live to stand trial for his crimes.

I looked up once and saw a black van pass by. I didn't get a good look at the driver, but there was body damage to both the right front and rear fenders. "That's Antony," I shouted as the van sped away.

Josh, Kiana, and I all rushed for her car, but it was hemmed in by other vehicles. We stood helplessly and watched Antony's van speed out of sight. Kiana called in the description, but we knew it was unlikely anyone would see it. It was a desperately busy day for the New Zealand police in Christchurch.

We stayed busy, keeping a growing crowd back and getting Cal out of the car. After they hauled Cal away in an ambulance, Constable Mench took a deep breath as he looked at his bloody hands. Then he said, "The dead girl in the house may not be who you think she is."

Kiana, Josh, and I both looked at him. I asked, "Why do you say that?"

He told us about the girl found in the hole in the Farndells' backyard.

It was all I could do to control my emotions as he described her to us. "That's Skylie," I said, so relieved I could hardly contain myself. "Why didn't you tell us earlier?"

"I was going to, but—" Constable Mench began before he was cut off.

"My friend in the gang said that Blanco had killed *the girl*. We assumed it was Skylie, the only girl we would have reason to think about," Josh said.

"So who's the dead girl?" Constable Mench asked. "Whoever she was, your friend might have killed her."

"Not likely. It was probably Blanco Wilson. But that can wait. We need to get to the hospital," I said urgently. "Right now!"

"Then let's go," Kiana said as Constable Mench looked blankly at us. "We'll fill you in later, Constable," she added.

As we attempted to free our cars from the traffic parked around the wreck, I saw a dark blue car from the corner of my eye. The driver had a head of bushy black hair.

"There's Keenan," I shouted as the car shot up the street. A moment later it was out of sight. "All of the bad guys are here," I said, wondering which were the most dangerous, feeling strongly that all of them wanted me dead.

We finally managed to free the cars and head for the hospital. Constable Mench, still confused, was taking a couple of other officers back to the house where the dead woman's body was. He'd left Raymond there to keep people away, but he'd told me he had to secure the scene properly, which was true. There were enough officers left at the accident scene that they didn't need our help to get Wilson Blanco's badly mangled body from the car. The tree Cal had driven into was on the left side of the car, the passenger side. The tree being on Wilson's side was why he'd died, despite the airbags, and Cal had survived with the help of the airbags—so far, at least.

Kiana drove as fast as the damaged streets would allow. While she drove, I called Inspector Keller. "I think we've found Skylie," I said. "She's alive in a hospital in a coma, but they think she'll live. Kiana, Josh, and I are headed there now."

"Who found her?"

"It's a long story. She got away on her own. I'll fill you in when I know more, but for now, you need to know that Wilson Blanco is dead and Cal Granberg is critically injured."

"What happened?" he asked.

"They came by the abandoned house where we think Skylie was held captive until she managed to escape. I guess they thought the aftermath of the quake would keep anyone from noticing them. We chased them, but Cal was going too fast and lost control of his car. He hit a tree and smashed Wilson's head into the tree trunk. Oh, and there's a dead woman still in the house Skylie escaped from. A team of officers is there now. The woman was stabbed in the chest. We think we found the knife she was killed with."

"So that's who Blanco killed," the inspector said thoughtfully. "I wonder who she is. I'm coming to Christchurch. I'll be there as soon as I can get free. Keep me informed."

"That's not all," I said before he had a chance to disconnect. "Both Antony and Keenan are also in the area. I saw them both, but there was no way we could go after either one of them."

My next call, as we worked our way through the streets of Christchurch, was to Captain Bertrand.

TWENTY-FIVE

"THE MAN WHO SHOT ME is dead," I said calmly as soon as the captain answered the phone. "And my old partner is close to it."

"Detective Denton, what in the world are you talking about?" Captain Bertrand asked.

By the time we reached the hospital, I had filled him in on our recent activities with as much detail as time permitted. "So is Cal going to make it?" he asked.

"We're just getting to the hospital now," I said. "I should know in a little while."

"We have warrants for Cal, Mike. If he lives, will you make sure the New Zealand police keep him in custody while we begin extradition proceedings?"

After assuring him I would and ending the call, I entered the hospital with Kiana and Josh. It was packed with people who had sustained injuries as a result of the earthquake. We asked for directions to Skylie's room. A harried receptionist gave us the room number, and we walked quickly that way. I couldn't get there fast enough.

As we rode the elevator, Kiana said, "We can check on Cal later. He obviously isn't in any condition to walk out of here before we get around to seeing him. Anyway, he's probably in surgery."

The door to Skylie's room was closed. I stopped in front of it and took a deep breath. Kiana stepped up, put a hand on my arm, and squeezed gently. I smiled at her, my thoughts on the girl who lay in a coma beyond that closed door. I wiped my misty eyes.

"She'll make it," Kiana said softly then let go of me.

Josh had been watching us, and he finally spoke. "Let's go in. I want to meet this sister I never knew I had, this sister who has stolen your heart, Detective." He grinned feebly and reached for the door.

I barely recognized Skylie. She was thin and pale. Her eyes were closed, and tubes ran from her to machines in several different places. Her face was badly bruised, and both eyes were swollen and purple. Her hands and ankles were swathed with bandages. I suppressed the impulse to cry out in anguish. As I stood looking down at her, tears streaming down my face, I knew I loved her. I closed my eyes and asked God to spare her life.

I felt arms around me. I opened my eyes. Josh had an arm around my waist from my right side and Kiana had one around me from my left. "She's beautiful," I said, for I was seeing her as she had been, and as she would someday be again, God willing.

"She's my sister," Josh said, his voice breaking up. "I never knew I had a sister."

"Hey, guys," Kiana said, her voice also filled with emotion, "she'll be okay. I know she will."

The three of us shuffled closer to the bed. I leaned down. "Skylie, it's Mike. I'm here. And your brother Josh and a friend of ours are here too."

I thought I saw one of her bandaged hands move very slightly. Josh saw it too. "Mike, speak to her again. I think she can hear you."

Josh and Kiana let go of me, and I leaned down closer still and touched a swollen cheek with my finger. "Skylie. It's Mike. I'm here. I've missed you."

This time I was sure the hand moved. I stroked her cheek. "I love you, Skylie," I said.

"I . . . love . . . you," the girl on the bed replied, her lips barely moving and the words hard to distinguish, but I knew what she had said. Her eyes fluttered, and one of them opened, the one with the least amount of swelling around it. "You found me," she whispered. Then her eye closed again.

"No, you found me," I said. "You got away."

A ghost of a smile then creased those swollen lips that I felt the urge to kiss. "I . . . look . . . awful." The words were coming easier now.

"You're beautiful," I said.

"Thank you," she whispered; then a cloud crossed her battered face. "Marama was . . . with me. The big man . . . was after her. He . . ."

"We found Marama," I said without going into any of the details. "She's fine." That was stretching it, but I didn't want to give Skylie anything else to worry about.

Skylie gave a slight smile.

"Your brother Josh would like to say hi." I removed my fingers from her cheek and stepped back.

Josh took my place. He touched one arm above the bandage and said, "I'm so glad to meet you, Skylie. I always wanted a sister."

That one eye opened again, and after a moment it focused on Josh's face. "You're my brother?" she asked.

"Yes, I'm your brother," he repeated.

"We had . . . another brother," she said, her voice very weak. "He's dead. He tried . . . to save me." Her voice was fading fast. "He's dead." A tear escaped, and then the eye closed.

Josh and I again traded places, and I said, "We'll let you rest now, Skylie. You get better quickly, you hear?"

"I hear," she said so softly I could barely make out her words. She smiled again, but it faded, and her eye locked with mine. She took a deep breath. I leaned close to her face. "Someone else . . . is dead." She took a couple of shallow breaths. Then she added, "You need . . . to go find—"

"We found her," I said, "Can you tell me her name?"

"A woman?" Skylie asked. "It was dark. The big man . . . threw the body . . . in." Her voice faded away, her eye closed again, and the muscles of her battered face relaxed. We watched her for a minute as she drifted to sleep. I wished I could too. My lack of sleep was catching up with me. Now that I knew Skylie was alive, I hoped I could sleep soundly.

The three of us stepped back as the door opened. "Hello, I'm this woman's doctor, Dr. Fletcher. Who are you three?"

We introduced ourselves. "Her brother and a police officer?" Dr. Fletcher said to Josh after the introductions.

"Actually, all three of us are officers," Josh said.

"That's good. You three have a job to do. Someone hurt this young woman very badly."

"We'll find them," I said in a tight voice.

He nodded. "Good. She's a strong girl or she'd be dead. What's her name?"

"Skylie Yates," I said.

"Skylie," he repeated. "It's good to know her name. I think Skylie will wake up before too long. Her vital signs are all good."

"She just spoke to Mike," Kiana said. "But she fell asleep again."

The doctor's eyes grew wide. "That's amazing. I knew she'd be okay. I guess what she needed was to hear the voice of someone she knew, someone she loved."

He asked us to leave a moment later while he examined her. "You can come back in when I'm done," he concluded.

We stood in the hallway outside of her room and talked softly. "She woke up because she heard your voice," Kiana said, her face filled with wonder. "Love can do powerful things."

My phone rang. It always rang at such inconvenient times. I had given my number to Constable Mench before we left the accident scene. It was him on the phone. "The dead woman doesn't have any identification on her. She'll have an autopsy, and we'll find out who she is through fingerprints or dental records or something. She should be easily recognizable to anyone who knew her. She had a kiwi tattooed on the back of her neck."

"Oh my gosh!" I exclaimed. "Her name is Sage Decorte. It was her apartment we searched this morning. Has the body been moved yet?"

"Oh no, where it's a murder, there are lots of officers and people from the crime lab here now. I've just been running back and forth between here and the accident site. They finally got that dead guy out of the car. He was pinned in bad. How's the other guy?"

"I don't know. We've been with Skylie Yates," I said. "We'll check on Cal in a little while."

"Okay, thanks," Constable Mench said. "Oh, and one more thing. We found a pistol in the wrecked car," Mench said.

"Great," I responded. "We'll need to do a ballistics check on it." I wondered if it could be the one that was fired at me the previous day. If so, Keenan wasn't the shooter—I doubted the gun in Cal's car was the one.

As soon as the call ended, Kiana said, "The dead girl is Sage?"

"It seems so," I said.

"I wonder why she was killed. She was clearly thrown in with Skylie much later than when Skylie was locked up," Josh said.

"But now we'll never know what she might have told us," I said. A thought struck me. "I wonder what she told Wilson Blanco to make him kill her. We need to talk to Cal. Maybe Wilson told him."

"If he can ever talk again," Kiana cautioned.

"And if he'll tell you," Josh added.

"Oh, he'll tell me all right," I said with an angry grimace. "I'll make him tell me. I think I'll go check on him right now. Skylie needs to sleep anyway."

The others decided to go with me, and as we were walking down the hallway toward the elevator, my phone rang once again. I pulled it from my pocket and glanced at it. "I don't recognize this number." I answered the call.

"Detective Denton, this is Constable Nico Portill," the voice on the phone said. "I just talked to Inspector Keller. He's just getting ready to fly out of Picton to meet you."

"That's right."

"He asked me to call you. I'm at the hospital in Wellington; Marama and Rongo Parata are both doing much better now," he said. "Marama said she thinks she knows where Skylie is, but I understand you've already found her. Is she going to be okay?"

"Yes, she is," I said confidently. "You tell Marama and Rongo that, will you? And if either one of them wants to talk, you tell them to call me. Rongo knows my number."

"I'll do that," he promised.

By the time I had finished talking to Nico, Josh and Kiana had learned that Cal was still in surgery but was expected to live.

"When he's well enough to talk, he's going to have to face me," I said.

We returned to Skylie's room. I sat next to her bed, but exhaustion got the better of me, and I drifted to sleep in the chair. When I awoke, drool was dribbling from my mouth, and I was momentarily disoriented. As I wiped the drool away with the back of my hand, I realized where I was.

Kiana was grinning at me from a nearby chair. "Have a good nap?" she asked, looking as fresh as a new rose blossom.

"Actually, I did," I told her, embarrassed over the drool. "Why don't you look tired?"

"I fell asleep for a little while myself, and so did Josh," she said, pointing at him. He was still asleep. "Inspector Keller just called. He'll be at the airport in a few minutes. Do you want to ride with me to pick him up, or would you rather wait here?"

"I think I'll wait here," I said as I looked at my watch. "Good grief, I slept more than two hours."

Kiana rose gracefully to her feet. "You needed it, Mike. You've gone through a lot these past few days. I'm glad you got Skylie back." There was a catch in her voice when she spoke again. "She's a lucky girl. I hope she knows that."

Smiling at her, I said, "I'm the lucky one. When you get back with the inspector, I'm sure he'll want a full report. I would assume that now that Skylie is safe, the focus will be on finding her brother's killer."

Kiana nodded. She was rubbing her eyes as she walked out. She'd barely left the room when my phone rang. I pulled it from my pocket and turned away from the door.

"Hi, honey, it's me," the voice of my ex-wife said. "I miss you. When will you be home? I can't wait to see you."

"I don't know, Macy," I said shortly. "I'm awfully busy down here."

"Don't sound so mean," she said, the old sulkiness I remembered so well back in her voice. "I love you. We're meant to be together."

I touched Skylie's hand and felt again a powerful surge of love for her. "Listen, Macy. That's not going to happen. I'm sorry things didn't work out for you with Reece, but I am not going to come back to you."

"But, Mike," she whined, "you've got to. I made a mistake. It was all Reece's fault." She went on for a couple of minutes, and I found myself thumping my foot on the floor in frustration. I tuned out most of what she was saying. But I tuned back in as she said, "I know you still love me, Mike. Come back to me."

"No, I don't, and I won't, Macy. I found someone else. I'm with her now. Please, don't call me again." I hung up before she could respond. I felt horrible being so cruel to her, but she had left me, and it had hurt. I was completely over her. I'd never hate Macy, but I'd also never love her again. My love was committed to the girl I was gazing at now.

"She was a fool," Kiana said from behind me. "I didn't mean to eavesdrop, but I don't know how that woman could have ever left you."

I was startled when she spoke. "I thought you left," I said. "I didn't hear you come back in."

"Inspector Keller got another ride. He'll be here shortly." She rubbed at her eyes again then pasted a smile on her face. "I mean it, Mike. She should have realized how lucky she was."

"I wasn't right for her," I said lamely. Kiana and I had spent a lot of time together, and I had eventually told her about my past. She knew about my son as well. Kiana was a great girl. Some guy would be lucky when he got her. I shifted the conversation to a more comfortable subject. "Should we go check on Cal?"

Josh had just woken up, and he joined us. Cal was out of surgery and in the recovery room. We were told that it would be at least an hour before we could speak to him.

When we got back to her room, Skylie was still asleep. We'd been talking softly, but I was half expecting our voices to awaken her.

"She looks a lot better," Josh said.

"She does, doesn't she?" I agreed. "Perhaps the IV fluid is making a difference already." There was a little normal color back in her face, that part of her face that wasn't bruised and swollen, that is. And she looked relaxed and peaceful as she slept.

Inspector Keller entered Skylie's room and greeted us cheerfully. Then he asked, "How is she?"

"Sleeping," Kiana said. "But she's looking better. We've been with her for two or three hours now. She's slept the whole time."

"That's good. You know, you three make a great team. And I have permission to use all of you to help me find our killer. I have some ideas about what we need to do next. Should we sit down somewhere and talk?"

TWENTY-SIX

"Sorry I'm so slow getting here," Inspector Keller said a couple of minutes later. "Before my plane got off the ground in Picton, one of the officers at the hospital there called me and said that the surviving gang member from the ambush was awake and willing to talk. So I went to the hospital. And it's good I did. He was scared and knew he was in a lot of trouble. It didn't take much to get him to turn on Hemana and his gang. The officers in Auckland rounded up some of the people as soon as I notified them of the information. They've arrested Hemana and several others."

"Have you got enough to hold them?" I asked.

"Yes, but we could use more." He turned to Josh. "What you learned during the time you were undercover is going to be key to their convictions, but I'm hoping we get a chance to talk to Cal Granberg. If we can get him to talk, I think we can put the finishing touches on the gun smuggling and the murder of your brother as well as your sister's kidnapping."

"Do you think my family's safe now?" Josh asked.

"I think so, but I can't be sure. Until we find and arrest Antony Bahr, there's still a threat out there," Inspector Keller said.

"And Keenan Chestain," I added.

"He's the one with bushy hair and a dark blue Honda?" Josh asked.

"That's him," I confirmed.

"I've seen him," Josh said. "It was after I met you and Rongo on the trail. He was parked down the road a short distance, just lounging in his car."

I shivered. "He seems to be keeping good track of me," I said, feeling lucky he hadn't killed me yet.

I didn't get a chance to mention that because just then Dr. Fletcher ran into the waiting room. "There's some guy in the room with Skylie. He won't let me in. I think he has the door blocked with a chair. I need your help."

My whole world turned over once again. There were two men who might be in that room, Keenan Chestain or Antony Bahr. I was on my feet and out the door ahead of the others.

I reached out and tested the door. As Dr. Fletcher had said, there was something lodged against it on the other side. The inspector stepped up beside me, and we both put our ears close to the door to listen. It wasn't Keenan. It was Antony! "Skylie, you will tell me where the money is, or I'll kill you right now."

Kiana and Josh had stopped right behind us, but now we all hit the door together, four strong bodies unified with one compelling purpose. It gave way as whatever was on the other side broke with a loud crack. Antony was holding a gun, but his surprise caused him to hesitate. By the time he started to turn the gun on us, my fist was connecting with his jaw. His head snapped back, and his grip on the gun loosened. Josh wrestled it away, and I hit Antony again. He flew back against the window so hard that the glass shattered.

He began to slide toward the floor as glass showered down on him. I let Josh and the inspector follow through with Antony. I turned my attention to Skylie. The tubes had been pulled out, and her face was pasty white. She was unconscious but still breathing. Dr. Fletcher was already desperately working on her. Kiana stood beside me, and we both had to move back as more hospital staff rushed into the room.

I was terrified. A soft hand took mine, and Kiana said, "She'll make it, Mike. Why don't we step out while the doctors help her?" She tugged gently. Numb with grief and fear, I went with her.

We stood together in the hallway for a couple minutes before Josh and Inspector Keller came out with Antony. He was struggling and cursing, blood pouring from his mouth and nose. My hand began to throb, and I held it up and looked at it.

"You hit him pretty hard," Kiana said with a satisfied grin. "He'll feel that for a long time."

"I hope so," I said angrily.

"Kiana, can you come with us?" Inspector Keller asked. "We are going to lock this killer up. Mike, stay here with Skylie. We'll be back."

The next little while was a blur to me. It was like I was enshrouded in a dense fog. I was aware of people rushing in and out of Skylie's room, but

I didn't hear their words or see their faces. It was Dr. Fletcher who finally brought me out of the stupor.

"Detective Denton," he said, placing a hand on my arm and gently shaking it. "You can go back in now if you'd like to. We've done all we can."

Those words sounded so final to me that I felt like I was going to collapse. Instead I stiffened my back, took a couple deep breaths, and then asked the question I feared the answer to. "Is she going to make it, Doctor?"

"I don't know. She's gone back into a coma, and for the time being, that's best. That man did a lot of damage to her. He must have struck her a time or two, and he disrupted the flow of medications into her veins. If she was conscious for any of it, and I think she must have been, then the fright he gave her was extreme. It had her heart racing at an alarming rate. That's why I think she was conscious. If she was asleep, it wouldn't have affected her heart the way it did."

Dr. Fletcher pushed open the door and ushered me in ahead of him. Two nurses were standing by the bed, and an orderly was cleaning up the broken glass. One of them looked up and told the doctor that Skylie's blood pressure was still dangerously high. He asked if it had risen since he'd stepped out. She told him it hadn't but that it hadn't gone down any either.

"Stay and monitor it," he instructed. "We've got to get another room ready for her. She can't be in here with that broken window too long, but I want her more stable before we move her. Call me if her blood pressure changes either way."

The other nurse reported that Skylie's breathing was still shallow despite the oxygen they were introducing through her nose.

"Increase the flow," he ordered.

I just stood there and watched and prayed and got angrier by the minute. I was angry at Antony for his brutality and greed. I was angry with Cal for helping get Antony out of jail. And I was angry at myself because I hadn't been standing here in this room protecting her. What had I been thinking? I knew Antony was in the city. I guess I just assumed he wouldn't try anything with four of us in the hospital. I would never forgive myself if Skylie died from the attack.

I paced the hallway outside her room for the next half hour. I was near the elevator when it opened, and the man who had been stalking me stepped out. I stepped toward him, my fists balled, but Keenan put his hands in front of him. "I'm not here to make trouble, Detective."

"The very fact that you're here *is* trouble," I said darkly.

He shook his bushy head. "I just want to make sure she's okay, that's all. And I wanted to talk to you. I'm sorry for the trouble I have caused. I know you love her."

"Yes, I do," I broke in, not convinced that he wasn't going to be a problem. "And she's not okay."

"I saw them take that man away," he said. "The one who shot at you."

I was stunned. My fists relaxed. "Shot at me?"

"Yes, when you were at that old woman's house," he said. "I tried to follow him so I could make sure the police caught him, but he got away. I'm sorry."

"Keenan," I said, "would you like to take a few minutes and explain what you've been up to?"

"Yes," he said. "Now that those men are all caught . . . or dead," he said. "I saw the crash. I saw them take a dead man out of it. I think he wanted to kill you too."

"There's a waiting room down the hall. Let's go there and talk," I suggested.

Keenan agreed, and after we were both seated, he began to talk. "I know Skylie loves you, Detective. And I know you love her." I said nothing, and he went on. "I love her too, but I finally realized I'll never be able to have her. So I decided that the least I could do was make sure she and . . . and you were both safe."

"You've been following me."

"Yes, I admit it. At first I was just angry with you," he said, "but I never intended to hurt you. Then when I learned she'd been kidnapped, I only wanted to see her found, to make sure she was safe."

I stared at the man. Surprisingly, I believed him. But then I remembered the notes Inspector Keller had found. "You left threatening notes in her house, Keenan," I said.

He shook his head, and his dark eyes grew wide. "Oh no, mate. You've got it all wrong. I didn't threaten her. I was trying to tell her she would have the one she loved—you. I would never hurt her. Never!"

I believed him.

He rose to his feet. I did the same. He extended a hand to me, and we shook. "May I see her for just a moment, Detective?"

"She's hurt badly," I said.

"I just want to see for myself that she's alive, and then I'll leave you alone—you and her. I promise, mate. Please," he begged.

We both peeked in on her. Keenan stared for a long time, and then he finally said, "She's got to be okay." Tears ran down his face. "Take care of her, will you?"

He left after that. I made no attempt to stop him. It was getting dark outside by the time the New Zealand officers returned to the hospital. I was sitting on a chair outside Skylie's door when they came up the hallway. "How is she?" Josh asked.

I shook my head and got to my feet. "Not good. The doctor's in there with her again. I should have stayed here and stopped Antony before he got to her," I said bitterly. "Did Antony admit to what he's done?"

"He denies everything," Inspector Keller said. "I mean, he doesn't deny being in her room, but he says he didn't kill Snake or kidnap Skylie. He even said he didn't shoot the officer in Los Angeles."

"We know that's a lie," I said. "There were witnesses to that one. So I think we can safely assume he's lying about the rest. Did you ask him if he shot at me?"

"No, I thought that was Keenan," the inspector said.

I shook my head. "It was Antony. Keenan saw him do it."

The inspector's eyes narrowed. "How do you know that?"

After I'd finished explaining, Inspector Keller said, "We'll check the bullet that struck Jane Somers's house against the gun we took from Antony. Then we'll know for sure. Now, are you doing okay?"

I nodded, and Kiana stepped close to me. "Mike, you need to eat. These guys will stay here and watch her while you and I go down to the cafeteria."

"She's safe now," I said. "I mean, she's safe from outside attack. We got the people who hurt her. I just wish we'd gotten them first."

"I'm sure you're right, Detective," Inspector Keller said. "But we'll stay here anyway, at least until you get some food in you. Then maybe we'll pay a visit to Cal Granberg."

The mention of my old partner's name made my blood boil again. "I look forward to that. That man has a lot to account for. Which reminds me, I need to call Captain Bertrand and tell him what's happened."

"That's taken care of," the inspector told me. "I called him a little while ago."

"Are you coming?" Kiana asked.

"No, I'm not hungry. I want to stay with Skylie," I said.

"We'll go with Kiana," Josh said. "And I'll bring something back for you."

Shortly after the three of them left, the doctor allowed me back into Skylie's room. I stood beside her bed until the doctor returned, so I was again in the hallway when the officers came back.

Josh handed me a sandwich and a bottle of water. "I hope this will be okay," he said.

"Thanks, it'll be fine," I responded.

I had nearly finished the sandwich before Dr. Fletcher came out of Skylie's room. I started to go back in, but he stopped me. "Her blood pressure is coming down, and her breathing is steady now. I'd like you to speak to her when you go back in. Even though she's unconscious, hearing your voice now may be soothing to her."

I looked at the others. "We'll wait out here," Inspector Keller said. "You take however long you need to. When you're ready, we'll go talk to Cal, if he's conscious."

Dr. Fletcher said, "I was told by a nurse a moment ago that he's awake now. You can go talk to him if you'd like."

"Go ahead," I said. "I'll catch up to you later."

"No, we'll wait for you. Cal isn't going anywhere," the inspector said.

I pushed through the door to Skylie's room and stepped beside her bed. A stream of light was filtering through the sheet of plastic that had been taped over the broken window. I gazed at her for a moment and then bent over and touched her cheek, like I had the last time. "Skylie, I'm here. It's Mike. I love you."

There was no response. I kept my hand on her cheek and gently stroked it. I said a few more words to her. The door opened behind me. I glanced that way.

Dr. Fletcher smiled at me. "Keep at it. I just want to observe for a few minutes."

I nodded and turned back toward Skylie. "You're doing great, Skylie. I'm proud of you. I sure missed you these past few days."

"Will you look at that?" Dr. Fletcher said. "When you spoke, her heart rate picked up slightly. She hears you and is reacting."

I spoke some more, and the doctor grunted his approval. Then he stepped out again. I stayed with her for a few more minutes, and then I said, "I need to go for a little bit, Skylie, but I'll be back soon." I backed up a couple of steps and then stopped as her right eye opened a little. I moved back to the bed and once again touched her cheek. "I'm still here," I said. "Are you awake?"

Her lips twitched, and she blinked.

"Hey, that's great, Skylie. I can't wait until you can talk to me. I love just sitting and talking to you," I said.

A tiny smile formed.

"Do you like talking to me?"

The smile grew a little.

"I love you, Skylie."

The smile grew bigger still, and her head moved ever so slightly.

"If you love me, blink your eye twice."

Two quick blinks followed, and I felt my heart soar.

"When I come back, I'll have your brother, Josh, come in again," I told her.

She nodded again.

"You'll like him. He's a great guy. He helped us catch the man who killed your other brother. He's in jail now."

The smile faded from her face, and she shook her head slightly side to side.

"Antony Bahr, that creep who harassed you in Los Angeles. We arrested him. He can't hurt you anymore. He killed your brother, and now he'll pay for that."

Again she shook her head. I was puzzled.

"What are you trying to tell me, Skylie?" I asked. "Aren't you glad we caught him?"

A slight nod.

"Me too," I said. "I just wish we'd got him before he killed Snake and kidnapped you."

She shook her head again, and then her lips began to move. "Not him," she said so softly that it took me a moment to understand.

"Are you saying it wasn't Antony that kidnapped you?" I asked.

She blinked twice. I took that as an affirmative answer.

"And it wasn't him that killed Snake?"

She blinked twice again.

I was suddenly very alarmed. "Skylie, you've got to tell me who did it. Are you sure it wasn't Antony?"

More blinks.

I took a deep breath. "Can you tell me a name, the name of the person who did it?"

Her lips moved, but no sound came out.

"Do you want to tell me later?" I asked.

She again blinked twice.

"Do you want to sleep again?"

She offered a slight nod. Her eye closed, and her face relaxed. I watched her for another minute or two. I also watched the machines that were keeping track of all her vital signs. I didn't see anything that alarmed me, so after a couple of minutes I slipped quietly from her room. But I was worried. Antony wasn't the killer. Whoever it was still roamed the country and was a threat to Skylie. Could I have been mistaken about Keenan? I wished I hadn't let him go.

"How is she?" Josh asked when I closed the door.

"Better. She woke up for a minute or two, but she's sleeping again now."

"Did she say anything?" Kiana asked. "She must have, and whatever it was is worrying you. It's all over your face."

"When I told her that you had arrested Antony Bahr for Snake's murder, she said, 'Not him.' She was too tired to say more."

The three officers were staring at me. "Detective, are you telling us that she says it wasn't Antony who killed Snake and abducted her?" Inspector Keller asked.

"Yes," I said. "She was only able to speak those two words, but she was able to answer me by blinking as I asked her about Antony. He didn't do it. The killer is still out there somewhere. I shouldn't have let Keenan leave. I must have been wrong about him. When she gets stronger, she'll be able to tell us who did it. Until then, she isn't safe."

"Let's find Dr. Fletcher," Inspector Keller said.

"Let me," Kiana said, and she sprinted down the hallway.

When she returned with him, Dr. Fletcher said, "Mike, I understand that Skylie spoke to you again."

"She did," I answered. "And she's still in danger."

"Okay, we have another room ready for her now, a more secure room, and I think she's stable enough to move. She'll have someone with her all the time, and if you want an officer there, you can do that too."

"That will be great," the inspector said. "We'll check back with you a little later. Right now we want to have a visit with Cal Granberg, who, incidentally, is one of the prime suspects." I looked at him. "It could be Keenan, but it could also have been Cal," he added.

"I'll stay with Skylie," Kiana volunteered. "You men go talk to Cal."

"Thanks," I told her. She and Dr. Fletcher entered Skylie's room.

As we went in search of Cal's room, the inspector said, "I don't think it was Keenan. I believe he told you the truth, but I am going to make a call and have an all-points bulletin put out for him just in case."

The inspector had completed his call by the time we arrived at the room where my disgraced former partner was lying in bed, badly injured but still alive.

TWENTY-SEVEN

CAL LOOKED TO BE IN pretty rough shape, but I was unable to conjure up any sympathy for him. He had brought his troubles on himself, and I was going to get some answers from him now. His face was damaged, but, unlike Skylie, he could at least open his eyes and was fully conscious. Both legs and one arm were in casts. His neck was in a brace. He lay helpless on his bed with the head of it elevated slightly.

"Hi, Cal," I said when those guilty blue eyes focused on me. "You've got some explaining to do. But before you and I talk, Inspector Keller, of the New Zealand Police Department, has a few questions for you. This is the inspector." I nodded at Inspector Keller and stepped back.

"Your other partner in crime, Wilson Blanco, is dead," the inspector said, "thanks to your reckless driving. Hemana and his gang, those that didn't die in Picton in the shootout, are in custody. The sole survivor of the ambush told us everything he knew. That, of course, includes your part in smuggling firearms to our country. You are under arrest at this time, Mr. Granberg, on several charges." The inspector then went on to list them.

Cal glared at us.

"Do you understand what you are being charged with?" Inspector Keller asked him.

"Of course I do," Cal said. "I'm not an idiot, but you can't prove a thing."

"I have a few questions, and my associate here," the inspector said, pointing at Josh, "may have some as well."

"Hello, Cal," Josh said. "You knew me as Gunner. My real name is Constable Josh Infelt. And of course, you remember selling me a gun, I'm sure."

Cal glared at him but said nothing.

Inspector Keller spoke again. "It would be in your best interest to shed the attitude, Mr. Granberg," he said. "Your cooperation in relation to our investigation of Hemana and his gang will be considered favorably by our prosecutors."

Cal was still glaring. "I have nothing to say," he said.

They asked him a few questions anyway, but he stubbornly looked away.

"Detective Denton, it appears he doesn't have anything to say to us. Would you like to ask a few questions?"

"I would," I said.

"I've especially got nothing to say to you," Cal said as his angry eyes met mine briefly.

"Your future is in my hands, Cal," I said. "I know you set me up the day Wilson shot me. It can be proved, but I would be willing to speak in your behalf if you'll help me now." He said nothing, but I went on anyway. "Cal, I want you to know Skylie Yates has been rescued and is alive," I said. "She's going to testify that Wilson murdered Sage Decorte, a woman to whom he sold the very gun he used to shoot me."

Cal's badly damaged mouth dropped open, and some of the glare left his eyes. "How . . . did you . . . know that?" he finally stammered.

"Good police work, Cal," I said. "We have the weapon as well. It was in the possession of her boyfriend, a man by the name of Jalen Lillard, better known as Snake."

"He's dead," Cal said. "He can't testify."

"Yes, I know that. I was there at the TopHouse when it happened. As I'm sure you also know, Hemana suspected that Snake, who was part of his organization, somehow got his hands on the money from a bank robbery in Wellington, a robbery that was carried out using guns that you provided."

"I don't know what you're talking about," Cal said defensively.

"You know exactly what I'm talking about. You sold the guns, and we can prove it. What did you think a bunch of cutthroats like Hemana and his followers wanted guns for? Did you think they were going to form a gun club and sponsor competitive shooting tournaments?" I asked facetiously.

He didn't answer, but the look of guilt that crossed his battered face was answer enough for me. "Tell me, Cal, exactly what your relationship to Reece Nesbitt was, how you knew him and what his role was in obtaining guns for you and Wilson to send to New Zealand."

Cal had the gall to chuckle. "Are you sore because he took your wife away from you?"

"I can't say it endeared him to me," I responded. "But that doesn't matter anyway. His crimes caught up to him, much like Wilson's did. Reece is dead. He died in a shootout."

Cal clearly hadn't known that. "Oh." The resistance began to ooze out of him.

"And for your information, the fake clerk of the court, Sam's wife, Jeanette, is in a lot of trouble. I don't imagine what she has to say is going to be very helpful to you. But I digress," I said. "Tell me what you know about Antony Bahr's escape from jail in Honolulu."

Cal did the best replica he could of a shrug of the shoulders as he lay there, slightly elevated on the bed.

"We'd like to have your version to go along with Jeanette's." I didn't tell him that as far as I knew Jeanette hadn't been arrested yet. I let him make his own assumptions, and that was good enough.

He finally gave up most of his resistance and admitted what he'd done. He ended saying, "If I were you, Mike, I'd keep a lookout for Antony. He doesn't like you at all."

"I'm sure he doesn't, especially after I bloodied his nose a few hours ago, just before Inspector Keller and Constable Infelt arrested him," I said. "He's making like a canary now, singing his black heart out."

If Cal could have slumped any lower in his hospital bed, I think he would have. But I wasn't finished with him yet. "Antony thought that Snake had taken the money from the robbery," I said. "I'm sure you are aware of that."

Cal said nothing, just looked around as if looking for a way to get out of the mess he'd created for himself.

I forged ahead. "Snake didn't take the money, Cal. And his girlfriend, Sage is dead," I said flatly. "But of course you knew that. Wilson told you."

Again, Cal looked at me blankly.

I tried one more thing. "Okay, enough of that for now, why don't you tell me why you tried to convince me that Skylie was in Picton and that—"

I never completed my question, for Kiana burst into the room, her face glowing. "I'm sorry to interrupt, but Mike, Skylie is awake and wants to talk to you. She says it's important, but she won't tell anyone what she has to say but you."

I turned to the inspector. "I'm through here for now," I said. "You and Josh can talk to him some more if you'd like to."

"Sure thing, mate," the inspector said with a grin. "I am going to explain very clearly to him what he is facing. I don't care if he doesn't want to answer my questions, but he will listen to me."

I had to jog to keep up with Kiana. The room they'd moved Skylie to was one floor above the one we'd been on. While we were on the elevator, Kiana said, "She's going to be okay now, Mike. We just have to make sure we catch Snake's killer before he tries to do something to her."

The elevator door opened, and we hurried to Skylie's new hospital room. I rushed to her bedside, and she smiled. In an amazingly strong voice, she said, "It's good to see you, Mike. I'll just be glad when I can use both eyes again—and when this one isn't so blurry."

I put my hand on her cheek. "It's good to see you too. Constable Lever says you have something to tell me."

"Yes, I do," she said. The smile faded from her face. "Antony didn't kill Snake or abduct me. It was Sage, but I think she's dead now. A big man came to my, uh, my dungeon, and he threw a body in there. There was a knife in the chest. I didn't know who it was until I got to thinking about it after I woke up. I remembered that you guys told me the dead person was a woman. I'm sure it was her."

"Yes, it was Sage's body, but why would she kill Snake and kidnap you? She was Snake's girlfriend. She even bought a gun for him. It was from the big man you just mentioned, Wilson Blanco."

She nodded her head. "Wilson Blanco," she repeated. "So that's who killed Sage?"

"Yes, it is, but he's dead now too," I said.

"Okay, I see now. Let me tell you what Sage told me. Like Antony and Hemana, she thought Snake had taken the money and hidden it. He told Sage he didn't, but she didn't believe him. She met him at the TopHouse when he came to see me."

"So she must have been the one driving the car that was stolen in Christchurch," I said thoughtfully. The New Zealand police had never figured out the stolen car.

"She took me away in Jalen's car," she said. She was thoughtful for a moment, and then she said, "Jalen wasn't all bad, Mike. He came to warn me that Antony and others were looking for me to try to get me to tell them where Snake had hidden the money, but he told me he hadn't hidden it, that he never even had it."

"I'm glad to hear there was some good in him," I said.

"Sage thought he was lying, that he did have the money and that he wasn't going to share it with her. I heard them arguing about it outside, and then they came in. Jalen was so nice to me, but Sage was angry. She kept mentioning the money. Finally he told her he didn't have it, had never had it, and to quit pestering him about it.

"I thought she'd decided to quit asking when she kind of moved away from us. He was telling me he'd learned about me earlier and had wanted to meet me and his twin brother. He said he hadn't been able to learn much about our brother, but when he heard Antony was looking for me, he decided to find me first. He said he'd protect me from Antony and Hemana and the others. He also told me that it was Antony's brother, Tristan, who warned him about Antony. Anyway, without any warning, Sage hit him over the back of his head with a big stick. She hit him really hard. I didn't see where she found it, and I didn't notice her approach us again. It was just so fast. Snake fell, and she grabbed me and threatened me." At that point Skylie started to cry.

I leaned down and kissed her cheek. "It's okay. It's over now."

When she got her crying under control, she said, "I'm sorry it all happened. I don't want to talk about it anymore. I want you to tell me about Marama and Rongo. I remember, when I was awake for a little while, you told me they were okay. But where are they? Why aren't they here?"

I explained as gently as I could, and she cried some more. "I'm really not a wimp, Mike. I don't want you to think I am. I'm sorry about crying so much."

When the inspector and Josh came in a few minutes later, Josh said, "So this is my long-lost sister. Hi, Skylie, I'm Josh."

We left the two of them to get acquainted, and the inspector, Kiana, and I stepped out into the hallway and went to a waiting room.

Inspector Keller asked, "Did she tell you who the killer is?"

"It was Sage Decorte," I said. "When she woke up, Skylie figured out who Wilson had killed and thrown in the room with her. All the time she'd been in there with the corpse but didn't know it was Sage."

"I never would have guessed it," Keller said. "And by the way, after you left, Cal finally buckled under the pressure."

"Did you get him to answer your questions?" I asked, surprised.

"Oh yeah, he talked to me," he said with a twinkle in his eye.

"What did you say to him?"

"You don't want to know, mate," Keller said with a smile. "I'll simply say that I convinced him it would be in his best interest to cooperate."

I nodded. "So what did he tell you?"

"First, he admitted that he and Blanco intended to sneak what Cal believed was Skylie's body out of the house and dispose of it. Cal wouldn't have known that the dead woman wasn't Skylie because he'd never seen either her or Sage, and Blanco didn't tell him it wasn't Skylie."

"If Cal thought Skylie was dead, why did he help Hemana set up the ambush?" I asked.

"Cal said that Hemana didn't know anything about Skylie or Snake or what had happened to either one of them. He just wanted to get his hands on you for messing up his gun running operation. Cal figured you would come, hoping she was there like he'd told you."

"That sounds like Cal. He still wanted me dead, didn't he?" I said.

"I'm afraid so, mate. And once again, we can rule Keenan Chestain out. I believe he told you the truth."

* * *

I slept in a chair in Skylie's room that night. The next day, Marama and Rongo were finally able to come to Christchurch. And to everyone's surprise, Jalen's parents, the Lillards, showed up at the hospital. They were a wonderful couple, and after meeting them I couldn't imagine why Jalen had turned so bad. While Skylie and Josh were visiting with the Paratas and Lillards, I left the room and spoke on the phone with Inspector Keller.

"They found the money," he said. "The bank president is doing cartwheels he's so happy."

"Where did they find it?" I asked.

"In Antony's house," Inspector Keller said. "Tristan had it in some boxes in the back of a closet in his bedroom. The boxes were covered with a blanket, and the clothes hanging in the closet hid the blanket and the boxes. Apparently the brothers each had their own space, and Tristan was confident Antony would never find it because he would never suspect Tristan in the first place. The one thing we'll never know is what Tristan planned to do with it in the long run. The only hint we have is that he had a visa for Australia in a drawer in his bedroom. It was recently issued.

Perhaps he planned to move there and spend the money once he was out of New Zealand."

"He should have left New Zealand before he let himself get involved in that ambush. Why did he do that?" I wondered aloud.

Inspector Keller grinned. "Whoever said criminals are smart or think that they're vulnerable?" He just chuckled. "I guess we'll never know."

EPILOGUE

EVERYTHING I COULD DO I had done. The case against Cal Granberg in Los Angeles was rock solid. Unfortunately for him, New Zealand also had a strong case against him. I left it to the higher authorities in New Zealand and California to work out the details of his prosecutions. As long as he was in jail, I didn't care where it was.

More important things took up my time. Captain Bertrand was anxious for me to go back to LA and continue what he said was my *exemplary* work there. Inspector Keller informed me that he and those above him in the New Zealand Police Department would do whatever they could to keep me in New Zealand if I would go to work for them.

Neither of those options were the most important things to me right now. No, Skylie Yates, my sweet Kiwi girl, occupied most of my time and the bulk of my thoughts. She healed quickly and was soon home in Wellington with Rongo and Marama. I spent almost every waking hour with her. Keenan Chestain came to the house one day and reaffirmed what he'd told me at the hospital in Christchurch. He didn't bother us again.

Pressured as I was concerning my professional future, I was anxious to see where things would lead with Skylie. I was in love with her, and she said she was in love with me. I believed her, and with that in mind, I invited her to the place where I had first met Josh. We planned to tour the Waitomo Caves, the Glow Worm Caves. But first I planned to take her on a relaxed hike through the trail known as the Ruakuri Bushwalk.

We spent a couple of leisurely hours letting the spectacular area cleanse us of the horrors we had experienced. Towering trees, the varied sounds of nearby wildlife, the rushing of the stream down a deep and rugged valley, a spectacular waterfall, small caves, numerous bridges, many ups and downs, an abundance of greenery—it all calmed and soothed us.

By the time we left the bushwalk that afternoon, I had popped the question, and she had given me the answer I had so hoped for. We were married in a little white chapel in Wellington a few days later.

The pressure regarding my professional future pressed more strongly on me after that. But the decision was no longer mine alone to make. While spending our honeymoon hiking and camping in the Nelson Lakes National Park, Skylie and I discussed our future together. We made a decision, one that both of us were content with.

Despite the terrible memories we had of the TopHouse, we decided to face down our fears and spend the last night of our honeymoon there. We arranged to stay in the room I had slept in. Neither of us was willing to spend the night in the room where the TopHouse murder had occurred.

We had dinner at the long table in one of the lounges, a table that seats eighteen people and was called the United Nations table. We were there with several other guests, but we had eyes only for one another.

Skylie and I finally were able to find peace in our lives. We bought a modest house overlooking the sparkling blue ocean in the beautiful seaside town of Picton, where I was employed by the New Zealand Police Department. We settled down, anxious to start a family. I loved her, she loved me, and I had never been happier.

ABOUT THE AUTHOR

CLAIR M. POULSON WAS BORN and raised in Duchesne, Utah. His father was a rancher and farmer, his mother, a librarian. Clair has always been an avid reader, having found his love for books as a very young boy.

He has served for more than forty years in the criminal justice system. He spent twenty years in law enforcement, ending his police career with eight years as the Duchesne County Sheriff. For the past twenty-plus years, Clair has worked as a justice court judge for Duchesne County. He is also a veteran of the US Army, where he was a military policeman. In law enforcement, he has been personally involved in the investigation of murders and other violent crimes. Clair has also served on various boards and councils during his professional career, including the Justice Court Board of Judges, the Utah Commission on Criminal and Juvenile Justice, the Utah Judicial Council, the Utah Peace Officer Standards and Training Council, an FBI advisory board, and others.

In addition to his criminal justice works, Clair has farmed and ranched all his life. He has raised many kinds of animals, but his greatest interests are horses and cattle. He's also involved in the grocery store business with his oldest son and other family members.

Clair has served in many capacities in the LDS Church, including full-time missionary (California Mission), bishop, counselor to two bishops, young men president, high councilor, stake mission president,

Scoutmaster, and high priest group leader. He currently serves as a Gospel Doctrine teacher.

Clair is married to Ruth, and they have five children, all of whom are married: Alan (Vicena) Poulson, Kelly Ann (Wade) Hatch, Amanda (Ben) Semadeni, Wade (Brooke) Poulson, and Mary (Tyler) Hicken. They also have twenty-three wonderful grandchildren. Clair and Ruth met while both were students at Snow College and were married in the Manti temple.

Clair has always loved telling his children, and later his grandchildren, made-up stories. His vast experience in life and his love of literature have contributed to both his telling stories to his children and his writing of adventure and suspense novels.

Clair has published more than two dozen novels. He would love to hear from his fans, who can contact him by going to his website, *clairmpoulson.com.*